STORM LAKE

STORM LAKE

a novel by Alan Loots

A-G
Andrew-Gray Publishing

Published by
Andrew-Gray Publishing

PO Box 71372
Des Moines, Iowa 50325

Cover design by Megan Walsh
Book design by Connie Kuhnz

Printed in the United States on acid-free paper
Library of Congress Control Number: 2007903965
ISBN Number: 978-0-9796196-0-1

First Edition
September 2007

Dedicated to Roger and Maureen

Acknowledgments

I am deeply grateful to first editor Shirley Koslowski, whose skills helped shape this book. She is a wonderful person and has become a friend. I am lucky. Thank you to editor, Phyllis Cadwallader, as well, for her valuable contributions. What an eye! Tom Bell read and critiqued a first draft, offering suggestions and support. His efforts are also appreciated.

Others who read, and in some cases, reread various drafts include Cindy Raabe, Susan Loots, Diane Marcus, Celine Little, Elizabeth Kushman, Rich Raabe, Joe Marcus, Alex Loots, Annie Lund, Bill Roach, Natalie Loots and Mary Laughlin. Thank you for your interest in the book and the writer.

Storm Lake

ﾉﾉﾉﾉ *chapter 1*

Michael Lund took a deep breath as he took in the warm April sunshine. Any other day he might have lingered where he stood and thought how nice it was that winter in Minneapolis was over. He looked at his watch and headed toward Seven Corners.

Lund's black cotton sweater, wrinkled khaki pants and Born shoes reflected his feeling towards the academic community . . . casual. He loved the concept of "student" and the continual process of learning from cradle to grave. There was, however, an itch.

Lund pulled sunglasses from a small pocket on the side of the black leather bag he used for a briefcase. His eyes adjusted comfortably to the sunlight behind the dark lenses as he walked across the concrete pathways past the Meredith Wilson Library and toward 19th Avenue and Mickey's Pub. Bag in hand and a youthful bounce in his step, he resembled a university athlete on his way to practice more than a faculty member with an appointment to meet a special agent of the FBI.

┄┄ chapter 2

Jesse Ford leaned back in his leather chair and traced the short scar on his left cheek with his index finger. He swiveled a half turn and focused on the portrait above the stone fireplace, allowing himself a brief visit with a person from nineteen years before. Even the gunfire outside his window did not intrude on his memories of Virginia.

Within a couple of minutes, Jesse turned back to the computer monitor. He was writing a letter to his new acquaintance in St. Louis. He knew the value of the training exercises the six-person team was completing just beyond his walls and the effectiveness of the good weapons and ammunition the team used, but he also knew carefully chosen words to the right person at the right time were equally useful.

Jesse resembled Paul Bunyan playing Chopin as his massive fingers glided over the keyboard. The light from the monitor reflected in the glasses that sat astride a broad nose below thick eyebrows. His face was well seasoned and large-boned, but not fat. The man's body followed the same proportions all the way down to his size fourteen waffle-sole boots. His light sandy hair and beard were short and dense; good genes.

Jesse's computer occupied part of an oak desk in front of windows that faced east toward the mountains. A photograph of the same woman in the portrait was displayed in a white frame next to the laser printer and fax machine. Another computer, along with other electronic equipment sat on a second desk nearby. Small glowing red and green lights signaled their readiness. On a third desk against the north wall were four black and white monitors, each showing an outside view from all sides of the house. The communications room operated twenty-four hours a day.

The room was western in decor and lined with wood paneling. Mounted deer and bear heads accented the walls. Old rifles with long barrels and worn butts were displayed beneath their victims.

During the day, the view from the windows offered a spectacular vista of the Wallowa Mountains. Jesse Ford owned the view and four thousand acres on the range's western side. His nearest neighbor was seven miles away. The nearest town was fourteen. He had fallen in love with this part of Oregon during high school when he was on a vacation with his parents to the Pacific Northwest. At seventeen, he thought he might some day move there to live for the rest of his life.

Gunfire continued at a safe distance from the house. Jesse called it the Command Center, not just because it was the largest building, but because it was the heart of the complex. He heard single pops and sputtering crackles from the weapons, followed by long pauses, then bursts of rapid fire lasting thirty seconds or more.

———

Five men and one woman each carried a semiautomatic pistol and a modified assault rifle. Under a heavily overcast sky they were being trained to use their weapons with confidence and accuracy.

The enemy could be found anywhere within a half mile of the Command Center. They were spread out, hiding in or behind natural structures or in the old barn next to the muddy creek bed. The enemy numbered only fifteen, but their strategic placement and complete silence challenged the defenders. Training exercises were conducted during the day and at night. One of Jesse's philosophies was "locate them during the day, eliminate them when it's dark."

Two of the defenders were Ford's sons, Barry and Tommy. They and their comrades eliminated six of the enemy before they reached the creek. Hot casings sizzled as a few of them fell into remaining patches of snow. Animals whose habitats were above ground had already raced from the area in a dozen different directions. They sought sanctuary in the woods far from the battlefield. The native creatures were not the targets of the shooters. They were observers and sometimes casualties of the war.

The army of six moved in a squatty jog to their next encounter. They wormed their way into a defensive position overlooking a small grove of trees not far from their first engagement. Their bodies were hot with sweat under dark blue clothing and their heavy breath blew white through the cold late-afternoon air.

As the defenders advanced, a large figure with a black face was observed clinging to a limb on one of the larger trees above them. His arm was still, but raised in a threatening gesture. He must have a gun. Two comrades reacted immediately to the towering figure. A pair of consecutive shots from an assault rifle severed the right arm above the elbow and the handgun's damage left a crater in his chest. The figure dropped in a heap to the ground.

"Excellent," praised Barry. "Again your reflexes and accuracy were outstanding. The Fort is proud of you." Barry stood out among the group. He was a slightly smaller version of his father, but still the largest of the team. His beardless face was not as weathered as Jesse's and his eyes not as deep-set, but they were just as clear and focused when it came to the business of The Fort.

"Yeah, great kill!" yelped Tommy as he stomped his feet in a war dance. "Let's bag some more garbage." Simply by looks, it was hard to tell Tommy was Barry's younger brother. He was shorter. His frame carried more weight, especially at his belt line. His hair, somewhere between sandy and blonde was longer and shaggy. He always seemed to be squinting, regardless of the time of day. The words from his mouth were usually as foul as his breath.

There were a few seconds of silence, until a half dozen or more of the enemy became apparent en masse behind a clump of trees and a large rock near the abandoned house. In the frenzied bombardment that ensued, tree limbs, bark and rock fragments flew in every direction. Weathered siding on the house flew away in small fragments. Within two minutes not one of the enemy was left standing. The ragtag enemy force lay slaughtered. Some were no longer in one piece. Others were simply full of large holes as they absorbed the hail of gunfire. The victors toasted with guns raised to the dark gray sky. This was a battle fought on American soil, for real Americans. The war had just begun.

———

Jesse J. Ford shifted in his chair and noted the silence. The battle was over and the men would be returning to base in their Jeeps after making a mandatory battlefield inspection. He would be there to greet them. Jesse had learned the value of praise from his father. It had to be timely and genuine. He proofread his letter as he waited for Barry and Tommy to join him at the house.

Dear Ted,

I just wanted to let you know how much I've enjoyed corresponding with you the past few months. It seems like we have quite a few ideas and goals in common. I admire a person who is willing to stand up for his convictions. With this whole country getting so damn mixed and mixed up, it's refreshing to meet someone, if only by long distance, who has such clarity. You should feel proud that you are a real American at a time when real Americans are needed.

For years, I and others, have been aware that America's white heritage and principles need defending. Now more than ever! We must *take it upon ourselves to eliminate that which is bringing America to its knees. "Pro-active" is the keyword for people like us.*

My sons and I want to extend an invitation to visit us sometime soon. As I mentioned in previous correspondence, this is an inspiring place to visit . . . or to stay a lifetime. There are strict rules for entering The Fort and staying, but I can assure you, our place is suited to your interests and ideals. It also might be a refreshing break from the painful divorce you said you just experienced.

Except for your transportation cost, your other basic needs here will be met. It would be our pleasure to have you as our guest.

Contact Barry, or me but do it by letter through a private carrier, not the U.S. Postal Service. As you see, we will no longer be communicating with you by e-mail or U.S. mail. Our privacy can no longer be assured. Could our freedom be next? We hope to hear from you soon.

God bless real Americans,
Jesse Jeremy Ford

Jesse moved the screen's pointer to File, Print and then he clicked.

————

"I thought you said there were fifteen," one of the men said to Tommy as they completed the body count. "There are only fourteen here, although there are a lot pieces."

Barry overheard the talk and took over the situation. He motioned to everyone to gather where Tommy and the other man stood. They looked on as Tommy separated the bodies with his foot. They were men and women, black and brown, a few whose faces vaguely indicated Asian or Hispanic or Arabic descent. Others were white and dressed in yellow. They were all garbed and made up like actors in a multi-cultural play.

The enemy was made up of an army of mechanized mannequins or human-looking stuffed targets. Those that were salvageable would be repaired for another battle with other recruits another day.

"I count fourteen, too," agreed the oldest son. He and Tommy then led the team to the top of the small hill nearby. Barry put his arm on the soldier's right shoulder and pointed to a lone distant figure standing to the left of the compound chapel. It was a mannequin dressed in black that was propped up and barely visible.

"There's always one more," he reminded in a grim voice.

The soldier took his shot.

~~~ *chapter 3*

John Kick looked at his watch and then glanced out the boutique window at the bar across the street. It was 4:13 p.m. and he was late by design. It was the small assessment test of patience used on people with whom he had appointments.

He had set up the meeting with Lund for 4 p.m. at Mickey's Pub, on Riverside Drive near the University of Minnesota campus. It hadn't been hard to learn some of Lund's haunts, and Kick decided it would be best if they met in a place where Lund was comfortable. He needed every possible advantage today if he was going to bring this assignment in.

Kick was under more pressure than usual from his supervisor, Raymond Stacey, the director of a special domestic anti-terrorist unit. Kick desperately needed a definite "yes" from Lund within two days. Overall, Kick had an excellent reputation as an agent, but a failed assignment and a reprimand in the space of two years jeopardized his special position with the Bureau.

After twenty-three years with the FBI he realized the grind was getting to him. He found himself fantasizing often about beaches, powerboats and the company of beautiful women. But a decent retirement would not be on the horizon for some time or never, if he screwed up again.

Kick had read and re-read the file on Lund given to him by Stacey. There was nothing out of the ordinary in his background except for the notation about the junior professor's career choice. He was the ideal candidate, just who Kick was looking for.

The file gave a detailed description of Michael Lund's years at the University of Wisconsin. Social Science degree. Bullet points included Lund being an outstanding athlete and an even better student. He'd completed master and doctoral degrees in criminology from Ohio State University nine years ago. He married Caroline Wright, a graduate art student he met at the school. No children. His father was deceased. The file also noted Lund's sandy hair and blue eyes. Another plus.

Kick pegged Lund as just another college instructor struggling for tenure and more pay. He couldn't understand why Lund would blow the opportunity mentioned in the file after graduating from Wisconsin. He obviously had talent and the desire. What happened? *That it happened* was the hook that would snare his catch.

———

Michael Lund sat at a small, round table in the back of Mickey's under one of the few lights bright enough to read by. A copy of *Twin Cities Reader* and a near-empty glass of tap beer on the table were his only company. One foot kept time on the wooden floor to "Light My Fire" playing on the jukebox. The song was one of many oldies from the late sixties through the seventies that the owner of the pub kept on the box. Students, faculty, university staff and the regulars from the neighborhood never bitched about the play list. The vintage jukebox, on free-play, was a moneymaker for Mickey. It made everyone stay longer and drink more.

Lund leaned back and scratched the back of his head. His thick hair wasn't long nor was it a business cut. Like his hair, most of his collegiate features had stayed with him. He tapped his ring impatiently against the cold and now empty glass, and checked his watch again.

The place was nearly empty except for a handful of male students getting a head start on their weekend drinking and two neighborhood regulars sipping beer and smoking at the bar as they mumbled at each other. Trendy old neon signs and posters on the walls added to the atmosphere. Lund liked the place. It reminded him of his hangouts when he was at Wisconsin. It even smelled the same.

"Year Of The Cat" followed the Door's tune. He began to suspect Kick would turn out to be just a brain picker wanting the latest theories on terrorism, serial killers or gang violence. This 'making a wish come true' *was* probably bullshit. It was Friday! He was finished with the class load and office hours for the week and he was ready to get home. He and Caroline had plans.

"No, thank you," he said to the waitress as she held up his empty glass and smiled. "When Al sings the last "Cat", I'm outta here."

As he put a tip on the table and bent down to pick up his leather bag, a man leaning over his table suddenly blocked the light overhead. The details of the face were hard to distinguish until the stranger straightened and moved slightly back and away from the fixture.

"Mr. Lund, I'm John Kick. I apologize for being late. I don't have a tardy slip."

The handshake was awkward, quick and extra firm.

"I just gave up on you."

"I would make a terrible student, wouldn't I?"

Michael watched as the agent pulled out a chair and sat down. He looked like he was in his late forties, slightly overweight, tall and tired. A small roll of flesh pushed out from above his white collar. His cranberry and blue tie went well with his dark gray suit. He looked like a salesman ready to have lunch.

"I don't have time for games," said Michael. "What can I do for you?" Michael waved the waitress away as she approached the table again.

Kick checked Michael's hair and eyes. "I can appreciate your rush," he said as he adjusted his chair closer to the table. "The daily grind can get to be pretty heavy, can't it? There has to be more than this, right?"

Michael was still and silent.

"Let me get to the point. And let me start by saying the Bureau and I truly appreciate your time," Kick continued. He folded his large hands together on the table and leaned in. Michael held his position, waiting.

"Fourteen years ago you applied to work for the Federal Bureau of Investigation. Apparently you saw something in the Bureau that appealed to you. Service to your country . . . and some adventure, too, I presume. Maybe you knew you had what it took to share in triumphs of protecting America from its enemies . . . outside and inside this country. Have I rung any bells, Michael?"

Lund didn't respond.

"It certainly wasn't the money, was it? Regardless, you were accepted. In fact, if you didn't know it, you were considered a star candidate."

Michael lowered his chin as Kick fiddled with a cigar he pulled from his coat pocket.

"Then for some reason, you pulled out just before you

were to go into training. And now, zipping way into the future, I understand you are still an assistant professor at the university." Kick emphasized the word 'assistant'. "And you have been an assistant professor here at U of M for the past how many years? It seems like a nice, safe place, but your salary is just a little more than what my niece makes teaching high school in Florida."

Both men stared directly into each other eyes. Kick leaned in further. Lund felt his jaws tense up and otherwise didn't move.

"It's logical to wonder how long it will be before you become a professor, even an associate . . . with tenure."

Kick didn't wait for a response. Michael motioned to the waitress and held up two fingers.

"Let's look at it this way." Kick's voice softened. "If I could guarantee that you could be the envy of the university faculty, more than likely gain a promotion, and at the same time earn triple your current salary in six months, would you be interested? If you were given the chance to see what you walked out on fourteen years ago, would you listen to an offer from the Bureau?"

Michael took a sip of his fresh beer. Kick sat back and watched the waitress return to the bar. "Very cute."

"How could I possibly be of value to the FBI?" asked Michael. "I just teach."

"I don't have to tell you that there's more threat to our country right now than ever before."

"Common knowledge."

"Yes, but you know more about domestic terrorism, radical and criminal groups than most in the country. You teach criminology so you know it from an intellectual point of view. But you also go after your research like you're in the trenches. You know and comprehend the reality of threats to this country from both sides."

"I would say that would merely be of limited value to the FBI."

"It would be quite valuable . . . if we were dealing with intellectual criminals."

"Are you? Is this country?"

"Possibly."

"Possibly what? Possibly intellectual? Or possibly criminal?"

"Intellectual, and we suspect criminal." Kick shifted back and forth on the hard chair.

"Come on. You mean to tell me that the FBI, with a two billion-dollar plus budget and twelve thousand agents, has met its intellectual match? That's crap."

"What large company or organization doesn't occasionally go outside of itself to utilize particular expertise? Your university is a perfect example. With all the brainpower here, and the huge staff, it still can't do everything. General Motors, IBM, even the President. We all need a little outside help now and then."

"So what are we talking about here? A religious cult or private militia computer hackers trying to break into government files?" Michael took a long drink of his beer and crossed his legs. Kick watched the body language.

"Recently, I read a piece you published not too long ago," said Kick. "It was called, 'When Cults Turn Criminal'. It's been read at the Bureau. You also wrote a piece a year before 9/11 about possible threats to the United States coming out of the Middle East. I don't think many people read that one."

"That's interesting."

"More than interesting. The conclusions you reached

on the religious cult and white supremacist group examples are invaluable. You may have a better read on these warped bastards than we do. You're a hell of a detective, Michael."

The praise was deserved. Michael prided himself on his methods and the amount of research on each project he decided to tackle. Risks meant better data. And better data bore better conclusions.

Michael held up two more fingers as the waitress passed by again and scooted his chair closer to the table. Three new customers came through the front door and settled on stools at the bar. Music continued from the jukebox.

"I'm not talking about computer hackers," said Kick. "Although the Internet plays a part in this situation."

"And what situation would that be?"

"Four months ago, one of our agents in St. Louis was online at home. In fact he's online most of the time. It's his job to constantly scour the Internet, searching for any Web site, chat room, bulletin board, etc. that might indicate a possible threat, large or small, to any citizen or the government of this country. Hey, this is a real growth area of the Bureau's business."

"There are dozens of Web sites and blogs out there set up by hate groups, militia organizations, the KKK, you name it . . . and they're all out in the open. Bright as daylight! Come on down!"

"We know. Everyone knows. And we monitor these groups and their Web sites twenty-four hours a day. It's the ones in the shadows that we are concerned about." Kick leaned in. "It's the ones who don't send their crap into cyberspace, who don't publish a newsletter or hold public rallies. It's the ones who are subtle, cunningly shy, but have a deadly agenda . . . like a sniper in tall grass. He's there and he isn't."

"Any *one* in particular?"

"Yes. Our agent ran across a chat room called "White Straight Arrow". Lots of common talk about terrorism, the World Trade Center attack, protecting our borders, immigration, gays, blacks, and on and on . . . many people offering their opinions on all of this stuff and more.

"He's been following this "White Straight Arrow" and has kept up correspondence for more than a month now. He concluded, and the company agrees, that one person is initiating all of this 'Arrow' dialogue stuff. A guy by the name of Jesse Ford is at the center of it. He operates out of a large, secluded ranch in northeastern Oregon."

"So what's so special about what this Jesse Ford does online? What is the hook that has the Bureau's interest? There are thousands of chat rooms and bulletin boards with thousands of messages and chats going on every day on every kind of topic you can think of. There is a ton of radical stuff on the net. It grows every day."

"This guy sounds different. He is different. He's smart. He's persuasive. He seems racist and militant, and we think he's beginning to recruit a racist, militant army using the Web."

"Are you serious?"

Kick nods immediately. "Listen. His public messages and dialog are really questions to anyone willing to read them and write back. He invites opinions about blacks, Arabs, Asians, Hispanics, and Jews, even gays. He leads people to discuss government conspiracy theories and the decline of freedoms. Select people who reply with bigoted responses are then contacted privately by Ford using e-mail."

"How do you know?

Kick takes a quick gulp from his glass. "Don't play dumb here. You know we now have some special tools at our disposal that we are testing. Dammit! We need these for the sake of our security. Anyway, once Ford has these think-alike people hooked, they become candidates for his organization."

"What organization? Are we talking Neo-Nazi stuff here? White supremacists?"

"We're talking about an intelligent, former military officer who we believe is beginning to build and train a racist army. Small now, but growing, we think. We hear Ford is a huge man, physically, and he's cunning. He also has a son, Barry, and from what we know, he's almost a clone of his father. And there's his other son, Tommy, who we are told, is as crazy as a friggin' bronco and unstable, a potential threat to almost anyone he doesn't like. One more thing . . . Ford has a lot of money. He made out big time on a business deal and on an insurance policy when his wife was killed several years ago. In short, Jesse Ford is a wealthy racist grizzly bear with brains who could become a threat."

Michael sat back in his chair and ran his fingers through his hair. "So your agent has been tracking and interacting with this guy. And you think Ford is forming an elite hate group, or army?"

"Yes, for the third time. The Bureau is concerned that Ford, his sons and anyone they recruit could cause a serious situation, if they haven't already. We need to know more about them . . . soon. The Bureau can't afford any more intelligence disasters. Our goal here is to try to stop anything before it happens."

"You can't send a team in unless there's reasonable cause. What have you really got on them?" asked Michael. "What you've said so far is pretty vague." Michael pushed his beer glass forward and scooted his chair back.

"Trust me. We took a quick look and we feel we have enough to send, not a team, but just one in . . . a special *one*"

"Excuse me." Michael abruptly stood up and walked away from the table toward the restrooms. His calculated move gave him a minute to think without John Kick scrutinizing every blink, nod and shift. Once inside, Michael pulled his cell phone from his pants pocket and called home to see if Caroline was there. She had just walked in the door and greeted him with a big 'hello'. He told her he would be home a little later than he'd thought, but assured her they were still leaving at six o'clock for their weekend trip.

"Something very interesting is happening right now," he related. "I'll tell you all about it when I get home."

"Love you," was her response. "Can't wait to hear."

He returned to the table, thinking of what might be coming next from Kick. The first thought that came to mind made him a little bit nervous. He sat down prepared for the pitch? He told himself not to show any emotion.

"Why not send in the agent who's been working the case?" asked Michael.

He's a terrific agent, but he can't be the one. He is fifty and he's black." Both men chuckled.

"You're right. Twenty-four to thirty-eight is good, although that's changing. More women are now joining these kinds of groups now. How deep did your guy get in?"

"After joining in the chat room a couple of times, he corresponded privately with Ford and his son, Barry, six times by e-mail. Mostly small talk at first. But then Ford started asking carefully phrased questions, hoping to get revealing answers. Our agent played it well. He fed the Fords a mild racist theme and his knowledge of weapons. This lit the fire. Six days ago, our man received an invitation from Jesse Ford . . . by Fed Ex . . . to visit The Fort, as Ford called it."

Michael now sat at full attention as he listened to the details and contemplated the progressions of the pitch. Kick paused and finished his beer.

"Radical ideas are one thing . . . and America is a free country. But add weapons to those ideas and we are more than interested . . . follow?" said Kick. He pushed his beer glass to the side and leaned in toward Lund. "*Just* between you and me, we had our Portland office conduct a little research and guess what it found? Several new buildings have been built on the property. Electricity usage tripled in one year."

"Not a crime."

"Three new water wells were drilled. Federal Express and UPS make deliveries to Ford's ranch every week. Who knows what kind of stuff is in those packages."

"You guys *have* been busy. Still not a crime or reason to go in, Mr. Kick."

There was a large explosion on the Ford's property about a month ago. It was called into the county sheriff's office by Ford's closest neighbor . . . several miles away. Propane tank explosion was the answer given. After that, Portland decided to get a little more hi-tech and take a closer look. Agents managed to get a long distance look at what they believe is a shooting range . . . excuse me, a mock battlefield . . . right in the middle of his four thousand acres. They've observed vehicles with plates from seven different states enter the compound during the past two months. Aerial photos indicated . . . "

"I get the picture," interrupted Michael. "Pretty classic. And the way they recruit online . . . ."

"Right! We're not dealing with a bunch of skinheads, or a band of sixty-year-old high school dropouts with shotguns, mean dogs and shit on their boots who want to terrorize anyone who's not white. What we've uncovered here is a potentially dangerous racist group, an organization with brains, money, a threatening agenda and a unique way of recruiting the cream of the crop, so to speak.

"You said that five times," said Michael.

"Hey, this is new territory. We need to see what's going on inside. That's why I'm here, Michael." Kick caught his breath.

"I'm listening."

"We would like you to start a dialogue with The Fort."

Michael stretched his legs under the table and folded his arms across his mid-section.

"Continue."

"We would provide you with copies of all the correspondence between Ford and our St. Louis man. You would see from those how he gained their confidence and what the tone has been. We don't care how you do it, as long as you stay connected to the Fords . . . and eventually accept their invitation and get in." Kick hailed the waitress for two more draws. "We will set you up with a new computer and a separate Internet connection, in case he corresponds again through e-mail. We will provide you with all the known information on Ford, his sons and The Fort that we have. There's not a great deal more data at this point. And that's why the Bureau needs someone to go in. Someone like you."

The waitress replaced their empty glasses with full ones. Kick gave the waitress a twenty and said it should take care of the last couple of rounds. He took a gulp and sat the glass down.

"You know how to use firearms," the agent said. "We will train you further . . . as far as you want to go. But we don't anticipate that you will be in a defensive situation during your mission. So, what do you think, Michael?"

"I'm married," Michael said without hesitation. "I wasn't fourteen years ago. We've been talking about having a baby. And . . . "

"Hey, we're not talking about a life-long career here," said Kick. "You gave up that idea a long time ago. The Bureau only wants you to correspond with the Fords, get on the inside for a short time and let us know what the hell's going on. Find out who is there and what their objectives are. What kind of firepower do they have and so on. Think of this as a summer research sabbatical out west, only without your wife. If all goes according to plan you'll be right back here ready for the Gopher's first kickoff of the season."

"And how much does this summer job pay?"

"I thought you'd never ask." Kick laid his unlit cigar in the clean ashtray, folded his hands and leaned his elbows on the table. "We estimate the entire operation would last about two months, maybe a little longer once you get linked up with the Fords. You can't seem too eager to get in. Ford's no dummy. But you can't take forever either.

If you can take them up on their invitation by the end of your semester that's fine. Early June would work, too. We are open to however you want to play it. We just can't wait too long."

"And the pay?"

"The pay. For your service, the Bureau is willing to pay you three times your current annual salary. One lump payment."

"Gross or net?"

"I'm afraid the IRS is still a fact of life. But don't just think of the payoff in terms of money. You have the chance to experience something you've probably wanted to do for the past third of your life. Not many people get a chance to fulfill their dream . . . and without any risk of losing what you already have. Once the operation is over, you can come back and leave it behind. I am offering you the road not taken."

Lund didn't blink as Caroline flashed through his mind. What would she say? She was a risk taker. She had the spirit that would give the unknown a chance. That's one of the reasons he was attracted to her in the first place.

"Think of the millions of people out there who wish they'd at least tried something way back when, but never did," said Kick. "How many people would love to be in a movie, once . . . fly a plane, once . . . or be an FBI agent, just once?"

Michael watched the agent's eyes and mouth. He looked for a dark side to the offer and its salesman. Kick's pitch was good and he'd hit most of the hot buttons. And he knew Kick knew he had been turned on. The agent pulled a small card from his shirt pocket and set it next to his glass.

"You understand that I'll need to think about it."

"Of course. Do you have any concerns that I can help you with?"

"None now."

"As you think things over, think about how valuable the experience will be. And about how it could advance your career. Even think about the money if you want. It takes a lot of it today, especially when you have a kid." Kick pushed the card across the table. "I have to fly back to Washington tonight. Call me at the second number on the card about eight o'clock your time Sunday night."

Michael stood, pushed the card into his pocket and picked up his bag from the floor. His knees were stiff and he was feeling the beers now. "That should be enough time."

Kick scooted his chair back, rose and offered his hand. "Thank you for your time, Professor Lund . . . by Sunday night then."

"Eight o'clock." Michael put on his sunglasses as he walked out of Mickey's. His step was quick as he headed toward his car, parked in a near-by campus parking lot. He was anxious to tell Caroline about his day.

————

Special agent John Kick sat back down and stretched his legs under the table. He pulled a chrome lighter from his shirt pocket and lit his cigar. He looked at his watch and then waved to the waitress with his empty glass. "Scotch this time." A circle of smoke floated above him.

————

Fourteen years earlier Michael Lund had wanted to be an agent for the FBI or a similar security organization more than anything else. Crime, criminals and the fringe elements of American society had always fascinated him. Logic and other skills needed to identify that fringe and to solve the crimes were deeply intriguing. His parents didn't try to limit his interest in these areas, but neither did they encourage it. When there was discussion about college choices, degrees and good career choice options, Mr. and Mrs. James Lund would steer it toward civil engineering, architecture, international business or finance. He listened, but fantasized about becoming an ace field man and working on a case like the one Kick just offered. He investigated career opportunities at the FBI, CIA, US Marshall Service and the DEA, trying to decide what agency would be the most fulfilling. His research led him to decide on the FBI. The agency's goals and his seemed better matched. He applied during his senior year in college, was accepted and then scheduled to begin training soon after graduation.

Twelve days after Michael's college graduation, his father died of a sudden heart attack at the age of 57. The event proved to be devastating to Michael's mother and extremely sad for Michael. He both admired and loved his father dearly.

Michael's mother never said it, but he knew she hoped he would stay close to home, at least for a while, until she was able to adjust to a life without her husband. This weighed heavily on him. He wouldn't be able to stick with the time-table initially laid out by his eventual employer. Maybe he could delay his training. These thoughts gave him fleeting moments of doubt about the FBI all together.

His decision was further challenged when close friends of his parents and even his own friends brought up his possible FBI career. These people, whose opinions were not solicited, but were respected, would ask him why anyone would want to be underpaid and overworked for the dubious pleasure of devoting their life to the worst America had to offer. He had also just met Caroline, and they fell in love. She encouraged him to do what he thought best for himself and his future. She said she would always support whatever his decision might be.

He was torn and tortured trying to decide what was best. It was hell. Maybe they were right. He pulled the plug on his career with the Federal Bureau of Investigation and entered graduate school in Columbus, Ohio. A short time later, he and Caroline were married.

Some days he knew his decision to walk away had been the right one. On others . . .

ww *chapter 4*

Michael and Caroline Lund arrived at the Riverside Bed & Breakfast in Stillwater a little after nine o'clock Friday night, an hour later than they had told Mrs. Kirsch, the owner, to expect them. Michael unintentionally drove slower as their discussion of the unexpected proposal from the FBI was continuous during the drive.

Miriam Kirsch was seventy-four and a widow who usually retired early with her herb tea, a hardcover book and the late news on WCCO-TV. Caroline offered the explanation that the traffic through the cities was much heavier than they had anticipated. But the owner wasn't much interested in big city gridlock. She was however, genuinely glad to see them again. Her keen eyes inspected the handsome couple. Her soft voice welcomed her guests into her home once again.

This was the Lund's fourth stay and Mrs. Kirsch had grown to enjoy their company. On their last visit, she said that they seemed a perfect couple, then, she asked if they planned to have children. She had three of her own scattered around the country. Her guests' responses were polite, but vague.

"We're still young." Michael would commit to no more than this.

"We talk about it all the time," added Caroline.

Caroline loved the sense of family, as did Michael, and both looked forward to creating and raising a child. But they had decided to leave the time line open-ended. Both agreed that if their family included just one child it would make them just as happy as having more. Or at least that was what they decided to think for the time being.

Caroline's mother was thirty-seven when she gave birth to her only child and Caroline was approaching this age. Caroline and her parents had lived in a modest house on ten beautiful acres of land outside Crosslake, Minnesota. Caroline thought little of the remarks her parents would often make about how young most of her friends' parents seemed. It wasn't until her senior year in high school that she felt any fear about the aging process and how it seemed to be slowly changing her mother. Although her father was three years older, he always looked healthier and acted immortal. Her mother passed away of breast cancer at 61. He survived her by only eight years.

The combined three deaths of two fathers and one mother in their families only strengthened Caroline's and Michael's commitment to each other. And although the passing of their parents was something sad they shared, it gave them a positive outlook on their own lives, apart and together.

Michael and Caroline didn't spend weekends in Stillwater during the summer months when the tourists were thick. They liked the solitude of the village when it was quiet, and the setting near the scenic St. Croix River that separated Minnesota from Wisconsin. Spring and autumn, especially early October, when the fall colors were spectacular, were their favorite times.

This trip had been planned as a belated celebration of

Michael's 36th birthday. Now the weekend would include a decision about the FBI's offer.

———

Caroline and Michael lay nude under layers of flannel sheets and cotton blankets. They had left the lacy curtains on the tall windows pinned back. The street lamps of Stillwater softly lit their small room as their hands and arms, glided over smooth warm skin. Their motions produced ripples in the white cover. Caroline's long blonde hair swept across Michael's chest. Michael rolled and responded with kisses on her flat stomach.

"Your skin is wonderful," he whispered. His lips moved to her shoulder, then to her ear and finally to her closed eyes. "I love you."

Michael's firm strokes down Caroline's back and legs transmitted the passion he had felt for her since they first met. Both enjoyed giving and receiving pleasure.

Their legs intertwined as their bodies joined. "I love you, too."

———

Caroline was first out of bed. Michael propped himself up to watch her walk through the beam of morning sunlight coming through their second floor window. She pulled on a clean pair of French cut underwear from her overnight bag and the black jeans she had thrown over the wooden rocking chair the night before. Michael exaggerated his stare as he watched her dress. She played along, taking her time as she slowly slipped on a silk T-shirt and white pullover sweater. She sniffed the air. "Muffins!"

"Are you sure you don't want to come back to bed?" Michael asked. "It's a lot warmer in here."

Caroline smiled. "Do you think Mrs. Kirsch heard us last night?"

"I don't think she would mention it if she did. I'm sure she has a lot of stories she could tell about her guests."

Caroline put on her socks and cross-trainers as she sat on the edge of the bed. She stood, pulled the covers off Michael with one yank and grinned. "See you downstairs, birthday boy."

———

They took the scenic route north on Highway 95 to Taylor Falls after a breakfast of blueberry muffins, scrambled eggs, oatmeal, juice and coffee fixed by Miriam.

"Are there any more questions you should ask this Kick guy before really deciding?" asked Caroline.

"Like what?"

"Like, what if you get to this Fort place and something goes wrong. What would happen if they found out you were working undercover for the FBI?"

"That won't happen. How could it? The sense I get from Kick is that the Bureau just wants me to get in, get the details of what's going on inside the compound and then get out. I would be briefed thoroughly before I went in and there would be contingency plans if something unplanned happens inside. But again, that's not going to happen."

"You don't think the FBI plans to arrest anyone, or try to break up the group?"

"Who knows? At this point they haven't broken any laws that anyone knows of. I think what I would find when I get there, is a bunch of weekend warriors only with no tolerance or compassion for anyone other than people like themselves."

"So you don't think there's any danger? And the assignment would be finished by the end of summer?"

"Sooner if I can help it. Unless there's something Kick isn't telling me, I don't see any real danger. Scary, yes. I admit I would be scared. But I really think I can do the job. I get in, learn all I can and get out. I tell the Bureau what I know and that's that."

"Is Kick telling you everything? Do you trust him?"

"He's a little cynical, like me, but I think he's being up front with me."

"Why is he cynical?"

"You get that way when you're in law enforcement for a long time . . . or teaching for that matter. Right? I don't think he's promising anything he can't deliver."

"You really want to do this, don't you Michael?"

"Even though it would be scary, I know I can pull it off. This is a one-time-only chance to experience what I let go of years ago. This is something I think I need to do."

Caroline put her hand on his knee. "Then, you should do it."

———

John Kick answered his telephone at four minutes past nine, Washington time. He satisfied several last-minute questions Michael threw at him. Caroline got on the line and asked a couple, too, just to make sure Kick understood that Michael was not in this venture alone. He even agreed to four times Lund's annual salary when Michael pressured him, although it was contingent on the approval of William Stacey. Kick expected the Bureau's new recruit to be well worth the money.

chapter 5

The same orange light of sunrise that swept across the Wallowa Mountains also bathed The Fort and the exspansive piece of land it sat on. It penetrated a window highlighting a single bed and touched the face of Michael Lund. He lay on his back with a heavy cotton blanket that was pulled up to his bare shoulders. With arms folded across his chest and hands interlocked, his eyes focused straight above somewhere beyond the high beam ceiling of the bunkhouse. Michael knew he should make two more secret telephone calls soon. One would be to Caroline whom he hadn't seen in fifty-four days.

He had arrived at The Fort almost eight weeks ago. Lund certainly didn't want to arouse anyone's suspicion the moment he got there, having followed the exact instructions Jesse Ford had given him two weeks before that. The instructions had included a list of items that he were forbidden to bring, such as a cellular telephone, camera, tape recorder, a laptop or pocket computer, illegal drugs and hard liquor. A favorite gun was OK. A bible, other books and prescribed medications were also on the acceptable list.

Upon arrival, three men immediately and thoroughly searched his ten-year-old Chevy Blazer, with scuffed Missouri plates, after he parked in front of the main house.

Lund was a little surprised that there wasn't a guard at the outer gate he had to pass through before he got to the house. Nor did he see dogs or a fence of any type securing the front of the compound. It seemed pretty laid back, except for the three fellows who quickly appeared as he drove up.

His truck and all of his travel bags were thoroughly examined. Lund was taken aback when one of the men asked him to remove his clothes. He was allowed to leave on his underwear and the large metal cross and gold chain that hung from his neck. He stood there in the late morning sun, almost naked as his clothes were squeezed, turned inside out and shaken. They also went through his billfold, at which point he was told they would keep his ring of keys and park his truck in a secure location on the property.

Once the search was completed and Lund put on his clothes, one of the men waved to the front on the house. Jesse Ford emerged, followed by Barry Ford, who both warmly greeted their newest guest. There was small talk and a lot of subtle evaluation on both sides. Finally, Lund was invited to join him in a private dinner with his sons that night.

Michael played the evening well and knew exactly the story of his fictitious life he had to tell and sell. He was comfortable using the name of St. Louis resident, Ted Grimes. He was confident he passed the test. A long prayer preceded the excellent meal.

Lund was assigned to the compound's "white" bunkhouse, a simple wooden structure whose exterior was painted the color of its name. The interior was lined with tongue and groove pine and was large enough to house eight residents in moderate comfort. Each "guest" was provided a single bed, a lamp and a dresser. His living area was flanked on both sides by six-foot-high portable partitions. Privacy was adequate. They shared a large bathroom containing a pair of sinks, stools and showers.

Jesse Ford called the white house residents "freshmen"— they needed to be closely evaluated and tested before becoming true Straight White Arrows.

"Distinguish yourself," Jesse Ford would say. "Prove your worthiness. America needs you."

"Honorable comrades" were promoted to the "blue" house, which had more creature comforts, including a small entertainment area with a stereo system and television. There, six men currently shared space built to house ten. The two bunkhouses were a hundred feet apart and were about four hundred feet from the Command Center. Another bunkhouse was under construction nearby. One of Lund's bunkmates told him it was being built for couples. He also told him two single women were quartered in the main house with Jesse, Barry and Tommy.

Michael shared the white house with four others. He felt certain there was an informant for the Fords among his mates, although he could still only guess which one it was. He speculated the family had been scrutinizing his movements and conversations continuously from the moment he drove into The Fort. He figured this was how the Fords decided who could stay and who would be leaving shortly after they arrived. Fifty-five days, tomorrow. So far, so good,

Michael turned his head on the pillow and checked the clock on the nearby dresser. It was a little before seven. His eyes returned to the ceiling as he rubbed his hand across the beard he'd started growing the day after he accepted the assignment from John Kick. The growth was now soft. He wondered what Caroline would think if she could see him with it. *Touching her body would be wonderful at this moment.*

"Better get your ass out of the sack," snorted one of his roommates, walking stiffly toward the bathroom. Gene Anderson was a stocky young man with a butch haircut and a raspy voice. He was always the first one out of bed. He had bunked with Michael since the beginning. "Better wake your lazy asses up," he repeated to everyone. " Don't you remember? Last night Tommy said there was going to be a special announcement today. Anybody wanna guess what it's about?"

Michael took the bathroom second and showered. His body was somewhat leaner than when he'd left Minneapolis. Physical training, with and without weapons, day and night, was the routine here. His face and upper body were deeply tanned from prolonged exposure to the sun at this higher elevation. He looked forward to the daily sanctuary of the private shower stall, lingering under the warm water for several minutes. He knew it was the safest place to think and plan.

He dressed for the unseasonably warm northeast Oregon morning pulling on jeans, a black tee shirt and hiking boots. The eastern side of the Wallowa Mountains was as pretty a place as he had seen. Summer here was usually cool and dry, just the opposite of the Midwest. He figured he'd probably have to change clothes twice today depending on what kind of training was scheduled—once for sure because of an eagerly awaited "fun night" trip into Baker City that evening.

As he and Anderson approached the small dining hall, they noted the daily activity board that hung next to the entrance. 'TBA' was written on it instead of the usual daily agenda.

"What did I tell ya, Ted," said Anderson. "I knew something big was going to happen today."

"As long as it doesn't spoil tonight," said Michael.

"You're ready for some serious fun, too, aren't ya? Let's

see . . . It's been at least three weeks since you and I've been to town."

"That's too long for me."

Gene threw his head back and inhaled as they entered. "Jesus, does that smell good." Blue and white house residents ate their meals at the same time, with at least two of the Fords joining them. Jesse greeted them with a raised coffee cup as the screen door closed with a bang. Four other men were just sitting down at one of the three long pine tables. Their plates were stacked high with pancakes and sausages from the buffet table at the front of the mess hall. Alice, a short, older woman and the cook, followed right behind the men with a pot of coffee and a pitcher of orange juice. She smiled and replied, "Nothing but the best for you boys," every time someone complimented her cooking.

Seated at the other table were Tracy and Celeste, the two women recruits who stayed in the main house. Barry sat across from them and looked up as Michael and Gene walked to the buffet table.

"Great morning, isn't it?" he asked.

"None finer," replied Gene.

"And a great breakfast once again, Alice," said Barry over his shoulder.

"Nothing but the best for you, Mr. Ford."

Michael filled his plate with pancakes and fruit and sat down next to Barry.

"Good morning," said Tracy.

"Mornin', Tracy . . . Celeste." Smiles were exchanged.

Celeste and Tracy looked as though they could have been sisters. But they weren't. They both had blonde hair, similar lean builds, and looked to be in their late twenties. Their eyes set them apart, though. Celeste's were warm and complimented her slightly softer looking face. Tracy's rarely blinked. Her look was more intense, street-wise and impulsive. Michael noticed Tracey's wedding band. And Celeste wore a three-inch silver cross attached to a thin leather cord around her neck.

Michael's other bunkhouse mates walked in, filled their plates and sat down at the table with him.

"Now that we're all here," Jesse said as he stood at the front of the dining hall, "I've got a special announcement to make. Something you've been wanting to hear for some time now, I'm sure."

Knives, forks and conversations were suddenly silent. All eyes were focused on their leader. Barry got up and whispered something to Alice. When she left the building, he positioned himself at the end of one of the tables that had a cardboard box on it.

Jesse's posture was one of commanding confidence as he looked intently at each of the comrades before speaking again.

"As you know, thinking alike as we do, sharing the same goals for our America, we are here to train. And we train in order to better serve and protect our country, our freedom and our way of life. Some of you are fairly new to The Fort. Others have been friends of ours for a longer time. All of you have trained hard. We are proud of you. America should be proud of you."

"Me, too." came a loud voice from the doorway. Tommy let the screen door slam shut and walked to the back of the room. He held a rifle loosely in his right hand with the barrel pointing downward. His boot heels hit the wooden floor, cutting through the silence. It wasn't unusual for Michael to see him with a rifle in hand or a handgun strapped to his side. Tommy propped the weapon against the wall and stood there with one boot resting on a chair. Jesse gave him a look that meant there would be a conversation between them later.

"Tommy is proud of you, too." said Barry to cover the awkward moment.

"It's time to use some of what we have all been training for." continued Jesse. " The Fort's leadership has identified a situation that has deteriorated to such a degree that action needs to be taken. This country continues to be infiltrated and overrun by foreigners whose only goal is to literally destroy America or bleed it dry by taking away our freedom, our jobs, our heritage. *And* America continues to be assaulted by those *already* in this country whose goal is to slowly eliminate the white race through their politics, inter-marriage and criminal behavior. We intend to take some action! We must take action. We are going to send these garbage people a serious message."

All eyes and ears were glued to the big man in front of them. Barry stepped forward and stood closer to his father. "Forty-eight hours from now," Barry said, "a force made up of three blues and two white freshman, to be chosen from among you this morning, will leave The Fort for a special assignment. Tommy and I will be joining you on this mission. In general, the operation relates to an American security situation some distance south of here. That's all I will tell you for now. The five of you will report to the rifle range at o-nine-hundred this morning for more special training. Just before we leave, you will receive a detailed briefing. We will return to The Fort in five days if all goes well. And we expect it will."

Michael's appetite vanished with the announcement. His stomach tightened. His mouth became dry. He'd known there was a chance it would come. He feared it from the beginning. If chosen, would he be required to seriously hurt someone? Kill someone? This situation meant making his first telephone call tonight even more crucial.

Michael learned quickly from the beginning that the Fords

took their mission of preserving white America seriously. He had overheard from others at the compound that there had been two previous operations. Where, and at what level of damage, he had not yet learned. Unquestioning loyalty and silence were the oaths taken when a recruit accepted Jesse Ford's invitation to become part of The Fort. Michael quickly assessed the odds of being chosen at forty percent, dependent upon whether Tracy and Celeste were in the pool of freshman.

Jesse walked to the table with the box and pulled two small American flags on wooden stands from it. He held them above his head and walked toward the reserve's table. Michael took a deep breath and lowered his chin.

"All of you have trained well. All of you have been considered for this mission. But only two whites are needed and only two will have the chance to distinguish themselves in the coming days. Our selection was based on assessing specific skills required to make this mission a success. For those not chosen, your chance will come soon."

Jesse reached over Michael's shoulder and placed one of the flags on the table in front him. The presenter's hand remained gripped around the flag's wooden base. Michael looked up. Tracey looked directly into his eyes and nodded.

"The first freshman chosen to join us tomorrow is . . . " Jesse slowly slid the flag away from Michael until it was within a few inches of Tracey. "Congratulations."

"Thank you." Tracey smiled proudly as she took the flag and raised it the air with both hands for everyone to see. Most of the men chose to look at her tight-fitting T-shirt instead.

"And the second one goes to . . . " Jesse said as he walked around the reserve's table. He looked at each one at the table, then placed the flag in front of Michael. "Congratulations, Ted."

Michael cleared his throat, giving him an extra second to prepare his response. "And *I* thank you. I will do my best for our country."

There were a few seconds of applause before the recruits attacked their food. Barry walked to the front of the room. Tracey grinned at Michael and offered a raised coffee cup in a toast. Michael lifted his cup, too, but could barely swallow the sip of hot brew. His stomach tightened even more as he looked at the flag again, fully realizing what it meant.

"Did you notice that these flags only have forty-eight stars on them?" asked Tracey.

"In fact, all of the flags at The Fort have just 48."

Michael barely reacted. His mind had jumped ahead to tonight, composing what he would say when he attempted to called Raymond Stacey, his telephone contact at the FBI.

"For anyone who is interested, the trip to Eagle River to-night is still on," said Barry.

Loud cheering and clapping followed the announcement. "Yahoo!" yelled Tommy from the back.

"There's a slight change in the plan, however. Because of the departure for some of us in forty-eight hours, Tommy and you will be going into town earlier, at seventeen hun-dred hours. I won't be joining you. My father and I have some business in Pendleton and we will meet you back here no later than twenty-three hundred. Remember, The Fort and this mission are not to be discussed with anyone."

"Everyone stand," ordered Tommy. "Everyone quiet."

The men and two women faced a large American flag at the front of the dining room. Next to it was a customized flag the same size sporting a large white arrow on a blue background with the words 'The Fort' printed on it. Jesse took a deep breath.

"Nothing we do here today or tomorrow is in opposition

to our founding father's laws and intentions," Jesse spoke. "We have the right to bear arms. We have the right to defend our country and protect our families from those who invade America from the outside, or try to destroy it from within, regardless of whether they attempt it by subtle or overt means. We are here to fight the liberal plot of those who want to make America, our homeland, the melting pot of the world. It is happening to Europe at a fast pace right before our eyes. The Anglo Europe we knew is nearing its end. We will not let America follow the same path. You and I think alike. We believe in the same things and we will protect our America as one united force. This is the creed of The Fort."

"This is the creed of The Fort," echoed sixteen voices.

"This is what I believe."

"This is what I believe."

———

"Don't shoot to kill," yelled Tommy. "Aim for the ankles and knees. They'll still be alive, but it'll be the last time the little bastards try to sneak into our country."

Tommy and Barry coached and commended each of the five specially-selected recruits as they scurried from position to position in the rifle training area. The unit of two whites, three blues and the Ford brothers wiped sweat away from their eyes as they aimed their rifles and fired low at the dummies far in front of them. All had practiced these maneuvers before, but only in the dark using night vision scopes on their long-range weapons.

Michael hung on every word Barry and Tommy said. From what he had heard so far, he deduced that the unit was going to carry out an operation somewhere along the U.S.-Mexican border. What kind of operation? Some of his questions were being answered right now on the training field. Shoot, cripple and frighten any Mexicans trying to get across. But don't kill them. The frightful message of "keep out of America" needed to be taken back home with them.

But exactly where would the operation be carried out? With all of the new border security being put into place, wouldn't they be taking a chance of being caught? Michael thought the answers might be found in the main house. Somehow, some-time today, he had to try to get into that house . . . without knocking. He had been in the main hallway a half-dozen times and had seen Tommy in front of or close to the two over-sized wooden doors. The room behind them, what Michael pegged as the communications room, should yield clues, if not hard answers to the details of their pending mission.

Michael looked at his watch and figured he had a mat-ter of hours to learn as much ashe could about the plan. The knowledge that he would be departing in about forty hours to take part in a violent, bloodletting operation sat like a brick in his stomach. How could he avoid going? Fake illness? Simply vanish from The Fort before morning? He didn't have long to come to grips with it all.

"Move your ass!" yelled Tommy. The command brought Michael's attention back to the training at hand. He posi-tioned himself at another location nearby. Tommy followed close behind and anchored himself just ten feet away. More dummies were in sight. Michael quickly locked his eye onto a dummy and fired. Accurate, as always.

"You bagged him good," said Tommy. "Just do the same when we get down there."

"Down where?" asked Michael.

"Can't tell ya yet. Let's just say we've got some good friends down there who think like we do and are gonna show us a secret location to do our business."

Michael's production of sweat doubled as he aimed and fired again. He yearned for a shower and his sanctuary.

"Remember," shouted Barry to the team, " the big difference between today and the real thing is that it will be dark . . . and it will be hotter than hell."

Barry looked at his watch and called Tommy to his side where they conferred, heads bent. Barry then turned and walked away from the group toward the main house.

"That's it," said Tommy. "Clean your rifles and check them back into the workshop. Then get ready to get loose. We're going to Baker City tonight! The train leaves at five o'clock."

The windowless workshop was really the weapons room where a vast array of guns from simple shotguns to high caliber assault rifles where stockpiled and maintained. Lund also identified many illegally modified rifles and saw materials and equipment on shelves he knew were for making explosives. The special room was part of a large barn that housed several of the Ford's vehicles not far from the blue bunkhouse. The entrance to the shop was fitted with a heavy steel door that remained locked at all times unless work was in progress. Only Barry, Tommy and a few Blue recruits worked in the weapons room. Michael was only recently allowed inside the workshop. He knew what he saw there would be of great interest to the FBI and the ATF. Explosive devices, detonated by sophisticated remote control, were among Barry's pet projects. Guns and knives seemed to be Tommy's specialties. Michael had seen Tommy use a favorite gun one time on several cats that roamed The Fort. "Population control," Tommy had explained, with a grin.

————

Michael made his move to penetrate the Ford house at 3PM. Barry's SUV was absent from its usual space in front of the house. Gone to fetch Papa Ford, he guessed. And the last he'd seen of Tommy was about 30 minutes earlier walking near the dining hall with Tracey. Just a little time and a little more luck were all he needed.

Slowly, Michael made his way toward the main house, casually glancing around as if he had no particular destination. He played it for the camera mounted high on the front of the house. He could hear faint voices far behind him from the bunkhouses, but he saw no one. He took careful note of the windows on the side of the house. Several were open because of the unusual heat. There was no indication that anyone was inside, although he knew there was a possibility Tommy would come into the house. If he did encounter him, he had a story he felt would work. It went something like, 'I knocked. In fact, I rang, too, but I guess you didn't hear me. I thought I might find you in the kitchen or something. Anyway, I thought I could offer some special help tomorrow on the mission. I'm only guessing here, but if southern Texas is our destination, I can help with the logistics. I used to live there.'

Michael had been there once. He visited the University of Texas at El Paso years ago as a guest lecturer. While there he spent four days with a rented car, a map and former colleague sightseeing in the Rio Grande area. Good enough.

Michael took a deep breath and visualized exactly what he must do in the next two to four minutes. He wrapped his fingers around the curved door handle and pushed the round latch down with his thumb. He added his other hand and pushed the thick wooden door open. It came freely with no creaking. His destination was the other side of the double doors on his right. Although his eyes and ears were on full alert, he tried to maintain a casual stance in case Tommy suddenly appeared. His story was ready on the tip of his tongue. He looked behind him as he approached the double doors to see if his boots had left any evidence. They hadn't. He tried the brass doorknob on the right. Locked! "Dammit," he whispered to himself.

Michael heard a door slam from what he thought was upstairs somewhere. A giggling voice followed, then Tommy's mumbling. Michael grabbed the left doorknob and twisted. It turned, and he was instantly inside the forbidden room. He left the door ajar just enough to see if anyone was coming. He heard footsteps quickly descending the staircase. Laughing voices sounded closer. From his sliver view he saw Tommy and Tracy, both without a stitch on, at the bottom of the stairs. Tommy pushed on Tracy's bare bottom, urging her forward as they hurried toward the open door at the end of the hall. Tracey turned and pulled Tommy inside the room. The door slammed shut.

Michael quietly closed the door and quickly surveyed the large comfortable looking room. Computers . . . LCD monitors, one showing a notice for newly arrived e-mail . . . surveillance monitors . . . books . . . desks with papers on them and mounted animal head-trophies made up the room's decor. A woman's portrait hung on one wall facing the largest of the desks. He needed to spend hours here. He calculated he had three minutes tops. A fax machine that started to churn out an in-coming transmission startled Lund, breaking his concentration. Should he read it? No. Let it be.

Michael carefully thumbed through a stack of papers next to one of the printers. A cursory look indicated various correspondence from across the country along with photographs of smiling men, and a few women, with and without guns. No time to digest further. His eyes scanned across the other desk as he leaned over it for a few seconds. The array of notes, letters and clippings was a distraction from his immediate objective. God! What a wealth of information! The insight. Invaluable research! Not now. The operation! Where were they going?

He walked toward a flat table under one of the east windows, careful to avoid being seen from outside. A large United States road map was taped to the surface. Three colored hilighters lay on top of the map. Michael traced the route from San Diego across the southern U.S. border to Brownsville, Texas. A transparent blue line highlighted the border from San Luis, south of Yuma, to Nogales to El Paso. Each town was circled. Written next to Yuma was "1075 miles."

Michael followed the blue line again with his finger and silently repeated the names of the three cities. He backed his way toward the double doors, trying to memorize everything he eyes focused on. Want to stay . . . but gotta go! I think I have enough.

The door at the end of the hall was still closed. The voices were wilder. All the better Michael thought as he quickly exited the command center and closed the door. He grabbed the door handle of the main door leading outside and pulled it open. He nearly tripped as he came face to face with Celeste who was about to enter. He stepped outside, blocking the doorway so she couldn't enter.

"Ted?"

Michael pulled the door shut quickly, softly. He looked at Celeste and put his index finger to his lips. It gave him an extra second to form a story.

"Hi," he whispered. "I should have knocked louder . . . I shouldn't have gone in."

"What?" Celeste took a step back and put her hands on her hips. She stared at him. Her eyes were soft blue and suspicious. "What are you doing here?"

"I needed to tell Tommy something. I knocked, but no one answered, so I opened the door. I took a couple of steps inside and then holy hell, I got a quick glimpse of Tommy and Tracy, well, kind of romping around in their birthday suits together in the doorway at the end of the hallway. They didn't see me or hear me, so I just hurried back out. It's none of my business. I guess I can ask him when we go into town tonight."

"I've gotten used to it," Celeste said. "It only happens when Jesse and Barry are gone."

"I see."

"Do you think I do that kind of stuff with him?"

"It's none of my business."

"Well, I don't," she said. "This place is a hell of a lot better than where I came from and I really like it here, but I don't do that kind of stuff. Don't repeat it, but the guy's a pri . . . never mind."

"Like I said, it's none of my business." Michael stepped away from the door. "Are you going in?"

"Like I said, I'm used to it."

Michael stepped off the porch and said he would see her later.

"Are you going into town tonight?" she asked

"I thought I might. How about you?"

"I think I will. Maybe we can have a beer together."

"Sure."

———

The barmaid brought two more pitchers of beer to their two tables. Gene Anderson was the first to refill his glass. He topped off Michael's and filled the empty glass Tracey pushed in front of him. Celeste's was tightly wedged between Michael and Tracey. Her pleasure was a gin and tonic that was nearly gone. Loud conversations and laughter mixed with the heavy smoke and country music from the jukebox.

The entire place was in a partying mood. The maid picked up two empty pitchers and several plates on which appetizers had once been piled. She took the money from Michael for the new pitchers and made her way through the shoulder-to-shoulder crowd gathered at the Time Out Sports Bar. Eagle River had been invaded by people from every small town in the area coming to have fun at the annual Eagle Rodeo.

Michael sipped his second beer while everyone else continued to gulp. He noticed Celeste began to slur her words as she started on her third drink. He pretended like this night was the party of the year and forced himself to interact with his comrades. But his mind was really reaching for the cellular telephone in a U.S. Post Office box four blocks away. The telephone and the key to a specific box had been arranged for him by the FBI before he left Minneapolis. Getting to the planted telephone the first time he made a call to Stacey over four weeks ago hadn't been a problem. He had found a way to get ten minutes by himself while in town with two others picking up a large quantity of frozen beef at a meat locker. No recruits from The Fort were allowed to go into Eagle River alone . . . groups of three or more, only. Needing to find a public bathroom 'quickly' then did the trick. But tonight, Tommy was trying to keep the whole group together the entire time. His excessive drinking and preoccupation with Tracey made his efforts less than effective, however. Celeste, too, might make a temporary escape a little difficult for Michael. She rode with him coming in and she sat by him at the table. She also touched him on the arm and leg several times when laughter was part of the conversation. She really didn't talk to anyone but him and now he felt she might be clinging to him all evening, and maybe beyond.

Tommy and the recruits all agreed they would drink for awhile at Time Out and then have dinner at the Pines Restaurant across the street. Michael glanced at a beer sign clock on the wall. He calculated he had less than two hours to make his call. He knew he had to keep his eyes and ears open for an opportunity. He would create one, if necessary.

"Gotta go to the little girl's room," whispered Tracey to everyone at the table. "Back in a minute."

"I'll go with you," added Celeste

They threaded their way through the dense crowd collecting stares from most of the men and some of the women as they passed by.

Michael quickly stood and pushed his chair under the table. "I'll meet you guys across the street in about twenty minutes."

"Where you goin'?" asked Tommy. "Don't tell me, I know. You're gonna walk around and look at the old buildings you think are so goddamn neat."

"You got it." Michael pulled a folded brochure from his back jean pocket and waved it. "Eagle River Historic District," he read aloud. "A walking tour. It's not just that all these buildings around here are old, it's the architecture and the history that took place inside and just outside of their walls. Anyone want to come along?" He already knew the answer.

"Hell, no," said one the other recruits. "Pass the beer."

"Twenty minutes." said Tommy as Michael walked away from the table and toward the front door.

Michael crossed Main Street and walked slowly in front of the Grand Eagle Hotel. He continued south past the Mint-Fox Building, rapidly picking up his pace once he was sure he could no longer be seen from the bar. He reached the U.S. Post Office on North Avenue, an extension of Main Street, in three minutes. He entered the empty public building, pulled the gold chain and the attached cross from around his neck and lifted it over his head. He held the top part of the brass ornament between his thumb and index finger of his right hand and pulled hard on one side of the bottom half at the same time with his left hand. The cross that appeared seamless snapped apart and one half became a key. He quickly inserted into the matching mailbox and opened the metal door. He pulled out a small cardboard box, opened it and turned on the power to the cell phone that was inside. Michael turned and faced the front entrance as he extended the short antennae. The telephone beeped a couple of times and the screen lit up. He punched one of the keys. A telephone number appeared on the readout screen, a temporary connection to Washington D.C.. He pushed "send" and moved slightly closer to the large front window to enhance transmission and reception, if possible. He could be seen if he was too close to it. His call to the FBI was carried across the country in a matter of a few seconds.

"Stacey here." He picked up half way into the second ring.

"Lund on this end. Can you hear me OK?"

"Sounds like you're next door. It's late. Good to hear from you. What's your situation?"

"It's later than you think and I've only got a minute." Lund's head kept moving, his eyes alert to anything that moved outside the large window. "I've been chosen for a mission. Either I've got to disappear or you've got to get me out of this mess somehow before we get there."

"Where's there?"

"We're scheduled to leave in 36 hours for the Mexican border. Barry and Tommy Ford, four others and me. Target practice on illegal Mexicans crossing over, I'm pretty sure. We'll be in two vehicles. A white Expedition and a silver conversion van. Weapons will probably be well-hidden in the van."

"Do you know the route?"

"Not positive, but a good guess is Interstate 84 and 15 south all the way to Yuma."

"What positions along the border?"

"I don't know. Could be anywhere from San Luis south of Yuma east as far as El Paso. They've got a guide who'll show them an unguarded position. And I don't want to be there. Got it?"

"Got it. Is all of your information documented somewhere at the compound?"

"Pretty much everything. This, other plans, correspondence, you name your evidence, it's all in what they call the command center . . . really just a big library in the house."

"Anything more on that weapons room you mentioned last time?"

"Explosives with remotes, illegal assaults and conversion work on very big guns confirmed. Now what about this mission I've been drafted for?"

"Can't let it happen." Stacey's words were decisive. "We'll have to stop it before it starts."

"I agree."

"But you are staying put. You're not going anywhere. What about security during the night?"

"There isn't as much as I expected, except a sentry posted on the drive from eleven to six in the morning. We all take turns. There are surveillance cameras on the house, but no one is usually watching them, especially at night."

"Is the sentry post that little shed about a hundred yards from the main house"

"That's it."

"We've got that logged from our other surveillance. I think we pretty much know the layout. Anything else?"

"Not really. I think they feel they are out in the middle of nowhere and they haven't put a full security plan into action yet. No alarms anywhere that I know of. No gates or fences to go through. A couple of flood lights light up the area around the main house and weapons room, though. You remember where I told you the main breaker was, don't you?"

"We do, but if cutting power ends up in the plan, we'll do it from a feeder outside of the compound. What about dogs?"

"One. An old one that sleeps any place it can find at night. The bunkhouse guys like it so I'll have it inside tomorrow night."

"Anything else we should know?"

"Just don't single me out?"

"We're not stupid. Just be one of them all the way through this. Do you understand?"

"Yes." Michael paced in front of the window as he continued to carefully note anyone outside on the street. "Have you talked with Caroline lately?"

"Yes, last week. She said to tell you when we spoke next that she was thinking about you. She's strong and doing just fine."

"It's good to hear that."

"We'd better cut it off. You've given me a lot do to. And you'd better get back out in the open. Don't worry. Whatever we do and whatever happens, you are one of them until the end. We'll use every possible precaution. If things start to get real nasty, just get your ass to a safe corner somewhere and stay put until it's over."

"Let's hope it doesn't come to that," said Lund as he walked toward the open mailbox.

"You've done a great job, Michael. Now just trust the Bureau. And good luck."

Michael pushed the 'end' key and immediately used the telephone's speed dial feature to access his home number in Minneapolis. Within a few seconds he heard ringing. He walked back to the window and held the telephone to his ear. He looked out and saw Celeste not more than 30 yards away, heading for the post office entrance.

"Hello." The familiar soft voice from Minnesota penetrated Michael's heart.

Celeste was fifty feet from the entrance.

"Hello? Caro—"

Power off. Shove the phone and box quickly back into the postal box. Shut door. Remove key. Stuff key in pocket and move away. Think of something.

"Ted?" Celeste said as she pushed open the door and saw Michael. Her surprised look turned into a large smile. "Checking out the FBI wanted posters?" She laughed, seeming not the least suspicious. Her walk was a little wobbly and her words came out slowly.

"Yes, and I didn't see your picture." Michael walked casually toward her. "How did you know I was in here?"

"I didn't. I was just going to buy some stamps. But since I found you I might as well go along on your old building tour the guys were pimping you about."

"After I find a rest room. I thought that since this was a public building it might have a public rest room . . . guess not though."

"Too much beer, huh?" She pushed gently at his right arm.

"Only a temporary crisis."

"I'll tell you what. Let's find a rest room someplace around here and then we can look at a few old buildings and then we'll join the rest for dinner." She walked to a stamp-dispensing machine and fed it a dollar bill. "Gotta write my mom and let her know I'm OK. . . . not supposed to send any letters out, you know . . . Fort rules. Don't tell, will you Ted?"

"Never." Michael couldn't think of any immediate excuse to gain another five or ten minutes of privacy to call Caroline. Maybe later.

"I want to buy you your next beer at dinner," offered Celeste sliding a small envelope into the outgoing mail slot. "We can celebrate the beginning of our mission . . . oops, we aren't supposed to mention that tonight are we? Have you mentioned it to anyone?"

Michael motioned to Celeste to follow him toward the exit door. "Rest room . . . a walk . . . maybe another beer and dinner. In that order."

———

Forty-eight men and women from the Bureau of Federal Investigation and the Bureau of Alcohol, Tobacco and Firearms were positioned within a half-mile of The Fort just hours before the White Straight Arrows of The Fort would depart on their mission of terrorism. Several of the specially trained force wore headsets fitted with microphones. Some held night-vision scopes to their eyes. All were outfitted in special protective vests. And their respective organization's abbreviation letters were imprinted on their back and chest. In distinct whispers, they communicated their on-going observation of the targeted area and last-minute instructions.

The multi-agency raid team knelt and squatted in six separate units under the moonless sky. Complete darkness and being 4:00A.M. were their allies as they waited, poised and ready to advance at a second's notice. The support team of fourteen Wallowa County law enforcement officials, two medics and more than a dozen vehicles waited a mile behind the front line on the main highway.

No surprises so far. No barking dog. Lund's description of The Fort's primary layout along with previous surveillance photographs and county building documents had proved accurate. There were the main house, two completed bunkhouses, mess hall, the weapons building, security shed, three small outbuildings and a number of false house and storefronts used for training. All windows in the main house and bunkhouses were dark, which the force commander hoped meant everyone was sleeping soundly. The targets were the main house, bunkhouses, weapons building and the security shed, which was up first.

Just as Lund had reported, floodlights, porch lights on the Ford house and on the bunkhouses were all that lit the populated area of the compound. They were bright enough to illuminate some of the compound's vehicles parked nearby. A large white SUV and a silver van were parked in front of the main house.

Twenty-eight hours and 12 minutes after Michael Lund's call to Raymond Stacey, the order was given to the special force to begin Operation Nightlight. Dressed in clothing as blue-black as the night that hid them, the first team of three FBI agents advanced on the sentry post. Team members worked themselves wide and far out from the shed and then inched their way toward the rear of the target. As they neared the post, they saw through their night vision goggles a man leaning back in a chair in front of the shed facing the long driveway. He wore a heavy jacket and a stocking cap. He held a lit cigarette in his right hand and a large rifle rested across his lap as he rocked back and forth on the back legs of the chair. Two agents poised themselves on the right side of the shed and the third was on the left. As fast as a fox can snare a squirrel, the sentry was down on his back, gagged and someone darkly dressed held his rifle. The man's arms were firmly and completely secured along with his legs, allowing just enough slack at the ankles to be quickly led away by the agents. Barely a sound was heard during the short and effective removal of the first target.

"Target one secure."

"Copy Team One. Good work."

Word from the commander was for the five remaining units to advance to their designated targets. A 'standby' was given to those responsible for cutting electrical power to the compound. Lund had reported to Stacey that many of the recruits slept with a gun near or under their beds. This made a simultaneous raid on the bunkhouses and main house an absolutely error-free necessity.

Eighteen agents were assigned to the main house. If alerted to a raid, the commander and his raid teams calculated the Fords would not hesitate to use an incredible amount of firepower. Their mind-set was adjusted accordingly. Timing, as in comedy, was everything.

"Everyone stand by." The commander checked the house front with his NV goggles.

Four dozen darkly clad figures armed with both weapons and the element of surprise froze in position waiting for the final order. The goals of their legally sanctioned mission were to subdue and secure all personnel at The Fort, to search and confiscate all materials related to the operation of The Fort including illegal weapons, and to take into custody everyone on the premises. The justice system would then decide whom would be charged and who, if any, would be released. Jesse, Barry and Tommy Ford were to be captured, separated from each other and removed from the area in individual waiting vehicles. The orders were to use whatever force was necessary to accomplish the mission.

"Stand by," the commander said firmly. "Cut power. Everyone, now."

The Fort went darker. Four special battering rams ripped doors from their hinges in tandem on all target locations. Inside the Ford house, Jesse flew from his bed and pushed a large switch on the wall. He pounded the wall and cursed as he saw from his window that the compound remained dark. Twelve agents raced down the hallway and converged on the three bedrooms on the first floor. Six more charged up the steps to the two bedrooms above. Two agents positioned themselves at the bottom of the stairs and two more remained at the entrance.

Jesse ran back to his bed, dropped to his knees and reached beneath the bed frame. Three agents, one with a large flashlight, burst into the room just as Jesse started to pull a shotgun from under the bed. His stunned face showed clearly in one of the agent's spotlight.

"Move one more inch and you lose a leg . . . two inches and you lose your life," barked an agent as he stood above him with his weapon pointed at Jesse. Another agent ripped the weapon from Jesse's giant hands. The senior Ford then lunged at one of the agents, only to fall back to the floor from a blow to the head from the butt of another agent's shotgun. One had his handgun pointed at Jesse's head. The other assured Ford, again, he would lose at least one leg if he tried that again.

Taking Tommy was a piece of cake. He reacted in slow motion, trying to reach a handgun on top of the nightstand next to his bed. Agents intercepted his clumsy hands and then pinned him to the floor. His breath was foul. He began screaming profanities.

Barry's room was next door. Barry woke to the crashing

door and his dad's shout. He immediately pulled a holstered handgun from a hook on the wall next to his bed. He leaped through his bedroom window, using a bed pillow to protect his face as the glass gave way. He literally fell at the feet of two agents stationed at the back of the house, prepared for just an attempt. Two handguns were trained on Barry as he hit the ground. An agent's foot pressed Barry's shoulder into the dirt as the weapon, still in its holster, was seized. Barry groaned and grabbed at his left shoulder.

There was little resistance from the two women on the second floor. Slurred screaming from Tracey filled the house and she was grabbed running down stairs and then hand-cuffed. Celeste also screamed, but stood still at the top of the stairs and waited to be led away.

Michael and the others in the white house found them-selves in arm locks with their faces pressed hard against the pine walls within seconds of being jolted out of bed by the invading agents. Michael's jaw and arm hurt at the hands of an FBI agent who held him, but the pain was overshadowed by the welcome realization that he could now secretly go home. The old dog was let out to continue its barking.

Fists and feet flew as the sixteen agents assigned to the blue house managed to neutralize The Fort's top recruits. Again, no shots were fired, but two FBI agents and two re-cruits were slightly injured in the fierce hand-to-hand battle.

By 4:53 AM, all White Straight Arrows in The Fort stood in a guarded circle between the main house and the barn. Michael Lund was among them. Jesse Ford and his two sons were handcuffed and each were under heavily-armed guard in separate buildings. Support personnel and vehicles sped to the main house and immediately began to assist.

After the compound's flood lights were brought back up, a thorough and careful building by building search continued until the commander felt comfortable that no one was left to be captured. Lund's prior report to Stacey indicated a total of sixteen subjects, including him, were living at the compound. Sixteen people would be taken away from the scene within minutes. First to be led from the compound were Jesse, Barry and Tommy. The recruits watched from a distance as agents toward the waiting vehicles pushed their handcuffed leaders.

"There is a traitor among you," screamed Jesse back to the circle of Arrows. " God will not forgive whoever he or she is . . . nor will He forgive those who have violated The Fort. I will return and you *will* suffer." Two agents quickly stuffed the ranting giant into the backseat of a car and slammed the door.

Barry said nothing as he was shoved into his designated car. Tommy echoed his father's behavior and screamed at the circle. "Someone's gonna pay for this! Somebody's gonna pay big!" One agent assisted another throwing Tommy inside the third car.

As the three cars sped away, they passed an older, four-door American car with its bright lights on slowly making its way down the long driveway to the main house. The operation commander knew it was not an official vehicle assigned to him and he drew his holstered revolver and ordered the driver to stop as it approached the center of activity. Five agents immediately surrounded the 1994 Chevrolet sedan and four pistols were aimed at the driver as the front window slowly came down.

"Oh, my," gasped the old woman. Alice Warwick's hands trembled as they clung to the steering wheel. She looked around and saw more men with more guns. The agents lowered their weapons as the small woman slowly rolled her window completely down and explained she was just coming in early to work.

"I don't think I wanna know what's goin' on here," she said in a tiny voice "I just wanna know if I'm gonna have to fix breakfast for everybody."

After copying some information from her driver's license and asking her a few questions, the agents sent the cook on her way.

The raid on The Fort was over, but Operation Nightlight wasn't. In fact, the most important work remained. The entire compound would be sealed and secured while experts meticulously combed every foot of the buildings and property for evidence linking the Fords and recruits to terrorist activities.

The United States and its citizens had changed the day New York City and Washington D.C. were attacked in 2001. No longer would terrorism, including the threat of domestic terrorism by Americans, be treated lightly and tolerated. Whether that terror is being inflicted on one person or several people, the United States government was now totally dedicated to investigating and hopefully preventing it by all means necessary. Swift prosecution of any person or group, regardless if their terrorism was based on religion, race or political view, would become the rule. The raid on The Fort would be a shining example.

Michael waited his turn to be placed in one of the prisoner vans. The other recruits showed a variety of emotions, from almost tears to anger, as they waited to be hauled away. Tracey stood erect and totally silent. She looked at no one. Celeste constantly looked at Michael. Her eyes were red from crying. She looked like she could collapse any second from emotional exhaustion. Michael avoided looking at her as much as possible.

The chaos that filled the compound moments before descended now to normal conversation between the many agents and local law enforcement personnel at the scene.

Dozens of official and unmarked vehicles remained scattered throughout the area, some with their headlights on and roof lights flashing or spinning in the early morning darkness. Men and women quietly came and went from building to building

Michael watched the FBI agents do their work. He could have just as well been one of them had he taken the road his heart said to take many years ago. Somehow, the importance of that seemed much less at this moment. All that was important now was that he was alive, he accomplished his mission for the FBI and that Caroline was waiting at home for him . . . waiting to hear his voice and the words, "I love you. I'm coming home."

~~~ *chapter 6*

December 2

Caroline tried to hold back tears for the second time as she sat alone in the high-back booth. Angelo's Restaurant was not terribly busy on this wintry Colorado evening. The dim lighting and recorded music playing added to her privacy. They also reminded her of her former life. A sip of her fizzy water as the waiter delivered the check helped with the moment.

She criticized herself for not looking forward the way she had told herself she must do. The nightmare of the past several months had to be stored and locked up somewhere, for a while at least, so she could face the future. And she did have a future, even though it was one she wouldn't have chosen.

Michael returned from the men's room and sat down across from his wife. He touched her face and gently checked a small streak of mascara with his thumb. She pressed his hand against her cheek.

"I'm sorry," she said. "I promised I would try to be stronger about all of this. I was thinking about the Twin Cities again and our friends. And you, walking across the campus."

"Caroline, I promise you that we are going to have a life, a good life together. I am just so sorry I did this to us. You are the strong one. I am so sorry."

"We decided together. You didn't do this alone, you know." She smiled at him. "You're right. The trial is behind us. Jesse and Barry Ford are in prison for a long time. You're going to be teaching again and I'm going to have a new job pretty soon. We have a nice home and we'll make new friends. You're right. We do have a future, and we'll make it a good one."

They leaned toward each other and kissed softly. Michael's eyes turned misty.

"Let's go home," said Caroline.

"Soon as I pay this, I'm ready."

"Be back in minute," said Caroline as she headed toward the ladies room.

Michael pulled several bills from his wallet and laid them on top of the check. He finished the last of his red wine and sat back.

Nine months ago Michael and Caroline had never imagined that they would be living in a new city with new names and identities. Michael's chance to be a part of an FBI operation and use that to further his professional career seemed to be a perfect opportunity, but now they wished the deal with Kick, William Stacey and the Bureau had never been made. The Lund's friends, careers and their life in Minnesota were now out of reach. Both hoped not forever.

Death threats had given them little choice but to go in the Federal Witness Protection Program immediately following the unusually speedy trial. A full-scale raid on Fort America hadn't even crossed Michael's mind until the night before it happened, nor was getting caught up in a planned act of domestic terrorism. He was only supposed to get in, get as much as information as possible and get out—that was the deal! And he was never told at any time that he would have to testify against the Ford's, who were indicted on terrorism, illegal weapons and conspiracy charges. But the Bureau and the federal prosecutors needed a swift victory. Lund, as a reluctant and disguised witness, was key in winning their case.

The three charges stuck for both Jesse and Barry, but evidence was weak for what prosecutors thought were previously planned and executed ethnic attacks in Detroit, Los Angeles and Alabama. Weak, too, was the evidence to convict Tommy. He walked. Federal prosecutors could not prove beyond reasonable doubt that he actually made concrete plans or had carried out terrorism, nor could he physically be linked with purchasing illegal weapons or altering others. Jesse and Barry were the president and vice president of The Fort. Tommy was the office boy. Even Michael's testimony couldn't directly connect Tommy to anything more than murdering cats and being present during training sessions.

Jesse and Barry Ford were convicted and both sentenced to eight years in a federal prison. Parole was possible in four years. Tommy returned to The Fort.

The Lunds were set up with new identities and lives, courtesy of the U.S. Marshall Service and U.S. taxpayers. Phillip and Diane Williams started life over in Colorado and would now only be known as Michael and Caroline to each other.

Caroline returned to the table and they left the restaurant. They had spent the afternoon visiting the Denver Library for the first time, followed by some window shopping at Larimar Square. As the stores began to close, they traded the frigid weather outdoors for the restaurant's steaming pasta and hot Italian bread before their drive home. Angelo's had become one of their favorite places when they visited Denver for one of their day trips.

Interstate 25 leads south to Colorado Springs. It was once a small city with a military base and a steady flow of tourists taking in the area's natural sites. Michael and Caroline had moved into a modest, but comfortable house in nearby Manitou Springs. They choose the Springs area from a short list of possibilities after learning their was a good chance of Michael securing a second-semester teaching assignment at Colorado College. And the outlook of satisfying employment for Caroline, if she wanted it, made the decision easier, as well.

Traffic was light. The Broncos were out of town. It was sleeting and getting dark as the weather deteriorated, not unusual for this time of year in the Denver area. The couple had been used to far worse conditions "back home". Interstate 25 was a picnic compared to I-494 in early December.

The moisture on the Subaru's windshield was enough to require wipers, but not enough to affect their speed. Michael kept in the left lane of the highway so he could pass any cars they might encounter. They engaged in light conversation while music from the car's stereo filled the spaces between their words and thoughts. There had been some off moments but, overall, the day had been special and the drive was relaxing. They each expressed some renewed hope for the future.

"It'll get better, Michael," Caroline softly announced as she put her hand on her husband's shoulder. "Better and better."

"I promise it will," Michael responded. He took her hand and kissed it. "I promise."

A large silver car that Michael had noticed behind them for several miles suddenly shortened the distance between them with an intentional burst of speed. The long four-door car's tires spit a spray of water as it approached the right side of the Lund's car. The silver sedan rapidly closed the gap until the cars were parallel. Then the cars touched.

"What the . . . !" shouted Michael. His pupils were large and black. Michael's eyes reflected his mind, racing at light speed as he tried to quell the fear washing over him, and to comprehend what was happening.

"Michael!" screamed Caroline as she leaned into to her husband. She gripped her seat belt with both hands.

Michael's head turned furiously back and forth from front to right several times as he tried to see through the silver car's heavily tinted windows and still keep his car on the road. The attacker's car broke away for a second then veered back at the Lund's car with a deliberate and harder hit. It forced the Outback onto the road's left shoulder where there was no place to go except across the median and into on coming traffic. Michael wrenched the steering wheel hard right as he tired to avert tragedy. The silver car pressed tighter. Caroline placed her trembling hands on her abdomen. With no cars in sight ahead of him, Michael sped up, then slowed down, trying to keep his distance from the other car. The other car immediately matched the moves exactly.

The driver of the attacking car then pulled away but remained almost parallel with them even as Michael slowed his car again. The dark window on the driver's side opened. The long barrel of a large handgun pointed directly at the right side of the Lund's car. Long blonde hair sticking out from under a yellow baseball cap worn backward blew around the driver's round face. A bushy mustache covered his upper lip. His sun-glassed eyes appeared frozen on his moving target and yet he steered his car perfectly in tandem with the other even as Michael slowed even more and veered left onto the left shoulder of the road. As Lund glanced quickly again at the other car he saw a flash as the large handgun fired. The window on Caroline's side exploded and she bolted forward. A massive wound to the back left side of her neck immediately left the dash and windshield streaked with blood. He prayed to any god there is or ever was that he would wake from this nightmare. His mind rejected the horror. Wake up! Wake up! He pushed the gas pedal to the floor.

Within a second another flash of light came from the driver's window. A large caliber bullet found its mark and the Subaru's right front tire exploded. A third flash, only softer and larger from the blackened back window this time caught Michael's peripheral vision as the silver car sped away. Michael tried to steer the car to a stop, but his efforts were useless and the car veered to the right, spun in a full circle and slammed head-on into a guardrail. Air bags instantly deployed.

Michael fought to stay conscious as surging pain enveloped his body. His left side was numb. Blood coated the car's dash, wind shield and its occupants. Caroline was lifeless as he tried to touch her with his right hand. His chest heaved as he saw what the bullet had done to her. He stroked her hair and then gently pressed the backside of his hand to her stomach. Tears whipped from his eyes as he thrashed his head about, screaming, screaming.

Their old life and their new life had come to an end. He knew why. He knew by whom.

Before blackness took him, he roared again. "Oh, Caroline! Oh, my son!"

~~~ chapter 7

Michael's injuries were serious enough that his doctors at Denver Hospital were not going to allow him to be moved from his bed for at least eight days. This meant Caroline's funeral would be delayed. Injections of morphine, stitches, constant changes of dressings and prolonged sleeping occupied his first three days. When awake, he struggled to regain some control of his limbs and of his memory of exactly what happened. He could do little of either. His only clear and constant thought when awake was that he knew Caroline had passed from his life in a very horrific event. Many times he wished he could join her in death.

By the fourth day, the patient, known only as Phillip Williams to his doctors, hospital staff and local authorities, became fully aware of his injuries. His left arm and three ribs were broken. His face, left hip and leg were sorely bruised black and swollen. His entire body throbbed with pain when the morphine would begin to wear off. The most serious injuries were those involving trauma to the head where it slammed into the driver's side window and the severe, compound fracture of his left clavicle. When he was able to slowly stretch his right hand to his left shoulder, he could feel it was deformed, almost collapsed and smaller.

His doctors told him that with their plan of treatment and long-term physical therapy, he should be able to function near normal within six months.

Michael's mother arrived in Denver from Milwaukee a day and a half after the incident. By special arrangement, she was met at the airport by a person from the Arapaho County sheriff's office and driven to the hospital. Her tears flowed at her son's bedside, so grateful Michael survived and so shattered and grieving at the loss of Caroline. Although numb with painkillers and always wanting to sleep, Michael realized enough that the trip from Wisconsin was a physical hardship on his mother. Her health had been deteriorating a little bit at a time, the result of early stages of Parkinson's Disease. She had moved in with her sister almost a year ago, which proved to be agreeable to everyone. Her mind was sharp and clear as she and Michael eventually worked their way through the necessary funeral arrangements. They came to a decision on what to do, but it wasn't a comfortable one.

The next day, John Kick appeared at the hospital.

"I got here as soon as I could," Kick told Michael. He methodically looked at the patient's wounds. "You look like hell, but you're alive. I'm thankful for that. But I'm sorry about your wife."

Michael responded with only a turn his head toward the window.

"I'll watch over your mother as long as I'm here," Kick added. "If there's anything she needs, she'll have it. I'm glad she's here with you."

Michael managed a weak "thanks".

Kick told Michael that he had heard the tragic news from Raymond Stacey. The Bureau Chief had been contacted by the Manitou Springs Police Department chief, who was aware that the William's were in the witness protection program. Kick mumbled on about how tighter security was needed for witnesses. He offered to do what he could to track down those responsible.

————

Michael was strong enough within eight days to bury Caroline in Colorado Springs. He had struggled very hard with the decision of where her body would be laid to rest. They had never discussed it. Both of her parents were buried in Crosslake, but there was no way he could travel more than a very short distance. He promised he would move her body to Minnesota as soon as he could.

The weather on the day of the service and burial was nearly the same as it was on the day Caroline was murdered. Michael heard, but barely listened to the soft monotone words at the funeral home where there were as many plain-clothed security people as mourners. His mind was back on I25, Stillwater, Minneapolis and a dozen other places.

At the cemetery he stared at the casket and prepared himself to say good-bye. He thought of Caroline's deceased father and mother, and his own father. He and Caroline had often talked about the possibility of an existence after death. She had frequently speculated about somehow seeing her parents again and how wonderful it could be. Michael hoped she was with them now in some unknown way. He wept for several minutes.

Conversation in the black limousine on the journey back to the Denver Hospital was mostly small talk. Kick was a passenger in the car to and from the cemetery.

"I'll be leaving early this evening for Washington, Michael, if I can get a plane out," said John. "I'll be checking in on you by phone from time to time, or in person if I get out this way. Stacey has me hopping all over the country. Stacey will have your security boosted to twenty-four hours a day for a while once you get back into your house."

"I appreciate you coming to see me, John. But I can't let you leave without telling you how incredibly angry I am. This wasn't supposed to happen."

"I know, Michael. Stacey knows. The Bureau will be working hard for answers."

"Does anyone really know . . . " Michael didn't finish the sentence as he turned to face the side window again. His eyes fixated at the gray horizon. He turned back to his mother beside him as she took his hand and gently squeezed. She looked at him. Her eyes were sad and comforting at the same time . . . eyes that only a parent could have for a son or daughter whose pain was go great. They sat in silence for several moments.

"Once you are doing better, I hope you continue writing your book," she finally said. "I think it's important, in many ways, that you do this."

"I plan to when I'm up to it."

"What book is that?" asked Kick. He repeated his question.

"I can't talk about it now. I'll tell you another time." His voice was harsh.

Mrs. Lund leaned toward Kick and whispered in his ear.

The young widower laid his head back as well as he could, turning slightly to one side. The tightly buckled clavicle strap was uncomfortable and restricting. He stared out of the window, trying to ignore the pain and listened to the hiss of the car's tires on the wet pavement. If only he could leap ahead in time. No, if only he could go back and change the past!

As the limousine approached the hospital, Michael repeated two questions over and over in his mind. Assuming it was a planned hit, who really was the target? How had they been found? Stacey and the people he and Caroline had talked with from the protection program had all assured them they would be safe. Every precaution would be taken, they'd said. And he and Caroline had believed them.

———

Michael returned to his house in Manitou Springs December eighteenth. His mother stayed with him through Christmas and into the New Year. The first holiday was a very depressing day and the second meant nothing. No festive lights, seasonal music or presents, except the love a mother displays for her only child during a time of extreme sadness. Mrs. Lund attended to her son's needs, trying her best to comfort him. They discussed the possibility of Michael remaining in the protection program and starting a new life, only in Minneapolis or Milwaukee. She suggested they contact Mr. Kick and ask him to assist in making new arrangements. After all, the Justice Department owed her son more than they could ever repay. Michael's response was that the Witness Protection Program meant nothing to him anymore. He would be completely on his own . . . his terms and solely responsible for his future.

———

The patient gave his mother disappointing news on January third.

"Mom," he said, as he sat in front of her at his kitchen table. "I've decided to stay here, as least for now. And you need to get back to Milwaukee, rest up and get on with your life after all you have done for me here."

She gently argued that she was up to any task that would help him further recover. He explained that he was pleased with his physical progress so far and that he wanted to continue his lengthy journey of recovery in Manitou Springs.

"I have a long way to go . . . physically and mentally, Mom," he further explained, "and I know it would be best for me to stay close to Caroline's grave and in this house where we started a new life. Besides, I want to continue writing my book right here."

His mother looked at and listened to her only child. Her eyes became misty and she reached across to hold his hand.

"I know this isn't what you want to hear, but I think it's best," he continued. My doctors are here, my psychologist is and my heart is, at least for now." He asked her to understand.

Michael's mother returned to Wisconsin on January fifth.

Alone, he began work on the silent promise he made to Caroline the day of her funeral. He would find and serve justice to those responsible for her death. Michael Lund had never broken a promise.

———

During the next several months Michael's life became very regimented, nearly obsessive. When he wasn't in physical therapy, he was writing. The book was progressing well. When he turned his laptop off, he became a nutrition fanatic and prepared foods and drinks to help re-build his body. Remedies to improve his spirit proved elusive, however, despite the help from his psychologist.

Security around his house remained even though there had been no threats against him. John Kick came to visit once and called Michael on several occasions over the next four months. These were usually conversations about Michael's physical progress and about his book. Michael gave him few details of the latter.

The agent would ramble on about the Bureau and its current working environment. Michael began to find his calls annoying. He still appreciated Kick's help after Caroline's death, but he simply didn't have time and tolerance for the whining, small talk and prying questions. Raymond Stacey also called . . . twice and briefly to check on his recovery and to remind him to call if there was anything he needed. What Michael needed, neither Stacey, nor anyone else could provide.

His teaching career mattered little anymore, although it did cross his mind that the second semester at the University of Minnesota would be coming to an end very shortly. He wished he was still there and that the life-long dream of working for a national security agency had never come true. These reoccurring thoughts plagued him, but he was beginning to learn how to shorten their stay and make them less frequent.

————

The documents he had been waiting for arrived May 18 from his trustworthy university colleague in Minneapolis. He followed the simple instructions that accompanied the official documents, and after withdrawing cash from his bank account he returned the signed papers and $4,000 in cash to his friend the next day via overnight delivery. Two weeks to wait.

ᴥᴥᴥ *chapter 8*

"Greta, give me another mic check," said Charlie as he put on his headset. "I want to see how much of the traffic noise is coming through."

"Houston police officials say the homicide may have been the result of a domestic situation," said the reporter. "Is that enough?"

"A little more. And bring the mike up a little more. This traffic seems to be getting heavier by the minute."

"Sure."

Greta Meyer swept her long, dark hair back. She adjusted the lapel microphone up a little closer to the next button of her dress and looked into the camera. The lens reflected confidence and professionalism.

"This afternoon, I also learned from an unidentified, but highly reliable source that Jackie Taylor may have . . . ."

"Good. We're live in three minutes."

The crime reporter at Houston's number two news station stood against a background of unkempt housing in the Fifth Ward. Weeds pushed through the cracks in the sidewalks and litter hugged the street curb. Abandoned cars with body damage or missing tires hid more discarded items behind them on the parking. A bent, rusted fence and untrimmed parking separated reporter Meyer from the crime scene, a dilapidated gray duplex.

The reporter in cosmopolitan clothing and the camera crew had drawn a crowd of onlookers. The crew from Channel Nine was doing the report from behind the yellow crime tape that stretched from the front of the residence to the trees at the edge of the yard. Greta Meyer, seen by many Houstonians as the best woman reporter on local television, was about to tell her viewers an ugly story of drugs and murder. The story was a commonplace one to the reporter and neighborhood alike. It was the second murder in greater Houston so far that day. The time was 6:04 PM.

"Stand by," said Charlie. "Watch my cue."

Greta stood with poised back and slightly tucked chin. Her legs were close together and the toes of her polished shoes straight ahead. She watched the camera lens and waited. One of the anchors at the station was reading the lead-in. She heard the intro through her earpiece.

"Ready . . . ," said another news crew member. His index finger waved her on.

"We reported to you at noon that the Houston police called the homicide a domestic situation. The victim was Jackie Taylor who lived with her husband in this duplex behind me. Taylor was the wife of Jerome Taylor, now being sought for questioning in the murder."

The video then switched from Greta to recorded scenes of Houston EMT personnel wheeling the body of the victim out of the residence on a gurney and into the back of a rescue vehicle. The reporter's voice-over continued to give details of the crime.

"The Harris County Medical Examiner told us Taylor's death was the result of bullet wounds to the head and chest. This reporter has now learned the likely murder weapon has been recovered. I am told it was found less than two blocks away from the crime scene after an anonymous tip and an intense search. The weapon is identified as a Sundance Boa, a small, twenty-five caliber automatic revolver." Greta was back live.

"This afternoon, I also learned from an unidentified, but highly reliable source that Jackie Taylor may have recently become an informant for the Houston Police Narcotics Division . . . and that Jerome Taylor and two friends of Mr. Taylor's were under investigation for drug trafficking in the greater Houston area. In addition, I have learned that Mrs. Taylor had filed for a divorce from her husband four days ago. Court records verify this, but Houston police officials have neither confirmed nor denied that Ms. Taylor was an informant. We'll have any new developments on this story on News Channel Four at ten. Greta Meyer, reporting."

Greta relaxed and walked a few steps into the shade of a large tree. It provided a small amount of relief from the mid-May sun, but did nothing for the humidity. Charlie joined her as the crewmember put equipment back in their mobile ENG van. The crowd that had gathered to watch one of Houston's star reporters started to dwindle.

Greta's entire week had been hectic. In fact, the two weeks of May sweeps so far had been hell, and she wanted nothing more than to go home and swim laps in the large pool at the complex where she lived with her seven-year old son, Ben.

She had to return to the station and, barring any new developments in the next three hours, help re-cut the Taylor story, so the rest of her Friday night and the weekend could be spent away from the business of television news. In fact, she planned to take a much longer break with Ben, right after he got out of school. She had two weeks of unused vacation that she was looking forward to.

The 6PM and 10PM newscasts on Channel Four enjoyed a ten and fourteen household rating respectively, just behind the top news station. News Channel Four was continually gaining because of the two seasoned and long-term anchors, and reporters like Greta Meyer. She had a genuine chemistry with viewers. She had the looks, but not the inflated ego. She had experience and intelligence, which enhanced her heads-up story investigations and reporting. A close friend on the Houston police force nicknamed her Detective Meyer.

Greta had moved through two smaller markets quickly and had been recruited by two Houston stations simultaneously. The best offer came from Channel Four and she took the job. It was fortuitous for both her and her husband Richard at the time. He worked for a small oil company in Oklahoma City where they had lived prior to moving to Houston. Through a headhunter, he secured a job with a larger oil company in the bigger city. The move couldn't have been better for all of them, including young Ben. But things had changed.

Tonight, Greta was exhausted as she finally passed through the security gate of her townhome complex on Memorial Drive. In a neighborhood of elegant custom homes and townhouses, she and Richard had bought a second story, three-bedroom townhome. Their son grumbled at first about the lack of a back yard of their own, but several swimming pools throughout the complex and more time for weekend trips made up for it. The family agreed townhome living was all right with them for now.

Greta walked up the single flight of steps to her front door carrying a bag of groceries from Randall's Market. She would be eating a late dinner alone, since Ben had been invited to spend the night with his best friend. Ben loved sleepovers.

Greta knew the friend's mother reasonably well and didn't have any doubts about Ben's safety.

She knew she couldn't hover over her son and control him all the time. She gave him enough freedom to be on his own so he would be able to survive in the violent world she witnessed nearly every workday.

Greta put the fresh shrimp in the refrigerator, along with a bottle of wine to chill while she swam. She psyched herself up for boiled shrimp on top of fresh, steamed asparagus, sourdough bread and white wine . . . her reward for completing fifty laps.

The townhouse was spacious and well kept, but sparsely furnished. The large screen television and stereo system were gone now, along with some of the living room furniture. The divorce had been finalized just two weeks before, and Greta and Ben hadn't the time yet to shop the furniture and electronic stores. They had an old portable TV and several books that occupied an otherwise empty built-in bookcase in the living room. She told herself she and Ben would fill the empty spaces with more books and CDs and a DVD player when she had some time. Ben had added an Ipod to the list.

She grabbed a large towel and her swimsuit from one of the master bath towel racks and opened the bedroom's double walk-in closet. A two-foot-wide, floor-to-ceiling mirror on the back wall divided the closet into two sections. Her business clothes were still densely packed on the right. With Richard's clothes gone, her casual clothes were loosely arranged on the left.

She undressed in front of the closet mirror, inspecting her face and her slender body. More than a few people in the past year or two had guessed her age at about twenty-eight, six years less than the truth. She had been carded at bars long after she was out of college.

Physical appearance was valuable to her television job, but, more importantly, it affected how she felt about herself. Her confidence level and her ability to face a situation with optimism and strength were at an all-time high. These traits had been tested strenuously during the past year and a half, ever since Richard had lost his job.

She slipped into her black one-piece swimsuit, and added a white cover-up from a brass hook inside the closet. She walked into the main living area and turned on a reading lamp that sat on a wicker end table next to the sofa. She then checked the latch on the double doors that led to a small balcony and turned on a floor lamp next to the front window. She liked everything brightly lit when she returned from the pool after dark.

She lifted a brass key from a hook inside the front closet and dropped it in her pocket. The key fit the new lockset that she had installed two days before final divorce papers were signed. The locks securing the door to the master bedroom balcony and the living area balcony had been replaced at the same time.

Eager to shake off the day's heat and stress, Greta opened the front door to the landing part way. Just as she reached to set the lock, the door was violently kicked open. She saw the cowboy boot as she fell back against the closet door and sank to the floor. The heavy door bounced off the wall with a loud thud. She gasped for breath. The large framed mirror crashed to the wooden entry floor. Mind racing, she tried to avoid shards of glass as she struggled to her feet. Her heart pounded as if it would push through her ribs.

The intruder quickly stepped inside and caught the heavy door before it shut.

"Going out for your midnight swim, Greta?" said the man. His half-closed eyes were glassy and blood-shot. His thick mustache and short hair were well groomed, but his yellow T-shirt and faded jeans were dirty. His chiseled face contorted as he towered over her.

"Richard!" screamed Greta. Her eyes widened even further and the color drained from her face. "Get out of here!" She stood up, arms covering her chest.

Richard closed the door with an exaggerated soft touch and locked it. "We wouldn't want to have all of the our nice neighbors hear us, now would we?" He put a finger to his lips. "We all know they've had a hard day at the office today, don't we . . . and they have to relax and unwind so they can go back to their goddamn jobs on Monday, right? Right?"

"What are you doing here?" Greta demanded. Still breathing heavily, she slid her feet inch by inch through the fragments of glass in an effort to avoid being trapped against the closet door. She looked directly into his eyes and said in a grim, level tone, "You are not supposed to come here anymore. Ever."

"Exactly."

"You're drunk."

"I'm just *relaxed,* like all of your fine neighbors."

Richard moved closer as she backed into the kitchen. She reached for the telephone at the end of the counter that separated the kitchen from the dining area. They faced each other on opposite sides of it.

"Get out right now, or I'll call the police again," she yelled, as her fear gave way to anger.

"Call the police? Why don't you call your little detective friend? Maybe he owes you a favor for screwing him. You do screw him, don't you Greta?" He suddenly realized Greta was in very close reach of the telephone, and his right hand dropped behind the counter.

"Get out, Richard! Just get out!" She grabbed the telephone, hugged it to her chest and frantically tried to punch 911.

Richard rushed around the end of the counter and ripped

the telephone away. The loose cover-up pulled off her shoulders as she twisted to avoid him. He threw the telephone like a baseball into the dining area wall and then backhanded a basket full of fruit off the counter.

She knew the rage, the twisted mouth, but she could never read how far he would go. "Get out!" She attempted to pull the cover-up back in place.

"Shut up, you bitch!" A jagged knife blade was suddenly in front of her face. "Shut up!"

Greta tried to throw herself over the counter. Richard slapped his free hand on her arm, pulled her back and locked his other arm across her throat. He ripped the white fabric from her shoulders, licking the back of her neck and pulling at the front of her swimsuit. She dug her fingernails into the arm covering her throat and gouged as deep and wildly as she could. A stench and a howl bellowed from his mouth. She tried to bite his arm but Richard forced her head back.

"Ben isn't here, is he?" as if the thought hadn't occurred to him until just then. "I want my son! I want him now!"

"He's not here."

"Where the hell is he, dammit?

"He's somewhere else."

"Where? Who's he staying with?"

"I would never tell you. Now get out! You know you're not supposed to be here."

Richard pushed the tip of the knife under her left swimsuit strap and cut it. "Tell me."

"Never."

He put the edge of the blade to her right shoulder and pressed it to her skin hard enough to draw a thin line of blood. She thought of the gun she had almost bought the week before. Her detective friend, Randy Quarve, persuaded her not to get it.

He cut her shoulder again, and drew blood further down her back as he tried to sever the other strap. Greta bolted when she felt his arm relax slightly. She tried to run toward the bedroom but his reach was long and quick despite his drunken state. He grabbed her long hair and forced her back into the center of the living room. She fought him fiercely with feet, hands and fingernails, but she was no match for a madman. He locked an arm around her waist and held the knife to her cheek.

"You took my life away." His lips were pressed to her ear. "And I want it back."

"I didn't. You did it to yourself."

"Wrong! You fixed it so I can't come home anymore. You fixed it so I can't see my son anymore. I don't have any money. I don't have a job . . . I want my life back!"

"You need help first. I tried to help you, Richard. I gave it everything I had." Tears rolled down her cheeks and onto the blade of the knife. Blood trickled down her arm from the cuts on her shoulder. "Things have changed, Richard. You've changed, and you need professional help."

"Shut up. I don't want to hear about change. Change! Change!" Richard threw her to the sofa and pinned her down. He grabbed a handful of her hair and hacked it with the knife. She fought to get out from under him. "Here's a change for those goddamn viewers who love you so much."

Greta thrashed and screamed as he sliced chunks of hair from her scalp. His knife caught the flesh low on the back of her head. Blood ran down her neck, onto her swimsuit and the sofa. He pulled and slashed until there was little hair left to grab.

At last Richard got off her, staggering as if about to pass out. Exhaustion consumed her, but she mustered the little strength she had left and charged him. Her nails dug into his face but her foot missed its target, his groin. He swayed slightly from her attack, but he quickly recovered and grabbed her again in a steel grip.

"Maybe your neighbors would like to see some changes, too." He hammered a fist into her face again and again, growling like a crazed animal at a kill site as she fell to the floor.

She struggled to get up, but collapsed into the blood and shattered glass.

"Richard, please . . . " Total consciousness left her.

————

Tommy Ford faced four armed recruits at The Fort. Each comrade was dressed in The Fort's traditional dark blue attire with a black armband. Sunglasses shielded their eyes from the sun as the three men and one woman faced eastward toward the Wallowa Mountains. The special meeting was being held next to the chapel since it was Sunday morning. The recruits gave the Fort's new leader their attention.

"I've got some important news," said Tommy. He scratched his short whiskers and kicked at the dirt. He searched for the words his dad would have used. "The traitor who was with us several months ago . . . the son-of-a-bitch who put my dad and my brother in prison, has fled from his federal protection in Colorado. This means he no longer has security guards around him. It means he's out there, somewhere in the open. Do we all know who we're talkin' about?"

The woman nodded her head and the men grunted.

"Then let me introduce you to your practice target for today."

Tommy turned sideways and pointed to a target dummy that had been propped up a hundred yards away.

"We will find this traitor and we will kill him."

ᴊᴊᴊᴊ *chapter 9*

The hawk was perched in the damp, green grass, one wing angled down, the other pointing to the full moon that lit the overgrown yard. The bird's narrow black and yellow body supported a bulbous head and a pronounced curved beak. Its large eyes were focused on the street just beyond the stone fence at the edge of the property. It gave the impression that it was there to defend, and if not to protect, then at least to warn of danger. Hawks are known for traits of superior observation, patience and anticipation, making them survivors in their naturally violent world.

Sweet fragrance from the flowering bushes that lined the driveway drifted across the vast lawn. Nearby, frogs double-croaked and bugs of diverse species whistled, whirred and clicked. The air was mild and still, without the humidity that would come later in the season. The big bird was motionless, too, waiting for its new master.

The hawk, a colorful yard vane, had once belonged to an alumnus of the state's largest university. But it sat now, abandoned, a wooden orphan fastened to the earth with a sharp metal stake. The mascot's most recent master had put the historic house up for sale three weeks before Christmas. He had tried living in the large stone home for almost a year after inheriting it from his uncle, the late Edward Hansen. Hansen had been a wealthy physician in the town for fifty-two years. Dr. Hansen's father had built the castle-like home in 1902. There was nothing resembling it in the entire county.

Its size and age were the reasons why the house had been on the market for nearly eight months. No one in the town of shopkeepers, summer resort folks and farmers could afford it . . . buy or rent. The town wasn't dying. Thanks to tourists it was holding its own. But there wasn't a soul in Rockwood, Iowa interested in paying even a reasonable price for a drafty stone mansion on the bank of Lake Emmet. It needed the right kind of resident... someone with special needs or with an unusual personality, perhaps someone from out of town.

Dr. Hansen's nephew, Chris, had received a telephone call May 10 from the local listing agent. He was lounging in the sun on the patio of his San Diego townhouse the day he learned the good news. Someone from Minnesota was interested in the old fortress, an offer of a twelve-month lease at $1,000 per month, plus utilities, with an option to buy. The agent said the agreement could be prepared and sent to California. Four months rent would be paid up-front. Possession date: June 2.

"Deal," said the nephew.

———

The Diamond cab drove slowly in front of the dark stone house. The cab's headlights augmented the old street lamps in brightening the deserted brick street. It was four hours before the town's thirteen hundred residents would be waking to commute to jobs in Spencer and Algona, or head to the fields with their machinery. Some would clock-in at the two local factories. Only the shopkeepers, the bank workers, retirees and those who lived leisurely around Lake Emmet had time this early to read *The Des Moines Register* or catch the latest Iowa news on television.

"This has to be it," said the cabby with an eastern European accent. "I don't see a house number, but it sure looks like how you described it. It is very large." The cabby strained his neck as he tried to see the entire house through the windshield.

"I'm sure this is it," said the passenger. He gestured to pull into the wide driveway. "Pull up a little."

The cab's lights illuminated a tarnished metal address plate mounted into a waist-high stone fence. 17 Lakeside Drive.

"Good," said the customer. "It wasn't that hard to find, was it?"

"I've been in this country for two years now and I've never been to this part of Iowa before. This is pretty far north. But I got you here okay. It's been an interesting night, yes?"

"You mean morning,"

"Yes . . . morning. It's been interesting."

The passenger let himself out the rear side door of the white Dodge Caravan. He was dressed for the weather in tan pants, casual shoes and a black knit shirt that hugged his lean chest.

The driver shut down the engine and grunted as he got out of his van. He tugged at his crotch and rubbed his eyes.

"I'll get big bag out of the back."

"Thanks."

Phillip Williams stood by the van's open door and let his head drop forward, then from side to side. He repeated the motion. The one hundred thirty-mile trip had taken longer than he had anticipated, due to the fact that little of the route was interstate highway.

He stretched up on his toes and followed with five knee bends and then moved his muscular arms in a circular motion like a swimmer doing the backstroke. It had been a marathon day, and night. He went through the routine again as he studied the house and its surroundings. He showed no surprise at what he saw, even though it was all new to him.

He reached inside the car and fetched a shoulder bag and a smaller rectangular case made of black nylon fabric. He set the smaller bag down gently on the ground near the car and quietly closed the door.

"Let me get those for you, too," said the driver as he bent down to pick up the nylon bag.

Williams abruptly intercepted the driver's reach, awkwardly grabbing the case as he juggled to hold on to the other bag.

"I'll get these two," said Williams. "You've done a good job."

"Thank you," said the cabby as he pulled a pack of cigarettes from his shirt pocket and shook one to his lips. He closed the van's back lid the same way Williams had closed the car door. "This is sure one quiet town. I think we're the only ones awake."

They walked the short sidewalk to the wide steps that led up to a covered porch.

"You can leave the bag here on the top step," said Williams. "I'll get the door unlocked while you figure the tab."

The driver walked back to his cab humming happily.

As Williams viewed his new home from a closer perspective, he noted that the cement steps and wood porch ran the entire front of the house. It reminded him of a lodge he had stayed at in northern Wisconsin with his family when he was a child. He pulled a brass key from his pants pocket.

"I hope you like high numbers." said the cab driver with a slight chuckle as he approached the steps. "The long mileage to get here and the high price of gas now you know."

"I'm ready."

"The total is three-hundred thirty-six dollars." He stood motionless as he waited for his customer's reaction.

"Sounds fair." Williams took his billfold from a back pocket and started counting bills.

The driver looked relieved as he handed him a receipt from his pad and commented again how quiet the town was. Williams counted out twenty-two twenties and handed them over. The cabby counted, mumbled and shook his head. "This is awfully generous," said the driver.

"You earned it. And I put in a little extra for your silence and my privacy that we talked about."

"I remember. Silence and privacy. Very important, I know. Thank you. Thank you very much. I and my family appreciate this."

Phillip Williams stood on the porch of his new home and watched the taxi's rear lights disappear down Lakeside. He turned and faced the mammoth house. How long would he be here? Would it all end here? If not, then where and when? Before he wondered further, he decided to deal with the more immediate needs. He had been up for twenty-eight hours. He was running on empty and needed sleep.

It took two trips to bring his belongings inside. Once the large wooden door was closed behind him he felt for a light switch on the wall by the door. He found not just one, but felt several switches in a row . . . seven in all. None worked.

Silence and a musty scent from another era greeted the new master of the house as he gently set the small nylon case on the wooden floor. Moonlight from narrow windows on each side of the door gave him a glimpse of the spacious entryway. He could make out a hall tree and a large rug.

The rental agreement had noted that the house was partially furnished. A bonus, but it wasn't a determining factor in his decision to take it.

An ornate light fixture hung from the high ceiling. Wide steps led to a second floor and the moonlight let Phillip see faint details beyond the top step. The house looked cavernous, but it immediately felt comfortable to him. The light from street lamps and the moonlight coming through upper windows gave a first warm impression.

Williams peered into the first door on his left. There was enough light to tell it was the kitchen. On his right was a small, square room, which he guessed to be a parlor or sitting room. The room's walls were lined with high empty bookcases and there were two chairs with a small table between them. A long window faced the street. He saw no lamps and didn't bother hunting for a wall switch.

A small windowless bathroom was next to the parlor. He hoped it was functioning. At the end of the hallway and beyond the staircase was a pair of closed wooden doors, at least twice his height. He pushed down on the brass handles and pulled. Although heavy, they opened easily. He took three steps into the immense room and, from what he could see, determined it was a library or a study.

There was a floor-to-ceiling fireplace made of stones, similar to those covering the house's exterior. An executive-size desk faced it. There was room on each side of the fireplace for a large painting. Behind him were bookcases like the ones in the parlor. To his left were two large windows, their tops curved and bare, inviting the moonlight in. Double French doors below the windows led outside.

Williams tried a table lamp next to a wingback chair by the fireplace. Then he tried a floor lamp next to a long sofa in front of the French doors, facing the center of the room. His attempts were futile, but he seemed little concerned. He was used to dealing with the unexpected. He believed surprises were a part of education. Expecting the unexpected was an advantage. The alternative could be costly . . . even deadly.

The bathroom proved to be in full working order, much to his relief. He brought his luggage into the library and set it out of the way in a corner. The nylon case went on top of the desk.

Phillip opened the French doors to an extraordinary view of Lake Emmet. He was sure he could see clear to the other side. He pulled off his shoes and socks before stepping out onto the rear porch. The deck was cool to his feet. The early morning air of an Iowa summer felt good in his lungs. It reminded him of his real home, one state to the northeast.

He rested his hands on the wooden railing that followed the porch to the ends of the house and scanned the horizon. A handful of distant lights dotted the far shoreline. They were almost washed out by a long, silver streak stretching across the water, the full moon's tail lying upon the still surface. Insects and frogs emitted sounds from the thick grass near the water's edge.

He took a last deep breath before he turned and went inside. He had started to reminisce about his boyhood summers in Wisconsin, but let it pass, knowing sleep was most important now. He could explore his house and Rockwood tomorrow and in the weeks to come.

He shut one of the French doors tightly but left the other slightly ajar to let the lakeside air infiltrate the house. A sweatshirt from his suitcase served as a pillow on the library sofa. He took off his knit shirt and stretched out. His eyes were fixed on the high ceiling above and his ears tuned in the faint sounds of summer outside, but his thoughts soon were of Caroline. His eyes closed and then pain would soon be gone for a little while. This is how it had been for several months.

Three hours later, when the lake had turned from silver to blue, a breeze blew across Lake Emmet and the wings of the hawk slowly turned.

chapter 10

Greta Meyer gently pulled the cotton blanket around Ben's small shoulders and up to his neck. She wanted to make her son feel secure and comfortable, the way she had felt when she slept in the same room as a little girl. With orange morning light coming through the bedroom windows, the mother gazed at her child and thought how quickly her baby had grown to be seven years. She paused and thought of how much she loved this sleeping child.

Ben's grandpa hadn't changed the room much in the past eighteen years, except for the mattress. Greta's mother and father had bought her a new bedroom set two years before she graduated from Rockwood High School. The rest of the house hadn't changed much either, just a little updating in the kitchen and the upstairs. George Meyer believed there was little reason to change anything just for the sake of making it look new. Pipes, wires and the basic structure were all that really concerned him when it came to his house. Nevertheless, he took pride in the home where he had raised his daughter and had seen that it was always well cared for. And of course, he had the town's newspaper to run.

Greta was thankful to have come back to her home of long ago. She and her son had left Houston temporarily, escaping from Richard, to this place where she didn't fear for their lives. And, with that sense of safety, she felt she had the power to protect them. In Houston no reasonable choices remained until Richard was caught, tried and put away. And far as the television station's general manager and news director were concerned, they were willing to give her a sabbatical for a few months. They needed her. Beside, her face wouldn't be healed for viewers until then.

"Do you want me to wake Ben?" asked her father as he entered the brightly lit kitchen. He had a little shuffle in his step as he ran his fingers through his thick white hair that never needed combing.

"I thought I'd let him sleep in a little this morning," said Greta. A spatula in hand, she stood over the stove. "If you guys are going fishing again tonight, he's going to need the extra rest."

"I looked in on him before I came down. He reminds me of you when you were about that age."

"I know. You've said that at least half a dozen times in the last two weeks," she responded with a warm smile.

"I can't help it. I look at Ben and I see you in him, the way you were when . . . . Anyway, are you sure that mattress is comfortable enough for him?"

"It's just fine, Dad. Mine is, too."

George nosed his way to the stove where Greta was watching over blueberry pancakes. The coffee maker on the counter was almost finished with its task. George sniffed the fragrant brew. "How come it always tastes better when you make it?" he asked. The table was set with green place mats, white plates with matching cloth napkins, and glasses of orange juice. A small arrangement of seasonal flowers from George's garden served as a centerpiece.

"When did you learn to be a chef?" asked George. He

poured himself a cup of coffee at the counter and sat down at the table. "I thought everyone in the big city TV business ate from a microwave or at those little deli places . . . when they ate. You're so skinny."

"I'm not. I'll bet I've already gained a couple of pounds since I've been here."

"It's because you cook like your mother did. And you've got more time now."

"I could never be as good as Mom. Mom was terrific at everything."

Father and daughter looked into each other's eyes.

"Still miss her, don't we?"

"Yes, we do, Dad."

They sat in comfortable silence and sipped their coffee. The conversation resumed as they sampled the pancakes.

The white curtains above the sink moved gently as a summer morning's breeze wafted through the open window. It was the kind of morning George and Greta had enjoyed many times when Emma Meyer was alive. Warm memories had risen above the sadness as the years passed. Their family of three had been as close as any family could be. Their number was still three, with Ben.

"I've got to go," said George. "I'm not finished with the next edition. And I bet Lucy and Peg are already at the office."

"What time are you and Ben going fishing?" asked Greta, removing dishes from the table. "He'll be anxious to know. You know how excited he gets when you guys go out together."

"Tell him exactly six-thirty. By the time we get on the lake and get our lines in the water, they'll be biting."

"That's what you always used to tell me. Those were great times, Dad. You guys are going to have to take me out with you one of these nights."

"Any time you wanna go. We'll bring the bait, you bring the coffee and cookies."

George gave Greta a kiss on the forehead and pulled on a navy blue sweater that hung by the back door.

"Listen . . . now that you're on the payroll for a couple of more weeks, I want you to find out about the sale of the old Hansen house on the lake. Ruby says it was kind of an unusual deal, but someone is moving in sometime soon, maybe even today."

"Who is Ruby?"

"Ruby Jenkins, Rockwood's top realtor and daughter of the Rockwood's only banker. Whoever bought it must be nuts. It's going to take a fortune to fix it up."

"Sounds like a slow news day to me, Dad," said Greta, deliberately using her professional news voice. "Will Ruby agree to an interview?" She winked and laughed.

"I'm serious," George insisted. "People are going to be curious. I bet the new people have three kids, two little dogs and a big boat. They probably made it big in the city, but couldn't stand it anymore and think life in Rockwood is going to be pure heaven. I thought we might as well put a few lines in the paper since it's the most unusual house in town.

"Any other major assignments today, sir?" she said with the same TV voice. "From the Houston police beat to *The Rockwood Ledger* lake patrol." She laughed again, but at herself, as she realized how her life had changed so suddenly and dramatically. Only for a while, she hoped.

"And sell them a subscription while you're there." He opened the back door. "I need every subscriber I can get. Sell 'em advertising too if they're business people. Great breakfast."

George smiled at his daughter and closed the back door behind him.

Greta discussed her assignment with Ben as he finished his pancakes and juice. He didn't mind going along, but he didn't want to walk to the lake, as his mother suggested. She listed all of the reasons why walking to the house down by the lake was the best thing to do. She had grown so tired of battling the traffic in Houston, the thought of walking to a destination sounded nothing short of wonderful.

Ben would walk, he said, if he could take a ball with him and have an ice cream cone downtown after their lunch. Greta agreed, aware that she'd been one-upped again.

Almost every place in Rockwood was within walking distance. Over thirteen hundred seasonal and year-round residents didn't take up much room. Her father had told her once that it figured out to be one resident to each acre of Lake Emmet. The Lake Road was only five miles full-circle. Greta had jogged the road once, with Ben along on his new bicycle. Grandpa George had bought it for him at Dalton's Hardware as a welcome home present.

Rockwood was a small town with big pride. It stood out from other rural communities in this part of the heartland because of its natural attraction, Lake Emmet, and its Native American Indian heritage. The lake was given credit for keeping the town's economy robust and its character interesting. Owners from around the state opened the summer lake homes as early as April. Anglers were usually the first to arrive for the season, reaping their rewards during the spawning season. July Fourth, the annual Water Festival and other community events during the year brought in weekend tourists. Local business people grew accustomed to the annual in-and out-migration and now depended on it.

"So, what do you think, Ben?" asked Greta as they began their walk.

He stayed two steps ahead of her as he tossed his blue ball in the air and caught it while trying to avoid stepping on any cracks in the sidewalk. He explained that he had to do it to win the game he had just made up.

"Think about what?" he finally responded.

"I mean, how do you feel about staying here with Grandpa . . . about living here in Rockwood for a while?"

"It's OK, I guess. I kinda miss my friends. But it's OK, I guess."

Greta thought she might have asked too soon. They had been in Rockwood only two weeks. She had told Ben it would probably be for just part of the summer and that they would then decide together what to do long-term.

The town felt safe. And Ben's safety was her foremost consideration when they left Houston. Let Ben enjoy the freedom, the space and his grandfather. It was good for both of them to get away from the hectic pace and their personal tragedy in Texas. She had seen enough pain to last a lifetime. But that was her job...reporting a lot of that pain. And she loved the television news business. Yes, Rockwood was certainly fine for the next month or so.

"Here, catch," said Ben as he threw the ball at Greta. The ball came toward her, breaking into her thoughts. She caught it and returned a perfect throw.

"Great, Mom!"

Greta smiled at her growing second-grader. He was slender, strong and really quite handsome, she thought. Like his father, but with a good soul. "Speaking of friends, maybe you'll meet some new ones this morning."

"I thought we were going on a big news story."

"We are . . . sort of. A new family may be moving in this morning, just a couple of blocks or so from here. And I thought we would welcome them to Rockwood and, at the same time find out a little bit about them."

"That wouldn't be news in Houston. This is going to be pretty boring for you, Mom."

"Maybe so, but we also might meet some interesting people. There might be kids about your age you could get to know. They might be a little afraid of moving to a strange town. Kind of like it was when we came here and you went to school here on your first day."

"I wasn't afraid, Mom. I just didn't know anybody but you and Grandpa."

"I'm sorry, Ben. I know you weren't afraid. You're the bravest boy I've ever known." She put her arm around his shoulders and pressed him to her side. He wiggled free and kicked his ball down the sidewalk.

Despite the trauma she and Ben had been through the last three years, and the uncertainty of their future, she was thankful to be here. Dad was healthy and as wonderful as ever, and Ben seemed to be adapting fairly well to his new surroundings and school, what was left of the school year. What a contrast Rockwood's quiet pace was to Houston's.

Greta threw her shoulders back and drenched her face and body in the warm morning sun. The gentle wind coming off the lake had its way with her short hair. It was no longer the long camera-ready style, but she thought the short look was attractive once she'd had it professionally styled. The scalp wounds and bruising were also looking better.

The summer clothes she wore showed off her healthy-looking figure. She was glad for the opportunity for outdoor exercise here. Sometimes, in Houston, she felt guilty going to exercise classes twice a week. It had meant spending even less time with Ben. Richard had even brought the issue up in court during the custody hearing. Time to forget big city news and perfect bodies and hairdos, she told herself.

Ben was a half block away, still kicking the ball. Greta increased her stride a little to keep up. For a moment she was absorbed by her immediate environment . . . not as a reporter gathering facts for others, but simply a person enjoying the simple pleasure of walking through a small town neighborhood.

Many of the homes in this Iowa resort town were older, but well cared for, and they lent an aura of stability and community. Lawns were trimmed and streets were clean. The few brick streets that remained reminded Greta of playing with her friends when she was younger. And the forest of indigenous oak trees and the sprinkling of pines planted by residents around the lake had grown taller than she had ever imagined they would.

The house she and Ben were looking for was less than a block away. They could see part of the lake straight ahead. The stone piers jutting into the water and the sandy beach had been among her most vivid memories of Rockwood.

"Is that the house we're going to?" asked Ben.

"That's it."

"Wow! It looks like something out of a horror movie or something." Ben urged his mother to walk faster. "You mean kids like me might be living there? Wow!"

"Hold on now," said his mother. "I don't know who is moving in or even if anyone has moved in. That's why we're here . . . to *investigate.*"

Greta even felt a twinge of excitement, too. She had been inside the unique house twice before, when her father had let her tag along. Something to do with a legal notice that had to be published, she vaguely recalled.

Some of their anticipation vanished as Greta and Ben approached the dark stone house. There was no activity . . . nothing was happening in the street, in front of the house or in the driveway. No boxes or furniture or people were to be seen. The house was somewhat secluded between the row of oak trees to the South and the bushes and fence in the front, but they hid no movement or household items waiting to be moved inside. The front door was closed and windows covered from the inside.

The reporter and her assistant approached the steps leading to the expansive front porch. Greta turned to Ben, expecting him to be disappointed.

"I guess we're just here too early, Ben," said Greta. "We can come back later today and see if they moved in."

Ben really didn't care about the house's new occupants at the moment. He was ready to explore a castle, look for its dungeon and discover treasure. After a quick glance through the front door window, he ran fast down the steps and around to the back of the house.

"Hold on, Ben. No one's home."

"Look at the lake, Mom. They even have their own little beach. That's not fair." Ben was like an puppy let out in the yard for the first time.

"Ben?" Greta lost sight of her son as he dashed further behind the house. Let him explore, she thought.

She walked down the front steps and onto the front lawn. Bending, she twirled the wooded wings of the hawk-shaped yard vane she discovered. Her clear blue eyes traced the exterior of the two and half story house. She tried to remember at what exact age she had been here. Ten . . . maybe eleven. One time was on business with her father, she was sure of that, and the other time was more of a social call.

Ben climbed the stone steps to the long porch attached to

the back of the house. Several uncovered windows reflected the morning sun, blue lake and sky. He cupped his hands around his eyes and tried to look through one of them. He moved to another window and then to a large set of doors. He stopped and his heart almost popped out of his mouth. One of the double doors was open about four inches. Exhilaration! Panic! Disbelief and luck . . . then indecision.

Ben peeked cautiously through the narrow opening. He saw a large desk, tall bookcases and a fireplace. A large oval rug covered part of the wooden floor. Not far from the open door he saw a big green sofa, its high back facing him. A tall lamp stood at one end.

Mustering courage, Ben slowly pushed open the unlocked door. It swung silently and easily although it was the heaviest door he'd ever encountered. He told himself that what he was doing wasn't wrong. Exploring wasn't wrong when you knew you weren't going to do anything bad. Besides his mom might be glad he found an open door. What if, instead of him, a bad guy found this door open? What if there was a really big storm and the wind blew it open and the rain came in and got everything wet? It was probably a good thing the door was found open by somebody that was good. Ben practiced the last thought in his mind in case his mother, who had not come around back yet, should ask.

Ben slid past the open door and into the quiet room. He knew he wouldn't go too far, at least not until his mother came. But he wanted to explore a little by himself. He held on to the back of the sofa as he scanned the high ceiling. He thought how much fun it would be to climb the tall bookcases.

Ben's fantasy was suddenly interrupted as a pair of large hands grabbed his wrists from the other side of the sofa. Before he could even gasp, he was pulled over the back of the sofa and found himself face to face with a man whose eyes sent terror racing through him. The unshaven man, dressed only in wrinkled pants, instantly moved to a sitting position. His eyes penetrated the boy's as if trying to comprehend the situation. Ben tugged and twisted to free himself. He knew he should yell. But fear prevented any sound from his throat . . . just like in scary dreams he had once in a while.

"What the hell?" barked the man.

Ben felt the strong hands loosen a little. "Help!" He managed a breathy "Mom!" and another "Help." The man released him and Ben ran as fast as he could for the open door.

"Wait. Wait a minute." Phillip Williams slid back down onto the cushions and rubbed his eyes. "Dammit!" He pounded the sofa once with his fist and ran his hands down his face as if it would help make sense of what had just happened.

Greta, panicked with heart racing, ran up the back porch steps and reached for her child.

"Run, Mom, run! There's a crazy guy in the house and he grabbed me! I bet he's a homeless guy or a killer, Mom!"

Twenty minutes later, Larry Champ, Rockwood's police chief, stood on the front steps of Phillip Williams' house, in response to an urgent call from a woman he had known since they had gone to high school together. The house's occupant sat barefoot on the top step. The Chief's service revolver was holstered to the side of his round stomach. His voice and his actions were calm, but he gripped a nightstick in his left hand. Champ's police car sat idling in the driveway. Sporadic radio chatter came through the open car window.

Greta's silver Volvo station wagon pulled in behind the squad car with a screech. Williams eyed the Texas plates. He remained seated on the top step, trying to see the driver's face through the windshield.

"That's him," shouted Ben as Greta turned off the car. "That's the guy who grabbed me and said the bad word, too."

She and Ben approached the stranger and Chief Champ. Champ motioned them forward. Williams stood, facing a very angry looking mother.

"That's him, Mom!" Excitement, not fear, made Ben take an extra step forward, to get a better look at a real criminal just caught by his mom's high school friend the police chief. Wow!

Greta was cocked and ready to fire. She glared at the drifter as she positioned herself between her son and his attacker.

"What's going on, Larry?" said Greta. Her eyes didn't let go. "Why no cuffs?"

Champ extended his hands, palms down, bouncing them a little, as if trying to calm down a crowd that was getting out of control.

"Greta, meet Mr. Williams." Champ waited for her response. None came. "Mr. Williams is the new resident of this house. He showed me the papers. He moved in last night."

"What?" Greta turned her stare from Williams to Champ, then to Ben. Her expression softened only slightly.

"My name is Phillip Williams. Actually, I am leasing the house for now, with an option to buy." The man moved forward to close the gap. He offered his right hand. She slowly returned the gesture and they shook hands.

"And this is young Ben," continued Champ. Ben moved front and center to meet Williams. "I can vouch for Ben. He's a great kid, just a little curious, like his mother." The chief grinned.

Phillip bent down to Ben's eye level. "Sorry I frightened you Ben, I was half asleep on the sofa. I heard something . . . I saw hands and I just reacted. Can I see your wrists?"

"They're fine," said Greta coldly.

"I hope I didn't hurt you, Ben."

"They don't hurt anymore," Ben said. He looked at his

mother. Her face hadn't warmed any. "I'm sorry I scared you, Mr. Williams. The door was open a little bit, but I guess I shouldn't have come inside. I just wanted to explore."

"No harm done," said Williams. "If I had found an open door to a place like this when I was your age, I've have wanted to go inside, too. Just like Indiana Jones."

"Who?" asked Ben.

Phillip stood up and faced Ben's mother. "I apologize for frightening your son, Mrs . . . ?"

"Meyer. Greta Meyer."

chapter 11

Kitchen lights in the stone house went on just before one o'clock according to Williams' watch, three hours after the police chief left. He'd spent intervening time investigating the house, top to bottom. He was pleased to discover everything seemed to be in reasonable working order. As for an air conditioner, there was none. And knowing if the furnace worked would never be relevant during his stay. He couldn't be sure about the telephone lines and the DSL services that he was supposed to have were working. The realtor had promised services would be activated before he arrived, but he had no telephone to check the line. He hadn't used his cellular phone for the past three weeks and wouldn't again for some time. He would try the Internet service later with his laptop.

The lakeside house and it contents were old and worn, but spotlessly clean. Best of all, it included more furnishings that he had realized the night before. There would be very little else he would need.

The furniture was from an earlier era. Most pieces were of interesting design, and like the house, comfortable and well lived in. Windows and doors opened and closed well and the plaster walls showed few cracks. In short, it was ideal.

Williams could tell the place had been built with views in mind. The back, including a large window upstairs in the master bedroom, faced the lake to the east. Below there was a broad expanse of lawn, overgrown now, that ended at the lake's edge. The large bedroom's east window looked over the street and the fenced front yard. The north and south lot lines were marked by stands of oak trees intermingled with lilac bushes. The front of 17 Lakeside Drive faced a row of well-kept homes on large lots across the street. There was distance and privacy from neighbors, but still a sense of neighborhood.

Phillip was hungry . . . and agitated. The two candy bars he had purchased at the Des Moines airport the night before were gone. Those and the water he washed them down with were the only nutrition he had in eighteen hours. Caroline had always told him that he became irritable when he was hungry and ate sugar. It was true. He needed to find a café somewhere in town soon.

The earlier incident in the house with Ben Meyer played on his mind, too. He replayed the scenario over and over again inside his head: the screams of the young intruder, the police chief pounding on the front door, and the confrontation with an irate mother . . . all within ten hours of arriving in town. "Jesus Christ!"

"Excuse me?" came an unexpected voice from the entryway. The words sounded more like a statement than a question.

Phillip was en route to the front door when he saw a woman in a dark green pantsuit already inside the house.

"I see you have a bad habit of leaving doors open," said the woman. "Just kidding." Parts of her body jiggled a little when she chuckled.

Williams said nothing, but offered a perplexed look at the short woman with a big friendly grin.

"Hi! I'm Ruby Jenkins from Lake Realty, and I have a hunch you arrived ahead of schedule," she continued. Her tone was cheerful and confident. "Welcome to Rockwood."

"Thanks . . . I guess." His voice had a slight edge. "I didn't count on so many people just dropping in right away."

"It's par for the course in a small town like this. But you're going to love it here. I'm sure you'll run into my father sooner or later, too. He owns the bank, you know."

"I expect I will, if I need a checking account." Williams' stomach growled. He was also aware that he hadn't shaved or put on his shoes. "What can I do for you, Ruby?"

"I have just two more papers for you to sign, now that you're here." She pressed her way past him and went into the kitchen as if she knew the house well. "It will only take a minute. I'll leave copies of it with you. By the way, where is your car? I wouldn't have known you were here except for hearing it from Chief Champ. My office is right next door to the police station."

"I don't have one yet. Actually, I thought I might try to see what life can be like not owning one." He quickly asked for the paper and a pen. She pulled a small file from her canvas bag and laid the items on the kitchen table and they sat down.

"You're really going to enjoy this house. The roof will last forever . . . it's made out of slate, if you haven't already noticed. The basement doesn't leak, and most of the plumbing and electrical have been undated in the last ten years. The furnace works fine, too."

Phillip listened to her enthusiastic appraisal as he scanned the documents.

"You only have neighbors on one side which makes for a very private residence. And there's a fabulous view of Lake Emmet. Best of all, it's mostly furnished . . . just like you said you wanted. No hassle, no fuss."

Phillip looked up at her only briefly as he flipped to another page.

"Will your family be joining you soon?

"My family will not be joining me."

"Oh, I see. Well, I'm sure you're going to be very happy here. Rockwood is a gem of a little town. Do you fish?"

"When time permits." His stomach growled again, louder this time.

Ruby looked at her watch. "I think you'll find the telephone lines are working now. I told them to switch everything on at noon."

She pulled a pink trim-line telephone from her large bag and put it in the center of the table. "It's kind of beat up. Sorry about the color, but it works fine. I didn't know if you might need one immediately, so I brought this just in case. A phone is the only thing the rich kid who owns the place didn't leave.

"Thank you. It's very thoughtful of you."

Williams found the last "X" on the last page and signed. He was sure the paper work was routine, but he wanted it totally completed so there would be no more surprise visits from the realtor and anyone else. Besides, he was starving.

Phillip handed the papers to Ruby and rose from the table. His tone and gestures urged her to complete her business and leave. But she stood and walked across the kitchen, opened the refrigerator and stuck her hand inside.

"It should be cold enough to use pretty soon. Do you need a ride downtown to the market?"

"It's nice of you to offer, but I think I'd prefer to walk. I might as well try out the no-car lifestyle right away. And it'll give me a chance to see a little of your town."

"You mean *your* town." Ruby picked up her bag and shook

Phillip's hand. She followed him to the front door. "You won't have to lock your doors here, but you might want to at least close them . . . just kidding." She laughed and waved as she walked down the front steps to her car.

———

Following a shower and shave, Phillip Williams stepped from his new home into the warm sunlight of an Iowa afternoon. He stood on the front porch and surveyed the yard and the houses across the street. The short night of sleep that was dotted with disturbing images of Caroline and the events of the morning had left him a little exhausted. He needed to walk. He needed to eat.

He bent down and spun the wooden wings of the yard vane as he walked across the front lawn to the side of his house. He continued around the house to the back yard. The thick grass gently sloped into Lake Emmet and it looked as if a small beach had once been there, but had long since eroded. He thought he could make out a small marina about a third way around the lakeshore on his right.

To his left were two, long, pier-like structures made of what looked like stone and concrete extending some forty yards into the lake from the shore. Each looked wide enough for at least four people to walk abreast and they ended in a wide circular area bordered by a railing. A tall light with a stone base stood at the center of the circle, towering above a series of benches overlooking the lake. A man in a small fishing boat was trying his luck at the edge of a nearby weed bed. He could also make out a good size beach where several children were playing. Lund couldn't help thinking *what a wonderful place to grow up as a kid.*

He surveyed the skyline and spotted the top of the town's

water tower peeking above the trees to the west. He walked down his driveway to the street, feeling he would find the business district and a café in very short time.

————

Greta Meyer jumped from her chair as she saw Phillip Williams walk past the front window of *The Rockwood Ledger*. A stroke of luck, she thought. She still needed to write the article about the sale of the Hansen house for next Wednesday's issue, but she had completely forgotten to ask any questions of Williams earlier. She also had some personal questions for him.

"I'll be back in a minute," she said to Peg Swanson, one of her father's two employees.

Peg acknowledged Greta's statement and disappeared into another room.

"Williams," shouted Greta, pulling the office door shut behind her. She walked quickly toward him. "Williams."

"I want to ask you a few questions," she said, as he looked over his shoulder.

Still walking, he noted the paper's name on the building from where she came. "A reporter," he said to himself. Williams pushed his clean, sandy hair back and adjusted his sunglasses. "I'm going to that café over there and I'm not stopping for anything or anyone." He spoke slowly and clearly without breaking his stride. He pointed at the Corky's Café sign down Main Street.

Greta followed just one step behind. "When was the last time you ate?"

He ignored the question. As they entered the café, he eyed a booth in the back. The handful of patrons stared as Greta followed him to the booth where she sat opposite him. Mid-afternoon in summer was not a busy time for either of the only two downtown cafes, except when it was raining or during the Water Festival.

Williams continued to ignore her as he scanned the menu. She stared at him, but it didn't crack his concentration. The scene echoed times with Richard when he would completely shut her out.

A waitress brought two glasses of iced water and drew a pad from the pocket of her light blue uniform. Phillip special-ordered three scrambled eggs, English muffin, coffee and milk. Greta asked for iced tea.

"Two checks, please," snapped the tea drinker.

"So. What's really going on here, Mrs. Meyer?" It was the first time he really had looked into her eyes. They were behind sunglasses the first time they met on his porch. She turned her eyes away for just a faction of a second, long enough for him to notice bruising around her right eye. He said nothing.

Greta took a deep breath. "Last night the old Hansen house was empty. Early this morning a homeless-looking man is living in it. He appeared out of nowhere, has no car, no belongings to unload and he . . . "

"And he has no food," interrupted Williams.

"And he had only leased the place."

"Ah . . . Ruby. There is an option to buy."

"And he frightened the daylights out of my son and me. And you don't think I'm just a little curious about you?"

"I didn't mean to scare your kid. He broke in. I was asleep . . . ."

"His name is Ben. And he didn't break in. He was just curious."

"Is this the way people in Rockwood behave when someone new moves in?"

"I'm not from here . . . I mean I am, but that was long ago."

"So most people here aren't like you, then? Good. I may have picked the right town after all." Phillip's voice took on a bitter tone. "And no, I don't have a pretty little homemaker wife and a two smart little kids . . . nor do I have a mini-van, a beagle, or a truck full of furniture and boxes on the way waiting to be carried in."

A few patrons' eyes and a few ears caught the drama in the back booth.

Greta leaned over the table and fixed him with an icy look. "Sorry to hear you're not Mr. Average. But you could at least act civilized."

"Hey, I'm not the bad guy here," shot back Williams. "As a matter of fact, I think you owe me an apology."

The waitress came to the booth with their orders. Greta scooted out of the seat.

"I'll consider an apology after I find out who the hell you are. And stay away from Ben."

She put a dollar on the table from her pocket, strode to the front door and out onto the sidewalk. Her face looked intense, almost fuming and she walked toward the newspaper office without a story.

Williams left nothing on his plate or in his cup. He left a two-dollar tip on the table and walked to the counter with his check.

"How was the food?" asked his waitress. Standing behind the cash register, her eyes locked onto his after glancing at his left hand.

"Good enough to come back," replied Phillip.

"Well, that's good to hear. Are you new in Rockwood?" She gave him a flirtatious smile and his change.

"I'm new and I'll be back," he said as he quickly pocketed the change and took a step toward the door.

"Thanks for coming. See you soon."

Phillip walked up, then down Main Street looking in all directions and taking his time. The business district was three blocks long and made up of mostly turn-of-the-century brick buildings, he guessed, trimmed at the bottom with stones, similar to the ones on the outside of his own house. The sidewalks and streets were wide, clean and free of parking meters. Appealing storefronts and the numbers of parked cars indicated Rockwood enjoyed a healthy economy. Phillip noticed only two empty buildings at the T intersection at the beginning of the first block.

He responded to half a dozen people who, in passing, greeted him with a "hello." Older men talked with one another next to their pickups. Kids ran in and out of Lewis Variety. Women shoppers exchanged comments, passed display windows and entered stores. He surmised that many of Rockwood's residents were working, but would be out in force on Saturdays like in most small towns in the Midwest.

Phillip remembered the time when he was eleven and he and his best friend, Alex, had walked around downtown Hayward, Wisconsin. He and his family were staying at a nearby resort on Middle Eau Claire Lake and had invited Alex along for the week. While the parents shopped, he and his friend were free to explore. Phillip remembered the smells of the bakery, the front windows of the candy and souvenir shops, and the warm sun making summer vacation official. There had been hundreds of strangers on the sidewalks but it was just a safe and simple adventure for a couple of young boys, a little magic not to be forgotten. Williams sensed a bit of that magic in Rockwood, too.

The manager of Sunshine Market at the end of Main was more than happy to deliver the $137.60 worth of groceries and other necessities Williams purchased. He paid cash and briefly talked with the two women cashiers. Everyone wants to talk, he thought. He refused a ride from the owner, Roger Daulkie, and told him he would meet him at the house.

After the kitchen was stocked, Phillip called the telephone company and convinced the appropriate person that, yes, he really did want his number unlisted. His priority for the rest of the day was to set up an office in the library with the executive desk as the center of operations. As he attended to his duties of getting his house in order, he replayed the details of the two preceding days in his mind. It was vital that his trail from Manitou Springs to Rockwood was as absolutely clean as could be. No one from the past, except his friend in Minneapolis, could know where he was. No credit cards. No cell phone and checks. Nothing that would give his identity away.

———

Dinner was a full plate of spicy chicken strips and rice from a skillet, and a cold bottle of beer that he enjoyed while sitting on his deck facing Lake Emmet. The water was calm and a small armada of fishing boats and their captains were on the hunt for fish not far from the southern shore line. With his plate and bottle empty, Phillip decided to walk part way around the lake. He figured there was no better way to get charged up before he started his writing for the night. He slipped on a light jacket, shut the front and back doors and bounced down the back steps toward Lake Emmet.

The June air turned cool as the orange sun retired from the sky. Williams caught himself again looking back to his younger days in northern Wisconsin. He remembered how he'd loved fishing with his father on a night like this. Their special times together were too few. But he could still smell the sweet smoke drifting across the lake from a fireplace and the cries of the loons. He had spent evenings like that with Caroline, too. Both loved ones were gone from his life, now. Both had left too soon. He could feel his eyes almost beginning to tear up, but immediately stopped the process with a reminder of why he was here and what he needed to do.

He walked as close to the shoreline as possible and studied the layout of the lake. He had to anticipate everything . . . take nothing for granted. He noted how quickly his mind moved from warm memories to strategy.

"Hi." came a soft, but distinct voice. Phillip assumed the greeting was meant for him and he stopped to find its source. He saw nothing but an older man getting set to launch a small fishing boat from the public access ramp. Williams walked toward the boat. The man stood up straight and watched him approach.

"Boo!" shouted the boy with a big grin as he popped up from inside the boat.

"Ben Meyer!" Phillip exclaimed. A youngster with a simple trick had made him smile. "I remember the police chief said he could vouch for you, so I guess I don't have anything to be afraid of." Phillip looked across the boat's gunwale and gave Ben a wink.

"There's nothing to be afraid of in this town, Mr. Williams. I'm George Meyer, Ben's grandfather. Welcome to Rockwood."

Phillip accepted his handshake. He was pleased at the friendly gesture, but felt a slight uneasiness being called by name from someone he didn't know.

"Word travels fast, doesn't it?" said Phillip.

"That depends on what the word is, Mr. Williams," replied Meyer. "Actually, Greta told me what you looked like. She wasn't wrong . . . has the eye of a good reporter."

"And just how did she describe me?"

"Well . . . she said you have a 'city look', at least she thought so when she saw you the second time. I think I'd better not tell you the rest."

"I can imagine. What happened this morning was unfortunate. I guess I should have expected the unexpected."

Ben sat in the boat, his eyes and ears glued to the stranger. "My grandpa runs the newspaper and he knows everything. We're going fishing now."

"I can see that. How many do you think you'll catch tonight?" asked Williams.

"Lots! Maybe more. Grandpa's the best fisherman in Iowa and he taught me."

"Sounds like you have the best grandpa in the world, Ben. And sounds like I ought to try my luck on this lake sometime."

"We'd better hurry, Ben, if we're going to get any fishing done," said George. "Your mom is counting on us to bring back dinner for tomorrow night."

Ben and George finished loading their fishing rods and tackle boxes. Phillip took a step back and watched the team in action. Ben and George verbally checked off life vests, seat cushions, bait, cookies and thermos.

"Are you going to be warm enough, Ben?" asked George. He put on a well-worn fishing vest over his plaid shirt. "It's a little nippier than I thought it was going to be. We should have brought your jacket like your mother said."

Williams wondered how involved he should let himself get with people in the community. He looked at Ben and then removed his navy jacket and offered it to the boy. He decided the gesture might neutralize the rough beginning he'd had with an obviously good family. "It's a little big, but it might help."

"You don't have to do that," said Ben in a grownup voice. "I'm not cold."

"I know, but take it's just in case those fish are really biting and you want to stay out longer than you planned." Phillip laid the jacket on the bow of the boat. "My dad always told me that when you fish for the big ones at night, you need a good knot on your line, a good jacket and good luck."

As George listened to Williams, he watched Ben's reaction. "Are you sure you won't need your jacket, Mr. Williams? It looks like you were just setting out for a walk . . . and it is getting cooler."

"I'm out for a short one and then I have to get to work. I'll pick it up some other time. Or just leave it on my front porch tomorrow if you're passing by. Don't worry about it."

"What kind of work are you in, Mr. Williams?

Phillip chose his words carefully. He shouldn't have mentioned anything. He'd have to be more careful. "It would take too much time to explain it now. You and Ben better hurry while there's still some daylight."

Phillip threw the bowline into the boat and pushed Ben and George out onto Lake Emmet. The old six-horse Evinrude purred after one pull. The fishermen waved as their boat glided across the water, the dipping sun at their backs. Williams returned the wave.

There weren't any loons and the pine trees were sparse compared to the lakes he knew in Wisconsin, but Lake Emmet reflected the same sky . . . and there was a faint smell of wood smoke . . . just like in Chippewa country.

chapter 12

Greta stared across the kitchen table at the navy jacket hanging on the back of a chair. As she sipped her morning coffee, she tried, as she had the day before, to decide what time would be best to drop it off at the Williams house. It had been sitting in the kitchen for three days now. Her father and Ben both offered to return it, but Greta insisted she was the one who would do it.

She thought again how George and Ben had described their reaction to Williams' jacket offer. Ben said that Mr. Williams really wasn't a scary guy at all, and Grandpa suggested they should look beyond the cover. Obviously Williams had made a positive impression on them. But neither was as curious about the stranger as she was. It was her nature. It was her job. She would give consideration to her father's advice, however.

"Yes, I'd like the number of the Phillip Williams residence in Rockwood," she told the operator. "It should be a new listing." Greta thought it best to let Williams know she was on her way.

"I'm sorry," said the operator. "but that number is unlisted. I am unable to give you that number."

"Damn." Greta regained a dial tone and called the news-paper office.

"Rockwood Ledger," answered Peg.

"Is Dad there, Peg?" She had to wait only a few seconds before George picked up.

"Hi sweetie," said George.

"Hi, Dad. I think I'm going to be running later that I thought his morning. Would you mind keeping Ben there with you until about one?"

"Not at all. Take your time. I'll take Ben to lunch. I owe him anyway. He caught the most fish the other night. We'll see you whenever you get here."

"Thanks, Dad. Love ya . . . 'bye." One day, she knew, she would sadly miss her father's comforting voice.

She walked upstairs with the intention of changing clothes. Or would the blue shorts and yellow knit top she was wearing be appropriate? It was summer, and it was going to be hotter than the day before all over Iowa, according to the morning's TV weather forecast. Besides, she would get more sun if she didn't change and if she walked to his house. What the hell. She bounced down the stairs, checked the doors and left with Williams' jacket.

Two coffee mugs and a pair of wire-rim glassed rested on the walnut desk beside a laptop computer, a mini digital voice recorder and scattered papers. Phillip sat at the op-erations center dressed only in green athletic shorts and a day's growth of whiskers. A gentle breeze blew though the library window, bringing with it the fragrance of late blooming bushes beneath the open window. He heard the faint drone of a motorboat. The French doors were open and pushed back, offering a view of the lake glistening in the morning sun.

He broke away from his computer with the sound of the doorbell. He tilted the laptop screen down and shut the double doors behind him as he left the library to greet another unexpected visitor. He grabbed a black T-shirt from the hall tree on his way. He opened the door with his shirt in hand, half expecting to see Ruby Jenkins. Phillip suspected he had not seen the last of her. The face he saw instead caught him off guard. He had definitely noticed her pleasant appearance the two times he had seen her, but today, he thought, she looked like summer itself.

"You are home," stated Greta. Her eyes moved from his face to his chest and back again as he tried to quickly put on his shirt. She looked down at his legs and feet as he wrestled the T-shirt over his head.

"I wasn't expecting anyone . . . as usual," said Phillip.

"I tried to call you first, but your number is unlisted."

"I like privacy. It's a hard commodity to come by anymore, don't you think?"

"I won't take much of your time. I just want to return your jacket and thank you for loaning it to Ben the other night." Her voice was calmer than it had been during their last encounter. "I'm sorry I didn't get it back to you sooner." She moved closer to hand him the jacket.

Phillip stepped back slightly from the threshold, opening a passage to the inside of the house. "I'm sorry . . . please come in."

He looked startled with what he had just said. For the past seven months or more he had uttered only angry words or no words at all, to almost anyone, except this mother. All he had wanted to do was to be left alone to grieve and to fan his hatred for those who had destroyed his family and life.

Greta caught the awkwardness in Phillip's face that lasted only a second.

"What about your privacy?" she asked with a smile. "I really don't think you want to be disturbed by having me come in." She removed her sunglasses, revealing thick eyebrows and thickly lashed blue eyes. He assumed a little makeup was applied on his behalf to make the fading bruise on her eye less visible.

"Yes, I like my privacy. And no, right now you're not disturbing me. Come in."

Phillip took his jacket and gestured again for her to enter. She accepted the invitation.

"I don't think it's changed a bit," said Greta as she glanced around. She walked across a thick, ornate rug that partially covered the hallway's wooden floor. "I remember the hall tree."

"You've been inside this house before?" asked Phillip. "Oh, that's right . . . you're not from here, but you really are, but from a long time ago. Right?"

Greta looked puzzled as to how to react, but then she let out a small smile and brief laugh.

"I visited this house when I was about eleven. I came with my father on business." She started down the hallway toward the large, double doors and looked from side to side. "There was a huge library down this way filled with books, and beautiful art on the walls. I sat in a chair next to a stone fireplace while my father talked with Mr. Hansen. I was even offered tea."

Phillip moved in front of her as they reached the closed library doors. "This room is private," he said, trying not to be too abrupt.

"Of course. Excuse me. I guess I got carried away with the past. The past . . . funny that it can be haunting or comforting, maybe both at the same time, don't you think?"

"Would you like some coffee?"

"I really can't stay long."

"I'll give you a small cup."

Phillip showed her the remainder of the downstairs and suggested having their coffee on the back deck. He led the way into the kitchen where he poured two cups from a metal percolator on the stove.

"I'm going to have to get the electric kind that uses filters. I'm afraid the stuff out of this pot tastes like coffee on a cattle drive. I can offer you tea if you don't want this stuff."

"This will be fine, thanks."

They walked from the kitchen out onto the long deck and sat facing each other at a white wrought iron table where they could see the lake.

"So you grew up in Rockwood, but moved away I assume," said Phillip.

"Actually, I was born in Des Moines. My father worked as a reporter for *The Des Moines Register* for eighteen years and then bought the paper in Rockwood when I was seven. I lived here until I left for college. It was a wonderful life."

"What college, if I may ask?"

"Columbia."

Phillip watched her fingers and wrist as she sipped her coffee. No wedding band.

"Milk or sugar? It's probably pretty strong."

"It is. A little of both would be nice if you have any. But it's really not bad the way it is."

Phillip returned from the kitchen with a quart carton of milk, an uncovered sugar bowl and a spoon. Greta was kneeling, pulling dead flowers from several clay pots on the porch. Phillip set the items on the table and took the opportunity to study her, unnoticed. He thought she was attractive. She reminded him a little of how pretty Caroline had always looked. She was probably a pleasant person, but he was not about to forget her snappish temper earlier in the week.

As he bent down near her, taking interest in her task, he noticed a small, but wicked looking cut on top of her right shoulder that was in its healing stage. Her summer top had shifted enough to expose it as she reached to pull out more dead stems.

At the base of her skull he saw an even larger and more serious looking wound, longer and wider than the other, at the base of her skull. And there was another smaller one about two inches above that. They weren't as initially obvious as the cut on her shoulder since they were partially hidden by her short, but thick, dark hair. *Yes, this is all connected with the slight bruising around her eye.*

Phillip said nothing. Instead, he mentioned the milk he brought out. Greta stopped, dusted her hands off and sat down at the table again. She commented on the potential of the house as she stirred a small amount of milk into her cup.

"Thank you," she said.

At that moment a large bee landed on the rim of the sugar bowl, less that two inches from Greta's hand, just as she was about to dip into it. She dropped the spoon and bolted back into her chair. The bee buzzed away.

"I'm sorry," Greta said. "I am very allergic to bee stings. Not a good thing to happen to me although I think I over reacted just now."

"No apology needed. I understand. A lot of people are."

Greta added a small amount of sugar to her cup, stirred and approved of the taste after a sip. Phillip studied her face in detail as she stirred her coffee again. He almost convinced himself there were more wounds, however faint, on her forehead next to the scalp line. He had seen enough to know.

"Would you like some cookies with the coffee? They're store-bought, but I have about six different kinds."

"Thanks for the thought but, like I said, I can't stay long."

"Before you go, aren't you going to ask me anything?" Phillip asked.

She looked surprised by his question. She took another sip, which gave her time to think. "Actually, I would like to ask you a hundred questions, Mr. Williams."

They looked deep into each other's eyes for the first time. Their faces showed a degree of awkwardness.

"What is your number one question, Greta? I'll answer one question."

Greta looked pleased that he had called her by her first name. She pushed her half-empty cup away and folded her hands. Her eyes searched his for honesty.

"Who are you and why are you here?"

Phillip straightened, paused and looked as if he were about to tell a long story. But he had no intention of doing so. He thought that what he was about to tell her would be enough to satisfy her curiosity and stop further questioning. "Those were two questions . . . but it's fair," he began. "I'm on the faculty at a university, which I won't name, and I've taken an extended leave of absence to finish a project I have been working on for a long time."

Greta took another sip of coffee without taking her eyes from his face.

"I moved here because I wanted to see what the Midwest is like, and because I stumbled across this wonderful old house. This looks like the perfect place to work, don't you agree? And I like being by the water. I though it might make a nice vacation home some day when I retire—that option clause Ruby told you about. Pretty dull stuff, really. A little bit unusual, perhaps, but I'm not the alien from *When the Earth Stood Still*." Phillip sat back and waited for Greta's reaction.

"What kind of project?"

"Ah, you have ninety-eight questions left. I can't tell you."

"You don't have a car."

"Is that another question, in disguise?"

"No. But I see you don't have a car," fired Greta.

"Didn't you walk here?" he responded.

"I have a car. But I like to walk."

"Maybe I have a car, too. And maybe I just like to walk."

"But it's not here. Where do you have it parked? Where did you walk from?"

"Ah. Sneaky. I won't tell you."

The throw-and-catch conversation started them laughing. Their bodies relaxed. Even so, Greta was aware her questions were bouncing off his wall.

"But someone like you just doesn't move to a small town like Rockwood, unless there is some very special reason. You *are* an alien!"

They laughed harder. Greta choked on her coffee. And then the laughter died.

"What about you, Greta? Why does someone like you move back here?"

Greta swallowed hard. The cheery look on her face disappeared. "What about me?" she asked defensively.

"Why does someone who is obviously a professional, a reporter of some merit I gather, someone young and attractive, probably with a promising future, move back to Rockwood after all these years? Do you see my point? I think you stand out as much as you think I do. We both have our reasons for being here. And they're personal ones that maybe, at least at this point, no one has any right to know about."

Greta searched his eyes for a long moment. Phillip looked slightly uncomfortable under her probing gaze.

"I would like to know your whole story some day," said Phillip. "But I don't have the right to dig. My story isn't for publication either."

"I started digging when Ben was frightened by you. He means everything to me, and I'll destroy anyone who tries to harm him. Can you understand that?"

"Perfectly."

Greta looked at her watch and stood up. "I have to go. I promised Dad I would pick Ben up at the paper around one, and I still have an errand to finish. Thanks for the coffee."

"This house really has a lot of character," said Greta as they retraced their steps through the kitchen and into the hallway.

"I was surprised when I moved in. I really didn't know what I was getting into."

"Would you mind terribly if I took a quick look upstairs? As a child I always wanted to see it. I won't take more than a minute. Oh, unless it's extra private. I forgot."

"It's OK. Do you want the tour?"

"Oh, no. Don't bother. I just want to take a quick peek and then I have to go. Back in sixty seconds."

She hurried up the wide stairs and disappeared. Phillip returned to the kitchen.

The second floor included three bedrooms, two baths and a sunroom. The two smaller bedrooms, although sizable, were nearly identical and rather disappointing. Each room held double beds without linens. Oval braided rugs, old furniture and dated lamps furnished the two rooms that were overall dark and drab.

The master bedroom was quite the opposite. Someone had decorated the enormous room with splashes of imagination, yet had managed to retain the almost regal appearance common to the rest of the house. A comfortable looking spread and pillows covered the oversized bed facing double glass doors. The view was of the lake and the tall trees. Windows overlooking the street were on the opposite walls. Above the bed was a ceiling fan with four small glass shades. The furnishings looked like they were from the thirties or early forties. The floor was covered in deep, creamy white carpet. Greta made all of these observations within a half-minute.

She noticed a professional-looking digital camera on the larger of two dressers. In the mirror above she could see a suitcase sitting flat, out in the open on a floral love seat under the window. The case's lid was not tightly closed and it would be quite easy to flip it open and look inside should anyone want to do that. Near the suitcase, was a large painted closet door. She quickly, but carefully opened it and found the space empty except for two pairs of casual shoes, and a pair of jeans and tan pants, along with one knit shirt on hangers. "I'd better hurry," she whispered to herself.

Turning her attention back to the suitcase, she brushed her long fingers across its top. Without further hesitation, Greta quickly lifted the lid. A hasty look revealed a disorderly pile of socks, underwear and colored T-shirts. There was also what looked like a small photo album tucked against one side of the case. She jerked back as she also discovered a handgun wedged in one of the front corners. Her heartbeat accelerated. She recognized the revolver as a Smith & Wesson semiautomatic. She had fired a similar one more than once with her friend, Detective Quarve, at a practice range in Houston.

She looked back at the bedroom door. No Williams. She left the gun in place but picked up the album without hesitation. She scanned the four pictures inside and saw the same beautiful young woman in each. They had obviously been taken at different times and places, but they were definitely of the same person. One photograph had snow-capped mountains in the background. In another the woman was in a swimsuit, sitting on a large rock in the water . . . somewhere along the Mediterranean perhaps. The other two were close-ups. Was she his wife? His girlfriend? Someone he had killed, or was going to kill?

She closed the suitcase lid and walked toward the door. On the way down the stairs her pace slowed to a normal step.

Phillip came into the entryway from the kitchen as he heard her hit the last step.

"That was quick. Another disappointment?" asked Phillip.

"Actually, no," Greta answered. "It was much different than what I thought it would be. But I guess that's a lesson we learn many times in life. The master bedroom was quite a surprise." She walked nonchalantly to the front door. " I have to get going."

"Thanks for returning the jacket."

She opened the door, said good-bye and pulled it closed behind her.

———

She kept up a rapid pace the entire way home. Three thoughts gripped her brain. The gun. The pictures. And Williams' explanation for being in Rockwood. She was angry again.

chapter 13

Detective Randy Quarve took Greta Meyer's call without hesitation. He and Greta had developed a close friendship during the past four years and he never refused a call from her unless he was in the middle of a crisis.

Greta's beat for the television station had been Houston P.D., and Quarve was the officer she'd ended up going to for more information on a homicide story the day they met. Their friendship was of mutual benefit to their professional lives. She was always accurate and fair to the Department in her reporting. And if Quarve needed something he thought was important brought to the public's attention, he could always call on Greta to see what she could do. In turn, he sometimes gave Greta more information than her competition. He told her he had confidence in her sleuthing skills. Like most good journalists, she was as much a detective as a reporter. She liked to dig, and dig deep.

Now, Greta was back on the beat again and this time from her kitchen table. She had dialed the familiar number and waited to hear the familiar voice.

"Detective Quarve."

"Randy." She smiled when she heard his voice.

"Greta! Where are you?"

"I'm in Iowa. I decided Ben and I needed to take a road trip to see Dad and get normal again. He's getting older and it's important to spend as much time as I can with him."

"Well, it's great to hear your voice. What's going on in Iowa?"

"What else? The news business. Dad and I are about to put the next issue of the paper to bed. It's a whopping ten pages this week." She laughed. It felt good to talk to a friend.

"There must be big news, kinda like Houston, right?" joked the detective. "I bet you're the best reporter in . . . what's the name of the town?"

"Rockwood."

"Yeah. Rockwood. Never been to Iowa, but I hear it's nice. No crime. No smog. No traffic."

"Rockwood isn't like Houston, that's for sure. The biggest crime recently was a bunch of high school kids putting fresh dog stuff on the front seat of the principal's car. It was sitting in the hot sun and the windows were rolled up."

Greta joined in with Quarve's hearty laughter.

"Actually, there is something that might be going on."

"Like what? It's not Richard again?" said Randy in a louder voice.

"This is something else."

"Good. Maybe that no-contact order did the trick."

"I just wanted to get your opinion on something, and ask you to do a small favor for me if you could."

"You usually figure things out by yourself, but if I can be of any help, you know I will. What's your situation there?"

Greta told Quarve about Phillip Williams' sudden appearance in Rockwood. And that he had told her he was on sabbatical from a university, working on a project he couldn't or wouldn't talk about. He didn't have a car, but he had a gun. He hadn't come with anyone and he hadn't brought much of anything with him, except a few belongings and photographs of a woman stored in a suitcase.

"And there is something about all of this that doesn't seem right to you, I assume?" asked Quarve.

"I guess I smell a story here, Randy. I'm not sure if it's a bad one or a good one."

"Do you know how he got there?

"No, I don't. One night he wasn't here and the next morning he had already moved in with little more than a couple of suitcases. But if I could find how he arrived here . . . that would be a start."

"I agree with you. So you don't think he drove himself there?" ask Randy.

"I really don't. And there isn't any bus service to Rockwood anymore," answered Greta

"Maybe someone dropped him off. He either hitch-hiked there or was brought by a friend, perhaps. Yes, a friend sounds more likely at the moment."

"It's possible. I'll do some checking," said Greta.

"Where's the nearest major airport?" he asked.

"Des Moines or Sioux City. And I know what you're thinking. A gun would have been detected at the security gate and I doubt he bought this kind of semiautomatic handgun here in Rockwood."

The detective further agreed with his friend. Greta quickly jotted down a list of inquiries to make about the gun and transportation. She knew she could put the puzzle together if she had a few pieces of it. She pointed out possible clues coming from the real estate transaction with Ruby Jenkins, references for his utilities and any possible mail being forwarded to his current address.

"You're good, Greta. I'll see what I can find about Williams from here and call you back."

She gave Quarve her father's new telephone number and confirmed if he still had her cell number. He had. He wished her a nice visit in Iowa and told her to never hesitate to call if she needed anything.

"Miss your stories on the news here," added Quarve. "Hurry back."

"Thanks. Give my best to Mary and the kids. Talk to you soon, Randy."

————

Rockwood's newest resident labored over his laptop for six days, a routine of writing and rewriting, walking or running and restless sleeping with quick meals in between. The entire story of his undercover mission at The Fort and the Ford family's operation and goals would somehow be published, he assured himself. Whether he would ever enjoy an academic career again, he really didn't care at this point. But the book would be his ultimate research that America would need to read. It would expose the racial madness of the Fords and other white supremacists like them.

The manuscript would also serve another purpose, as well, something that would produce a quick return for his efforts. It would help bring Caroline's murderer out into the open.

The writing was going well, but his sleeping wasn't. When Williams wrote, and then tried sleep, he relived long and short pieces of the past. The replay of Caroline's murder always led to vivid images of the Fords. He saw Jesse's eyes, eyes that always seemed to be looking into the past while his voice prophesied a new world order in a voice that ranted and at times whispered in a deadly tone. And the image of Tommy Ford would live forever inside Phillip's mind. He was a ticking time bomb. His small close-set eyes and constant toothy smile were unforgettable. Tommy was a reactionary. His mouth never ceased pouring out anger and plots.

Phillip had long speculated about the reasons Jesse, Barry and Tommy had become staunch fanatics. Why would men like Jesse and Barry, both intelligent people with valuable life skills, be so devoured by hatred toward anyone who was not white? He had found a possible answer in the data file John Kick had given him soon after accepting the assignment. Jesse Ford's wife was been killed in a night armed robbery attempt during a family trip to Washington D.C. in the eighties. According to the file, two black men, armed with knives, tried to rob Mrs. Ford as she and a young Barry walked one night to a restaurant near their hotel. Mrs. Ford was stabbed when she refused to surrender her purse with the family's trip money inside. Jesse, who was not far behind with Tommy, tackled one of the bandits but suffered a deep slashed across the face during the scuffle. In his furious defense of his family, he crushed the attacker's skull and broke his neck. Then Jesse erased the man's face on the bloodied sidewalk as the accomplice fled.

The file went on to note that Ford was involved with several minor racial incidents over the years, especially when he was in the military. Jesse never remarried. He took the life insurance money and the hefty proceeds from the sale of the family's business and went west with his sons. He apparently became a man possessed with a distorted view of safety and revenge. Jesse took it upon himself to lead the charge for America, not against crime and violence, but against race and diversity. It gave him purpose.

Williams couldn't prove it, but one of his theories was that Jesse somehow gave the order for the Colorado hit from his federal prison cell . . . payback for testifying against him and his family. But how did Jesse or Barry know it was him who was the prosecutions star witness? Everything about him was completely disguised during the trial, he thought. Besides, he was arrested at The Fort like everyone else. But he had thought Jesse possessed an extra sense.

The other theory, the one that Phillip thought even more plausible, was that psychotic Tommy, acquitted and free, had acted on his own. Jesse's youngest son was capable of destroying without a hint of remorse. Phillip remembered the time he saw Tommy carrying a rifle and chasing a cat around outside the sleeping quarters, saying he was going to give it a second asshole. He did, and had laughed about it.

Phillip understood Jesse Ford professionally and personally. That was why he was writing the book about The Fort and what it stood for. His book would expose the Fords and people like them along with their murderous madness.

chapter 14

John Kick entered Phillip Williams' Manitou Springs house for the first time since the security team assigned to watch over Williams had reported him missing. An agent from the Denver office had carried out a preliminary search of the house, but found no clues to indicate when and why Williams left. Kick was asked by Raymond Stacey to lend his expertise and sift through the house once more since he was returning from the western part of the country anyway.

Kick had always been surprised that the Federal Protection Program had set Williams up in such a nice place . . . not that he didn't deserve it, but it was actually a little better than his own home in Washington. But then a Bureau salary doesn't go far in a city like D.C. and it doesn't help when you're paying alimony, he thought ruefully.

Kick was looking for anything that might tell him and the Bureau where their witness went, something that the first agents might have missed. Somehow Williams had slipped away without causing an immediate alert of his security patrol. The car was missing, too.

The special agent had retrieved Williams' mail from the Manitou Springs Post Office and brought it to the house with him. Mail delivery had been stopped until further notice, twenty days before. No forwarding address. The stack included a utility bill, several pieces of junk mail and two magazines. There were no personal letters. The utility bill was from the telephone company and was Kick's best hope for a clue. But once opened, it itemized no long distance or collect calls. Lund's cellular telephone bill did not detail individual calls. Further investigation into his cellular service may offer a lead if Lund was still using it.

Kick entertained the idea that Phillip had become so depressed and reclusive that he finally broke and drove away to who knew where, or committed suicide in the mountains. Or, he may have started thinking and acting like a professional operative again, this time with an agenda. But he certainly wouldn't have gone to Oregon to seek revenge against someone he wasn't sure had anything to do with his wife's death. Or would he?

Kick walked through the nicely appointed house, making mental notes of what he thought of importance might be missing. He had been in the house a couple of times after Caroline's funeral and he was trying to remember what he had seen. He knew the desk in one of the bedrooms had been turned into a writing space with a laptop computer which was now gone. *The book.*

In the living room, with his cellular telephone to his ear, he looked out the picture window at the foothills.

"Raymond Stacey please," said Kick.

He paced, waiting for his supervisor to answer. It annoyed him that Stacey always kept him waiting when he called his office. He assumed Stacey had a private number, but he was not privy to it. It was just Stacey's goddamn way of doing business with him, he assumed. It reminded him again that he should have been the one sitting behind Stacey's Washington desk pushing buttons for the special section of the counter terrorism division.

"Stacey," announced the man from Washington. His voice was calm and clear.

"It's Kick. I'm in Colorado." The agent pulled at his collar and loosened his red tie. He was sweating in the closed-up house. The extra weight he had gained the past two years made his clothes fit tighter and further added to his discomfort. Stacey had made comments to him about agents staying in shape in order to be at top performance. It was just one more little thing that pissed off Kick about his boss.

"Williams has been gone about three weeks as far as I can tell. He hasn't been seen in the immediate area. Everything I remember seeing here is still here, except for his car and a laptop computer . . . maybe a few clothes."

"So how does it read to you?" asked Stacey.

"It looks like he just left, plain and simple. No signs of force or foul play, as far as I can tell. I don't think he was taken and then taken out, if that's what you mean."

"Dammit, John, we try our best to protect people like Lund, I mean Williams, whatever, who have been of service, and then they go and pull silly crap like this."

"Things have been pretty tragic for him, sir."

"Don't remind me. I've read all the reports more than once. I wish we had the evidence to nail the bastards who did it."

"Agents are still assigned to the case." Kick switched the phone to the other ear and wiped a line of sweat from below his sideburn.

"I know. But by the time we get a break it may not make any difference to the guy."

"It's possible he finally flipped out and drove himself over the edge of a mountain or blew his brains out somewhere," said the special agent. "We've seen that kind of thing happen before."

"Could be. Would he have tried to go back to Oregon,

Kick? You know more than anyone about this whole situation. Do you think he'd go back?"

"That crossed my mind, too. But I really don't know. I'm sure he thinks the Fords are behind the hit, as opposed to being a random incident. So that might give him the motivation to head to the Northwest and try to take out Tommy Ford, I guess."

"Do what you have to Kick to track Williams down," ordered Stacy. "If he did himself in, well, so be it. If you believe he's going after the Ford kid, find him before he gets himself killed and causes a big stink. The Bureau can't stand anymore smell. I don't think he'd stand a chance considering the shape he's probably in. Besides it would look pretty ugly for us if one our informants started shooting up eastern Oregon."

"I understand. I've already got some ideas."

"Glad to hear it. You're a good agent, Kick. You deserve every dollar you make and probably more. Keep in touch."

John Kick put the receiver down and took off his suit coat. He scoured the house once again, but found nothing more to point him in a particular direction.

~~~ *chapter 15*

The last things Phillip remembered of his twenty-eighth night in Rockwood were waves of exhaustion and his unmade bed. He had been on a roll, but his vision kept blurring as he tried to focus on the small screen. He intended to rest for only a few hours before continuing with the manuscript. Now the bedside clock stood at 11:47AM. He had just slept over twelve hours, the most at any one time since his arrival.

He watched the activity on the lake from the French doors in his bedroom. There were just two jet skis cruising in the distance. Lake Emmet was void of fishing boats at the moment. The public beach was full of activity, however, with children running and splashing through the shallow water.

It was a warm and sunny Friday. Phillip decided he would try to take the photographs he would need very soon. It would be a good way to break up the marathon writing sessions of the past week. The manuscript was ninety percent complete and he was pleased.

As he sat at the kitchen table with coffee and a toasted English muffin, he inspected his digital camera. He brought the newly purchased Nikon with the long-range lens with him from Colorado. As a test, he pointed the zoom lens toward the lake through a window. He focused on a boat on the water, bringing it as much as nine times closer. The camera was the perfect tool.

On leaving the house, he encountered the boy from up the street he'd hired to mow his lawn. The thirteen-year-old entrepreneur was temporarily removing the wooden yard vane before he started work on the front yard.

"Take good care of my pet hawk while I'm gone," said Phillip.

The young man smiled but didn't seem to think much of his employer's humor. Phillip knew about the Iowa Hawkeyes because they played the University of Minnesota in various Big Ten sports.

"I'm a Iowa State Cyclone fan," said the boy.

"They're good, too. By the way, where can I find the cemetery?"

Phillip was given complicated directions, but finally determined the cemetery was close to the high school, three blocks past the water tower. Phillip would find it easily enough. He put the graveyard on his mental list of several Rockwood destinations he would complete during the afternoon.

————

Williams had come to enjoy walking up and down both sides of Main Street. He always noticed how clean and well kept the area was. He learned that Rockwood, like most small Midwestern towns, had not grown much over the past twenty years, but it never flirted with demise either.

One morning, he briefly mentioned his impression about the town with Hazel Daulkie, co-owner of the Sunshine Market. A veteran resident, she philosophically compared Rockwood to a stone in a river. She said there was constant turbulence surrounding it, but the rock would only change slightly throughout the years. It just slowly got smoother and prettier.

Phillip carried that thought with him as he walked into Dayton's Hardware, on the same side of the street as *The Rockwood Ledger*. He wanted to look at fishing tackle and find a Rapala lure, one like he'd used when he was younger, fishing Wisconsin lakes. He wanted to give one to Ben. He thought a lot about Ben. He certainly knew little of Greta's past life, but he was sure Ben had been a witness, maybe a victim, of someone's abuse.

At times, Phillip also thought recently of Ben's mother in a way that surprised him. Caroline had been dead not quite nine months, but when he walked the streets of Rockwood on sunny days it seemed like several years. When he wrote or tried to sleep, it felt like only days. The time warp played with his mind constantly.

"That's a good one," said Gary Dayton. The owner's voice brought his customer out of deep thought.

Phillip held a small, clear-topped box with an orange Shad Rap inside as he stood before a wall entirely covered with fishing tackle.

"I have the exact same one in my tackle box," said Dayton.

"I'm glad they still make the ones I used years ago," added Phillip. He opened the lid and dangled the lure at eye level.

"The fish are still the same, too." Dayton's remarks got a chuckle out of his customer. "They're catching some nice bass on these when the conditions are just right. You don't want too big a one, though."

Phillip bought a fishing license and an orange Rapala.

His next stop was the newspaper office. He walked into the *Ledger* office expecting to see George running around in a visor, looking the part of a small town newspaper editor.

He knew the old-fashioned image was outdated, but somehow, it fit the town.

"Mr. Meyer?" asked Phillip to an empty office. "George? Are you here?" he called again in a louder voice. He walked to the long wooden counter just inside the front door. Several copies of the latest edition sat in a stack at the end of the counter. A box, with a slot in its top and the price of the paper was placed on top of the stack.

Three desks, all with computers with large LCD monitors, telephones and lots of paper were on the other side of the counter. The front area of the building appeared to be mainly used for editorial, customer service and bookkeeping. There were doors that he presumed led to another work area further back. The ceiling lights were all on. Music played from a radio.

Phillip heard the slam of a door or a cupboard from a back room. Before he could again let his presence be known, Greta appeared engrossed in a legal size piece of paper she held in one hand. A diet Coke was in the other. She obviously hadn't heard the visitor. She choked on her drink as she saw the man with the secrets standing at the counter, camera slung over his shoulder.

"Oh!" Greta set the Coke can on a desk and covered her mouth.

"I didn't mean to startle you," he said quickly. " I was looking for your father."

Greta recovered and laid the piece of paper on the desk and walked to the counter. "Sorry about that. He and Ben are out having an ice cream. Peg has the day off. Can I help you with something?" Her manner was all business and eye to eye.

"I was going to ask your dad . . ." he started to say just as the telephone on one of the desks lit up and rang.

Greta walked slowly toward the telephone as it rang again. She stood by the desk.

Another ring. Greta looked at the flashing square light as it rang a fourth time. Phillip observed. The small machine next to the telephone clicked.

"Thank you for calling *The Rockwood Ledger.*" George Meyer's friendly voice made the announcement on the answering machine indicating no one was available to take their call and if they left a number and message, someone would call them back.

Greta's eyes turned slowly from the telephone to Phillip. He saw something strange in her look. They waited in silence. No name or message was left, only the loud click of the calling party's receiver as if it was slammed down. She dropped her head slightly and walked back toward Phillip. Greta hesitated, then softly cleared her throat.

"I am recently divorced," she said. "I brought Ben here seven or eight weeks ago from Houston. Richard, Ben's father is under court order to not contact us anywhere, any time, in any way."

"Do you think he knows you and Ben are here?" asked Phillip.

"I don't know, although it wouldn't be that difficult for him to figure out." Her voice went from soft to strained. "Rockwood is certainly one place he knows I might come."

"And you think that was him on the phone?"

"I don't know." Her facial expression and tone changed even more. "Why all the questions?"

"I'm just trying to understand your situation."

"I don't need your understanding." Her intensity made the marks on her face slightly more visible.

She turned away from him and took a deep breath. Phillip watched her back as her rib cage expanded.

"I'm sorry. What I need is to be free from my ex-husband."
She walked to the desk and sat on a corner facing Phillip and
sipped her Coke. She wasn't crying.

"There have been at least ten calls like that in the past two
weeks," she said. "The telephone number at our house was
changed to an unlisted number when Ben and I first arrived.
Whoever it is hangs up when Dad answers or the machine
picks up."

"You're assuming the person only wants to speak with
you directly?" Phillip took his camera from his shoulder and
laid it on the counter.

"Or just hear my voice so he knows that I'm here. But I
won't ever answer the telephone. Not this one or the one at
the house. I don't answer my cell, either."

"What if Ben or George needs to call you?"

"We have a signal." Greta looked at her watch and stood
up. "Well, enough of that. It's only speculation at this point
anyway, isn't it?" Her voice sounded somewhat stronger.
"What was it you wanted to see Dad about?"

"Nothing in particular. I was going to show him my digital camera and see what kind of equipment he was using for
the paper. Just small talk and to say hello."

"What are you going to photograph?"

"Actually, I haven't shot any yet. I thought I would explore
Rockwood and see what interesting things I can find. I've
been impressed with what I've seen of the town."

"Are the photos part of the project you're working on?"

"For pleasure."

"I don't think you'd tell me anyway, would you? Private,
and all that."

"You're right." Phillip put his camera back over his shoulder and thanked her for the information. He turned to
leave.

"Oh. I also wanted to give this to Ben." He put the small paper bag on the counter. "Would you give this to him?"

Greta peeked inside. "That's thoughtful. He'll like it."

Williams left the newspaper office and walked toward the edge of the downtown area.

"Phillip? Phillip." He stopped, turned and saw Greta jogging behind him, carrying the paper bag. He waited for her to catch up with him.

"Why don't you give this to Ben yourself . . . tonight . . . at dinner, if you aren't busy."

———

Rockwood's city park was located on Hillside Street between Sixth and Seventh. A short row of two-story houses built on elevated terrain in the 1920s overlooked the park's playground, a shelter house and benches. He was told by the area's mail carrier that if you knew who lived up and down Hillside, you would know the history of Rockwood, the good and the stormy. The homes, many still occupied by the original owners or their descendants, were well maintained with healthy lawns and thick hedges between neighbors.

The third house from the corner of Seventh and Hillside was the smallest, but the best preserved on the block. It was painted light yellow with window frames and porch trim in bright white. The high-pitched roof was gray slate, complimenting the structure. A thick chimney made of football-size stones added the finishing touch to a house that could have been a storybook illustration.

A woman with white hair, wearing a calico house dress, was tending the large flower garden next to the front steps. Phillip guessed her age at close to eighty as he tried to unobtrusively watch her through his zoom lens from a bench across the street. He steadied the camera by resting his elbows on his hiked-up knee as he zoomed in all the way. The thin woman's face was long and bony, and her movements were energetic. She obviously took pride in her home and her health. Phillip had seen her twice before, at the same time of day, when he had jogged past her house. He had never spoken to her, however.

The woman stood up from her bent position, brushed off her gloved hands and looked up into a tree. Good! Her distinct face became a digital image. Good again, and again. It was a face you were not likely to forget, and a person who would not likely forget you. One more close-up captured. Phillip then pulled back a little to get more of the house in the frame and gain more depth of field. Three more shots. Good enough. He straightened himself out and walked in the direction he thought would lead to the cemetery. He checked the digital images as he left the first of two photo locations. Most were quite acceptable.

Williams reached his destination more quickly than he had expected. The first thing he noticed was that the Hansen family who built the stone house on Lake Emmet was well represented in Rockwood's burial field. The dynasty's tombstones, monoliths compared to most of the other markers, stood out under the four massive oak trees that towered above. The lower limbs of the quartet had been trimmed away, up to about a two-story height. A gentle breeze carried a sweet scent from flowers and bushes planted to enhance the peaceful place set aside for the dead. Phillip saw nor heard any other visitor as he walked.

He took time to read several of the headstones, looking closely as if searching for a particular one. Near one edge of the cemetery, where the earth edged higher, he stood and took several carefully framed shots from different angles of two particular tombstones. He turned his camera off, slung it on his shoulder and left the cemetery.

Phillip reached his house in short time. The lawn trimming met with his approval and the hawk had been reinstated in its guard position. He walked into his house through the unlocked front door, hurried upstairs and into the shower. He looked forward to the dinner that evening at the Meyer home.

––––––––––

"Twenty dollars worth," demanded the driver to the attendant standing in the doorway. "And clean the bug shit off the windshield. I can't see a goddamn thing." The customer got out of his car and walked into the rural service station. A sign on the front of the building said FULL SERVICE AT SELF SERVICE PRICE.

"Good morning," said the clerk behind the counter. He received only a grunt in response. "We've got a special on coffee this morning."

"Where's the men's room?" The man looked around, found the symbol on a door at the back wall next to a row of coolers and walked to it without waiting for an answer.

Three minutes later he walked out and asked the clerk if he had any fresh coffee. He picked through a bin full of specially priced candy bars as the clerk told him about the special again.

The man followed the cashier's gesture to a self-serve coffee counter. He chose the largest carry-out container and filled it with the steaming brew. "What's the forecast?" he yelled over his shoulder.

"Cloudy . . . just cloudy, I think. No rain until tomorrow they say."

"Good."

The clerk tallied up the customer's gas, coffee and pile of junk food. "Anything else for you today?"

"Gimmie a couple of those donuts," the driver said, pointing at the plastic display case sitting on the counter. "They better not be old."

"They were delivered fresh this morning."

The man paid cash. He didn't hear the cashier thank him. He did, however, question the outside attendant about the windshield as he got into his car.

He threw a road atlas from the front seat to the back and made room for his provisions. He clenched one of the donuts in his mouth as he started the car. He drove North on the mostly deserted two-lane highway.

~~~ chapter 16

The dinner guest walked with a quick stride to the address Greta Meyer had given him . . . six blocks from his stone house. Phillip was now familiar with the layout of Rockwood and he knew precisely where the Meyer family lived.

William's step was hurried because of the blackening sky to the southwest. He wasn't afraid of heavy rain or high winds. In fact, as a child he had loved to be outside in the center of it all if he could get away with it. But tonight he preferred not to arrive at the special event as a wet sponge.

It was the first time since arriving in town that he had put on long pants and a shirt with a collar. He carried a small paper sack with the fishing lure for Ben and a bottle of wine.

As he approached the Meyer home, Phillip realized he felt a little nervous. Something like the first day of a new academic year. Or maybe like meeting the parents of a girl you were picking up for the first time.

He analyzed that it was really guilt. He had accepted an invitation to a social event for the first time since Caroline's death. And it was a woman who had invited him. But actually he felt a slight respite from the agony of the last several months. *Was it a temporary crack in the wall of despair? Was the grieving process slowly changing? Most importantly,*

would his agenda be jeopardized because of the subtle se-
duction of this pleasant town and this particular family? He
weighed the last thought carefully and tried to discard it.

Phillip knocked on the Meyer front door at a few minutes before seven. George greeted him in an apron and with
a smile. "Welcome, Mr. Williams."

Ben popped out from behind George as Phillip entered
the house. "Boo!" said Ben.

"Boo yourself," grinned Phillip. He slipped the wine from
the paper bag and handed it to George. "I don't know if you
enjoy the stuff, but I took a chance."

"You didn't need to do that. But yes, I do like wine. And
so does Greta. Thanks, Phillip." George ushered his guest
further into the living room.

"And I have a little something for you, Ben." Williams bent
down and handed the bag to the wide-eyed boy.

Ben's fingers searched the bottom of the sack and pulled
out a small box with a plastic lid. "Look, Grandpa!" Ben studied the box and tried to pronounce the name on the side.

"Rap-a-la," helped George. "Every great fisherman . . . and
woman . . . should have at least one of these in the ol' tackle
box."

"Thanks, Phillip . . . I mean Mr. Williams," said Ben.

"You're welcome, Ben. I had one like this a long time ago.
I caught some big ones with it." Phillip briefly, but carefully,
recounted his wonderful times fishing as a boy and how
Rockwood and its lake somehow gave him a little bit of that
same feeling, even though it was in Iowa.

George and Ben took turns explaining how Lake Emmet
had been formed by glaciers and that it was only one of a
few natural lakes in Iowa.

"That's probably the reason it feels that way to you . . . all
natural," said Ben.

Greta stood in the kitchen doorway watching the three fishermen talk shop. The look on her face seemed to reflect pleasure in seeing Ben enjoying the interaction with another adult male.

Phillip turned and saw Greta watching them. Her white pants and red top were eye catching. A tied scarf used as a belt around her thin waist matched her black sandals. Her dark hair and tanned face finished the look. Greta noticed Phillip's eyes paying her appearance special attention.

"Hello, Greta," said Phillip.

"Welcome to our home, Mr. Williams. Any problems finding us?"

"No. I'm beginning to know my way around town pretty well. Your home is very nice." His polite gaze took in the furniture and the decorated walls.

The furnishings were of an older era, but well cared for. A spinet piano occupied a corner, its top crowded with framed photographs and a few glass pieces. A television sat on a table in another corner with a sofa and a recliner in front. The walls were accented with wildlife prints and large framed photographs. A picture of a woman hung above a small brick fireplace.

Greta told Phillip that the photo was of her mother, Emma, who had died several years ago of cancer. Then she urged everyone into the dining room. "I think we're about ready."

"Whoever the chef is, it certainly smells great," Phillip said, sniffing appreciatively.

"This is a group effort tonight," said Greta. "Ben and Dad caught the fish—"

"Two nice bass and a whole lot of crappies," interrupted George.

"Dad cleaned and fixed them. He also did his special potatoes. Ben set the table and I fixed the salad and dessert."

"I should have contributed something, too," said Phillip

"The wine," said George. "Besides, you're our guest to-night." He showed Phillip to his place at the table.

"I truly appreciate your invitation," said Phillip.

He knew he was letting himself be slowly seduced by an attractive woman, a storybook grandfather, and a young boy he imagined his son would have been like some day. The only thing missing in this picture, he thought, was the music and the cute dog under the table.

Greta disappeared for a moment as the others sat down. Light, classical music came softly from the living room as she returned to the table. George offered a short verse of thanks after Greta sat down. Phillip bent his head slightly in respect for his hosts. His eyes remained open, but he listened.

Greta poured three glasses of wine and passed the platter of hot fish to Phillip. It was followed by a large bowl of potatoes. He wondered how long it would be before the first question was asked.

The guest was not shy about filling himself on the fresh fish, pan-fried with lots of black pepper, fried potatoes with Parmesan cheese, and spinach salad. He thought the meal lasted an eternity, however. He was used to working at his computer much of the day and into the night, taking only a few minutes to fix and eat food. The exception was an occasional visit to Corky's for a big breakfast.

He asked question after question of George about his newspaper career, the history of Rockwood and Lake Emmet. All the subjects were dear to George's heart, he was sure. Ben soaked it all in. Phillip asked Greta a question about her mother. What was she like?

"Wonderful," she answered warmly. "Simply wonderful."

Phillip threw out small bits of information about how he came to be a resident of Rockwood living in the Hansen house, and a little about his writing. Greta had heard the brief sketch all before. He explained he was in the midst of a special project for a university he couldn't name, and that part of his work involved writing a manuscript related to a segment of social behavior in modern society. His revelations were carefully worded evasions and every adult at the table knew it. Despite the game, all four seemed to enjoy dinner and each other's company.

George's suggestion to move into the living room was music to Phillip's ears. Greta said dessert would be served shortly, and she disappeared into the kitchen. Ben helped clear some of the dishes from the table and then joined grandpa and Phillip.

Mr. Meyer introduced his guest to the family photographs on the piano and walls. Most, spanning several years, were of Greta and Emma. They moved to comfortable chairs where a thick scrapbook and a photo album waited on the coffee table. They told the story of Greta, the only child of George and Emma Meyer. The last few pages of the album were candid shots of Greta at her job in Oklahoma City, just before she was married. There were also a half dozen more recent pictures, of Ben, and Ben with his mother. There was no mention or pictures of her former husband.

The warm air that had filled the living room before dinner was now cooler as the men talked. The air movement was stronger than before, as it passed through the room from the front screen door to an open side window. George excused himself and checked the combination temperature-barometer-humidity gauge near the front door.

"It's dropped nine degrees in the last hour," announced George.

Ben disappeared for a few minutes and reappeared with his fishing tackle box. He planted it on the floor in the middle of the room. He wanted to show Phillip everything the box held. An ancient, moist odor slipped out like smoke from a genie's lamp as the plastic treasure chest was opened. Phillip joined Ben on the floor. Together they explored the treasures.

"We're going to have to make room for your new Rapala," said Phillip.

George picked up that morning's *Des Moines Register* and settled back in his recliner with a sigh. "What paper did you used to read, Phillip?"

Phillip immediately knew Grandpa, the ex-reporter, had not lost his touch.

"I've always enjoyed the *New York Times* and I'll pick up a copy of the *Washington Post* once in awhile. But you know I dropped *The Times* several months ago and I think I want to start up with the *Rockwood Ledger.*"

George knew Phillip, the professor or whatever he was, had been around the block, too.

"You don't need any advertising space, do you?" joked George.

They discussed the media business and the fierce competition today for advertising dollars. George gave his opinions on large media mergers, broadcast versus cable television, small town newspapers, and the Internet, which he confessed he knew little about. "I just can't see anyone sitting in front of a computer monitor for hours reading a book or a complete newspaper. You need to hold what you are reading and smell the ink."

George related that there had been offers from newspaper chains to buy him out, but that he could never convince himself he would be better off without it. Family, his small newspaper business and fishing were the most important components of his life, in that order. "It's a wonderful life."

Phillip looked at Greta squarely. "That's really not necessary. You're all settled in here. I can walk. It's only water. It'll be something interesting to remember."

"Lightning is not interesting," said Greta. She returned his gaze. "It's no bother at all. I think you should just say yes."

"I'll help Grandpa with the dishes so Mom can take you home," said Ben. "I think you should say yes, too."

Phillip smiled at Ben as if he were taking advice from an old friend. "OK, but only if I get to go fishing with you and your grandpa one of these days."

"Ab-so-lute-ly!" said Ben.

Greta and Phillip made a dash for her car in the driveway. He was drenched in eight seconds. She fared better, wearing a nylon jacket with a hood. "Whew!" they said almost in unison. Greta threw back her hood and wiped her forehead with her hand once inside and then started the car. Lights on. Defroster on high . . . outside air.

Visibility was not more than eighty feet as they pulled away from the Meyer house. Rain hit the windshield in waves. Street curbs disappeared under the rushing water, and brilliant lightning back lit the trees, their branches whipping with the wind.

"Just like Houston," said Greta to break the silence. "The storm, I mean."

Phillip pushed his wet hair back and apologized for getting the interior of her car wet. The semi-fogged windows and the humidity made the inside of the car seem small. He could smell the fresh scent of whatever perfume Greta was wearing. It made him feel like he was sitting too close to her. He was slightly anxious and didn't know why. And why did he find himself looking at her hands on the steering wheel, or stealing glances at her face as she concentrated on the road? What was going on here? With less than a block to go, the rain diminished slightly. Visibility increased a little and

"Boy, did you just see that big lightning?" exclaimed Ben. He backed away from the picture window, but a small circular fogged spot remained for a few seconds. He moved closer to his grandfather's recliner as a gentle rumble followed the quick shots of light. George got up and checked his weather station again. The faint odor of earth smell drifted in from the open front door.

Greta joined them and offered a choice of chocolate cake with, or without mint ice cream. Before everyone had time to place his order, the telephone rang. There was a telephone on an end table in the living room, but during the second ring George said he would get it and walked into the kitchen. Greta remained quiet through the third ring and then ask Ben about the ice cream offer.

"Greta," came George's voice from the next room.

Greta repeated everyone's wishes and returned to the kitchen. Ben and Phillip heard raindrops connecting with Greta's car in the driveway. The curtain bordering the open side window danced in the breeze. Lightning highlighted a tall tree outside the window.

"Who was it?" asked Ben as Grandpa rejoined them. George put his hand to the window screen to see if rain was intruding. He said he couldn't feel any.

"It's that Randy fellow your mom knows," answered George as he sat down in his recliner again.

"Randy Quarve! He's a cop in Houston. He carries a big gun and everything."

George watched Phillip's reaction as Ben spoke about the policeman. The guest felt his host's probing eyes, but wasn't sure if George's "Randy" remark was a subtle warning shot on behalf of his daughter. Regardless, he knew Greta was talking with a police officer of one of the largest metropolitan areas in the country, and that officer could have access to data from law enforcement agencies all over the country. Perhaps they were only discussing her former husband. That seemed more likely. He would wait and see.

Greta stretched the extra long cord across the kitchen to in front of the sink. She turned her back away from the living room and her guest, holding the receiver closer than normal to her face.

"I hope I'm not disturbing you."

"No, it's fine," said Greta in a soft voice.

"This won't take long. I just wanted you to know I haven't forgotten you."

"I know you haven't. I'm sure you are as busy as ever."

"Busy? I don't know what's going on lately. It seems like every wacko in the city has come out of the closet these past few weeks. Jesus . . . this is going to be a long summer."

"Nothing changes, I guess." Greta glanced over her shoulder and saw Phillip and Ben sitting in the next room. She tried working with the dessert as she talked. "So you've come up with something?"

"Not yet. But you and I know it's a process of elimination. What I did do was look through a lot of national data files. No one with the name and description you gave me pops up anywhere so far. But I have calls into a couple of people in D.C.. I've got a few contacts and a few favors owed to me. Maybe something will break there."

"I appreciate anything and everything you can do, Randy. Call me if you come up with something . . . anything."

"Will do. Say hello to Ben for me."

Greta hung up the receiver and quickly closed the kitchen window. Wind was blowing rain onto the windowsill. She dipped the ice cream and carried the dessert tray to the living room.

"Here we are," she said.

"Yum!" said Ben as he saw the size of the servings.

George had just returned from upstairs a he'd closed all of the windows. The lightning had grown more frequent and closer together. coming down faster and heavier.

"We need the rain," said George. "I'll bet the fa smiling tonight."

"Have you even been caught in a storm on the George?" asked Phillip.

"Grandpa has some great stories about storms," said his mouth full of cake.

"Even though Lake Emmet isn't all that big, you'd b amazed at its fury when a major storm breaks," said George.

"He even saved a paralyzed girl and her mother once when they were in a rowboat out on the lake during a really big storm." added Ben. "It was dangerous!"

"Sounds like your grandpa is a hero," said Phillip to Ben.

"We need more people like him, don't we?"

Listening to the conversation, Greta looked pleased with what she saw and heard. Phillip was keenly aware of Greta's observations of him during the evening. He was evasive, but still felt he gave enough for his host family to be comfortable with him.

Phillip stood and put his empty plate on the coffee table. "Thank you for a very nice evening," he smiled. "Dinner was great and the company was even better."

"Don't you want to wait until the rain lets up?" asked Greta. "It's coming down pretty hard."

"I really can't. I have to get back."

"That's right," said George. "That manuscript you're working on . . . must be awfully important."

"To me, it is," said Phillip. "I hope it has an impact some-day. Do you have an umbrella I can borrow?"

"I don't think an umbrella will do much good in this storm," said Greta. "Let me drive you home."

the windshield was cleared. The atmosphere inside the car felt calmer, too.

"You learned a lot about me and my family tonight, didn't you?" said Greta. Her eyes searched for William's house as she spoke.

"From your dad, yes. I think he's very proud of everything you've ever done. But, if you noticed, I didn't ask one direct question about you."

"I noticed. But you really didn't have to, did you?"

"What's your point?"

Greta found William's driveway and pulled up as close as she could to the walk leading to the front porch. She put the transmission in park and turned to her passenger.

"I'd like to ask you two more questions," said Greta.

"That will bring it down to ninety-six, right?"

"I'm serious. Just two. That's all I ask . . . for now. It's only fair, right?"

"An eye for an eye, an answer for an answer? It that what you mean?"

"Yes."

Phillip turned his head to look through the window. His breath made a circle of fog on the glass and obscured the view of his house. "Ask."

Greta took her time. "Are you married?"

Phillip faced Greta. He realized he hadn't talked to anyone at all about the loss of Caroline, other than his mother and Carrie McGaw, his psychologist in Colorado Springs.

"I was married," answered Phillip.

Greta listened intently. Her eyes did not blink as she watched his face.

"My wife was killed in an accident last year. I was married over ten years."

Greta responded after a moment's silence. "I'm so sorry. I can empathize only a little with what you've gone through, but I haven't experienced that sort of sudden loss. My mother's death was long and drawn out. It was painful, but expected. I suspect there's a big difference. I am sorry." A long tear traced down her left cheek.

The wind had calmed and a hint of pink peeked from behind the scattering clouds. The rain dwindled to a light shower. The grass and the wet streets and rooftops reflected the last few minutes of daylight. The first big storm of summer had ended.

"OK. Next question," said Phillip.

"That's not necessary."

"Go ahead. You said two. You've got another one coming."

"Not tonight, but thank you for telling me about your wife. I can understand how you might want to get away to a place like this and concentrate on your work." Another tear started downward.

Phillip didn't react to her understanding. Instead he gently put his thumb to her left cheek and wiped away the tear, then faced forward. Greta remained still and silent for a few seconds.

"I hope you had a nice evening," she finally said. "I know Ben and Dad enjoyed your company."

"It was an evening I'll remember." Phillip smiled at her as he opened the car door. "Good night."

"Good night, Phillip."

Williams closed the door as Greta put the car in reverse. She slowly backed out onto Lakeside Drive. He didn't go up to the front porch, but walked slowly around behind the house and down to the lake's edge. He stared into the choppy water. The sprinkling rain matted his clothes to his skin. Like a living statue, he closed his eyes, remained motionless and visited his past.

 chapter 17

The fourteen-foot boat slowed to a troll and bobbed slightly in its wake thirty yards from shore, not far from the Surfside Ballroom that sat on the eastern bank of Lake Emmet. Tall leafy trees anchored on the bank provided patches of shade for the vessel's three mates. And two large decaying tree trunks submerged in front provided a good place to try one's luck. A quartet of fishing rods and a landing net were propped against the boat's stern pointing to a cloudless sky that signaled another hot Iowa day.

"This is one of my favorite spots," said George. "See that old dance hall over there, it's the old Surfside Ballroom. It still has a dance every Saturday night. Big band music . . . dancin' music like Miller, Goodman and Dorsey. I have a lot of memories from that place. Not many like this one left around the country."

"I've seen it only from the outside on my runs," responded Phillip. "I'll have to give it a closer look sometime."

"Grandpa took me and Mom to the dance two weeks ago. We had a great time. Maybe we can take Phillip with us next time, Grandpa."

"Greta hadn't been there since high school," replied George.

"We did have a fun time. And if Mr. Williams would like to come along sometime, Ben, he'd be more than welcomed."

"I think I'll have to sleep on that one, Ben."

George shut the motor off and lowered the anchor and its nylon rope over the side. The line went slack as the weight touched bottom. "Nine feet . . . maybe ten," reported the captain to Ben and Phillip. He then slowly released the anchor rigged to the boat's bow. "I think we'd better use both of them right now. We've got a little bit of wind this morning, but we should stay pretty steady."

The Editor in Chief had organized this fishing expedition especially for Phillip. Although Williams had fished lakes a hundred times since he was a child, he graciously let his host act as the fishing master. He decided to take the time for this outing, that it wouldn't much delay his first order of business in Rockwood. The last time he'd sat in a boat with a fishing rod was with Caroline, two years ago on Pelican Lake in northern Minnesota. It seemed like ten years . . . and it seemed like yesterday. He could hardly wait for his first cast.

"Which rod to you want me to use?" he asked.

George didn't answer, but handed a rod with a spin cast reel to Ben, who in turn passed it to Phillip. "Here, this one's yours," the boy said.

"Thanks."

"No," said Ben. "We mean it's really yours . . . to keep."

"What?" Phillip's reaction was one of genuine surprise.

George passed a small, plastic tackle kit the size of a cigar box to Phillip. "Here, this goes with it. It has the basics."

Ben's face was all smiles as he watched Phillip's delight. "Grandpa said you needed one. He said he bets fishing will take your mind off things."

"It's nothing fancy," said George quickly. "But we took up a collection at the Meyer house and thought this was something you could really use now, since you live right on a lake."

Phillip opened the tackle kit and shook his head. He took out a new Rapala. The rest of the items in the box, as George had said, were the basics. "Thank you very much. I'm really speechless."

"Just catch lots of fish with it," said Ben.

"And speaking of that, let's get at it," added George. "The wind's picking up a little more and I feel lucky this morning."

"Grandpa says the fish bite better when it's a little windy. Don't you, Grandpa?"

"You never forget a thing I say, do you? Unless it's wash your hands or time for bed."

Phillip and Ben carefully attached their prize lures to the ends of their lines. George opted for a small silver spoon tipped with a night crawler. Ben didn't care for live bait yet. But George put him in charge of keeping the worms in the shade and the leeches they brought in fresh water so they would stay at their wiggling best. He also had oatmeal cookie detail, ones Greta had made for the crew. Ben threw his first cast with a skill that could only have been taught by a patient grandfather.

"So what do you think of Rockwood now that you've been here for awhile?" asked George.

"It's different."

"How so?" George looked straight ahead with his mind divided between his line and Phillip's answer.

"It's half farm town, half lake town. The landscape is somewhat plain, but the people aren't. It's just different... but I like it. I wouldn't call it a diamond in the rough, but maybe a ruby or a topaz."

George chuckled. "What don't you like about it? I only ask because I'm always curious of what outsiders, excuse me, newcomers, think about my town."

Phillip cast again and began a slow retrieve. No one had a bite yet. "I didn't think I would meet and have to deal with so many people right away. I came here to get away from people and concentrate on my work."

"And the best thing about Rockwood?"

The newcomer thought for a few seconds and lost concentration of his retrieval. "Besides the lake . . . all of the people I've met and have had to deal with right away. George, I think I'm being seduced by it all."

"What does seduced mean, Grandpa?"

"Got one!" shouted Phillip. His rod curved toward the water.

"Wow! That Rapala really worked," shouted Ben.

"I bet it's a beauty," added George.

"Ben, grab the net and help me land this big fella," said Phillip. He played the fish with great pleasure and skill.

Ben pulled the long net from under the middle seat and dropped the netting and metal rim into the water as Phillip worked the fish toward the boat. Ben's eyes were fixed on the fish struggling to escape from the treble hooks and the painted piece of balsa wood that had lured him.

"Remember how you did it the other day, Ben." said Grandpa.

The fish dove deep as it was pulled closer to the side of the boat. The rod bent more, but didn't break. Ben dropped to his knees and bent over the side. He gripped the net handle tightly. The boat rocked as Ben searched the clear water for the catch. He worked the net to get it underneath the fish. Phillip and Ben worked together and shouted to each other they were close to landing the prize.

Phillip cautiously brought in a little more line, bringing the fish closer to Ben's net.

"Now!" said Phillip.

Ben pulled up with both hands and the netting surrounded the catch. The excited boy almost fell overboard as he stood up to bring the fish inside the boat. "Got it!" George grabbed the back of Ben's shirt and pulled him back. Ben didn't even notice his grandpa's concern.

"What do we have here, Ben?" asked Phillip as he untangled the fish from the net. He held him up by the bottom jaw.

"Bass. Big one!"

"Two pounder, I bet," said George. "Nice fish."

"He's a fighter, isn't he, Ben?" Phillip released the fish into a large bucket filled with water that was in the boat. "Thanks for the help."

"Anytime."

Phillip watched the sleek creature try to swim in its new and confining environment. Alive, but no longer free as it was a moment ago. It took a chance and lost. Williams knew this same scenario would soon be played out on land, but there would be different bait and a different prey.

———

At her makeshift office at the kitchen table, Greta was enjoying the same perfect summer morning as the three fishermen. It was Saturday and she sat cross-legged, still wearing the oversized Mickey Mouse T-shirt she had worn to bed the night before.

Her office consisted of a reporter's notebook, address book, pen, pencil, her new cellular phone and a laptop computer. A full cup of coffee completed her array of necessities. She tapped the tip of the pen as she organized her thoughts.

She thought about the trio on the lake. Actually, she focused on Phillip Williams and tried to imagine what the atmosphere was like in the boat at that very moment. She had known him for only six weeks, yet she found him often in her thoughts. Her feelings for him had ranged from anger to sympathy. She didn't know what to think of his mysterious presence in Rockwood. She did know she didn't fully buy his story.

She had to learn more about him before his unforced influence affected her and her family further. That was part of his magnetism, she thought. Williams didn't force himself on anyone. He just emitted subtle signals that were hard to ignore.

Greta looked over her notes on the Phillip Williams story. She flipped through several pages of the notebook she had been writing in off and on the past weeks. There were more questions than facts or assumptions. How did he get here? There wasn't bus service to Rockwood anymore, and she doubted he'd just walked into town late one night from off the highway. He hadn't driven a car here, unless it was hidden in the garage or some other place, which she doubted. That left being dropped off by someone, a friend or someone for hire.

She called long distance information for the general number of the Sioux City airport. She felt positive he had come a long distance, although she sensed he was a Midwesterner, but not from Iowa. No southern, northeastern or Chicago accent. He was definitely not from Texas. She called the airport and finally connected with the person who could tell her about incoming flights. She was told the latest arriving passenger flight on the night she was interested in was at nine-thirty. She also called the cab company in Sioux City, but found no one who remembered logging any fares to Rockwood six weeks or so before.

Greta left the kitchen and located an outdated edition of the Des Moines telephone directory on the shelf of the coat closet by the front door. She returned to the kitchen table, took two sips of coffee and opened the book to the advertising section.

She placed one finger beneath the number for the Diamond Cab Company, punched the eleven digits and counted five rings before the line was answered. A woman greeted her in a hurried monotone voice. Greta carefully explained she was trying to track down an eccentric friend and who may have hired one of the company's cabs for an unusually long ride late one night several weeks ago.

"Do you recall anything like that at all?" she asked. Her voice sounded concerned and convincing.

"Do I recall?" laughed the woman. "It made Almir's week, and then some. Yeah, I remember. We all do."

"So Almir was the one who drove Mr. Williams on June 2nd?"

"I don't know if his name was Williams, honey. I don't think Almir ever knew. Big tipper, Almir said, and a nice guy, but I guess you'd know that, being his friend, right? Say, this fella isn't in any kind of trouble, is he?"

"I really don't know. But it would help me if I could just find out where Almir picked Mr. Williams up and exactly where he dropped him."

"I suppose I can help you out. Hold on a minute." The woman put Greta on hold.

She had enough time for another sip of coffee before the woman in Des Moines picked up the line again.

"Yep. June 2nd. Fare was picked up at Des Moines International at 10:41 PM. I think all passenger flights are in for the night about a half hour before that, but Almir sometimes waits for the stragglers . . . passengers who take their time or have problems with luggage or something. Fare was taken to Rockwood . . . up in northwest Iowa. Does that help you?"

"Yes. Yes, it does. Would Almir happen to be coming into the office anytime today?"

"Oh, no. He's on vacation with his family until Monday. I think he's spending that big tip." She laughed along with someone else in the background. "You can try back then if you want, honey."

"I might do that. You've been very helpful."

"Glad to help."

Although Greta was pleased to have landed some key information, she was puzzled about the pick-up point. How had Williams managed to smuggle a semiautomatic handgun onto an airplane? Questions still outnumbered answers.

The ringing of her telephone broke the silence in the kitchen. After four rings she knew it was not Ben or George calling. Only a few, including Larry Champ and Randy Quarve had the new Meyer number, and George wasn't here to answer it. She stared at the telephone and counted nine rings before it stopped.

Greta picked up her cell phone and punched in a Houston number.

"Randy?"

"Greta!" said the detective. "How did you know I'd be in the office today?"

"You're always in the office. Say, did you just try calling me?"

"No. Anything wrong?"

"No, just didn't get to the phone in time. No big deal. If it was you, I'd thought I'd just call you back to say hello."

"I'm glad you did because I've got something, but first, I'm really pissed at you."

"Oh, no. What's the matter now?" Greta pulled at the front of her T-shirt as she sat down.

"I mean I'm really upset. I thought friends confided in one another."

"What's this about, Randy?"

"You didn't tell me the truth."

"About what?"

"The real reason you left Houston. You said you were only taking a long vacation in Iowa to be with your dad."

"That's true."

"That's only the tip of the truth. You didn't just leave... you took a long leave of absence from the station because of that bastard husband of yours almost killed you."

"Ex-husband."

"The son of a bitch, whatever."

Greta didn't speak. She realized the genuinely upset person on the other end of the line was someone who really cared for her and Ben. "I'm sorry, Randy." Her voice cracked a little. "I didn't want to get you involved. It was too much for me to handle and I couldn't think of anything but to get away." She wiped her eyes with the back of her wrists. "I'm sorry I misled you. You're a fine and true friend, and knowing that is very important to me."

Both remained silent for a few seconds.

"I know that. I didn't mean to upset you. But I get so dammed furious about Richard and the way he treats you ... and Ben."

"I know. I'm hoping that's all behind us now."

"I finally found out what really happened from your news director at the station." Quarve's voice was calmer now. "I hoped that after the judge issued the restraining order things would be better."

"It wasn't. But it hadn't gotten any worse until the night he broke in."

"Why didn't you call the police? Me? I personally would have done something very unpleasant to the guy."

"I know. I was afraid of what you might do. And I didn't want to take a chance on getting you suspended. Besides, if I filed charges, Richard would have been back to kill me. I was so afraid for Ben."

Quarve acknowledged her reasoning. He told her he'd visited Richard's apartment several times the previous week and had staked it out on his own time. But he never saw him.

"Sorry I yelled at you, Greta," the detective said.

"And I'm sorry I worried you . . . I really am."

Then Quarve changed the subject. "As I said, I've got a little something on this guy in your town."

"Good. I've found out some things too, but I can always use your help. I appreciate all you're doing, Randy."

"That's what friends are for."

Greta turned to a blank page in her notebook, ready to write. "What do you have?"

"Only one of my contacts came up with any leads. A detective friend, who worked for us here four years ago, is now with the FBI in Washington. I don't think you knew him . . . good mind, real eager type. He owed me. Anyway, he said I should think in terms of the Federal Witness Protection Program and then he asked me what state the Broncos are based in."

"That's it? That's all he knew?"

"I said that's all he could tell me. He knows more, but he's an agent watching his butt, like most do today. But he said enough to lead me somewhere else. I called Denver P.D. and they were a little more willing to talk."

"Good." Greta crossed her legs. "What did they have to say?"

"Late last fall, a Phillip Williams and his wife were driving south out of Denver on I25. Mrs. Williams was killed. They apparently lived in the Colorado Springs area."

This confirmed what Williams had told Greta about his wife's death, but the location was new information.

"Let me rephrase that," added the detective. "Mrs. Williams was murdered on Interstate 25."

"What?"

"According to Denver, someone pulled along side their vehicle and shot Mrs. Williams through the window. Their car crashed and I guess Mr. Williams had half the bones in his body broken. He almost died, too."

"Jesus!"

"No suspects. No arrests. Case still open."

"They were probably both under protection, but which one was the witness? And they wouldn't be using their real names."

"I don't know," said Quarve.

"So, he fled because he thought someone might be trying to kill him," speculated Greta.

"Sounds like your story."

"No comment."

"But it might have been a random event. I doubt it, but it's possible. You may have a runner right there in Rockwood, Greta."

"Anything else on Williams?"

"No, but I'll keep digging. And Greta, promise me you'll come back to Houston someday soon. The woman who took over your beat isn't half as good. I bet the ratings are gonna take a dive."

"I plan to come back, but I don't know if that's possible very soon. I know I'll have to make decisions in the next few weeks. Hey, thanks again for all your help. I've got some more ideas to go on now."

"You know you're welcome. Keep me posted about

anything strange going on with Williams. And don't let any-thing happen to you . . . Ben needs you."

"Don't worry, Randy. Bye."

Greta's excitement about Quarve's information was over-shadowed by the knowledge that Phillip's wife had been murdered. It made her forget the telephone call she hadn't answered ten minutes before.

She sat at the kitchen table, both hands wrapped around her lukewarm coffee. She wondered what Phillip Williams' real name was and what he or his wife had witnessed.

~~~~ *chapter 18*

A brass table lamp and the glow of a laptop computer screen faintly lit the voluminous library as the writer sat at a desk surrounded by empty bookcases and naked walls. A telephone and a tiny short-wave radio, antenna raised, sat next to the computer. Faint sounds of insects outside and lakeside amphibians blended with Thursday's early morning news report from the BBC.

The screened windows and French doors were open, allowing the humid summer air to enter. On the desk, a bottle of beer with clinging beads of cold moisture sat next to a steaming cup of coffee.

Darkness encased the stone house as Williams re-read the confidential investigation reports from the Denver P.D. and the FBI for the second time that week . . . the tenth time since Caroline's death.

The conclusions reached in both reports said there was insufficient evidence for an arrest and that the investigation was to continue.

John Kick was responsible for getting him a copy from both agencies. Raymond Stacey had insisted Kick stay close to the investigation for a while. Stacey wanted to reassure

Williams that everything possible was being done to find the killer or killers.

Phillip never once considered the murder a random crime, unrelated to his undercover work for the Justice Department. It was far too planned and well executed. Neither he, nor anyone else from the Bureau, had a clue as to how he and Caroline had been found. Every possible detail had been taken into consideration with the U.S. Marshall's Service from the extinction of Michael and Caroline Lund of the Twin Cities to the legal creation of Mr. & Mrs. Phillip Williams of Manitou Springs, Colorado. They parted with every possession that linked them with their pasts and had abruptly severed relationships with everyone they knew, except Michael Lund's mother. But Williams knew, more than the Bureau, not to underestimate Jesse Ford.

Kick agreed with Williams that the motive would have been revenge if indeed the hit was ordered by Jesse from inside federal prison or by Tommy acting on his own. It was an assignment probably carried out by members of the White Straight Arrows and not by Tommy himself. Tommy did not fit the description of the trigger/driver with the backward ball cap, mustache and toothy grin. Tommy also had an alibi. The car and its driver were never located. The handgun was never found. The only witness, an elderly man driving I25 South at the same time, simply echoed Williams' description of the silver four-door car with the almost-black window tinting.

The only piece of physical evidence was a slug recovered from the left front door panel just below the window of Lund's car. It had passed through Mrs. Lund first. The slug was identified as coming from a .357 Colt Python. Investigators agreed that a second shot had been fired into the right front tire, but no second slug was never found.

There was no evidence of a third shot being fired, or at

least being fired and then hitting the car, even though Lund insisted he saw a shot-like flash from the back window of the other car. The rear-window shot theory was all but dismissed after reviewing Lund's conflicting recollection of whether the heavily tinted window of the other car was actually rolled down. During the investigation, Lund overheard a Denver policeman say it really didn't matter, since the two shots apparently did the job anyway. *Or did they?*

Michael and FBI officials speculated that, if the Fords were behind the incident, Michael was probably the target and Mrs. Lund was a casualty of war. If that were true, would the assassins try again? And when?

Phillip received the last update on the investigation a week before he fled Colorado. There may have been another since, but if it existed it would be sitting in his Manitou Springs Post Office box along with his other mail.

The miniature clock on the radio read 1:49 AM. Williams had been working for nearly seven hours on the second draft of the final two chapters of his manuscript. He was tired, but pleased with the day's work. He finished the bottle of beer in one swallow.

Parts of the investigation reports would be used in the concluding chapter of this book on the Fords and The Fort. It would not, however, be the end of the story, for that was unfolding right now, never to be read by anyone. Williams still had not decided on the title.

———

It was a long journey for the man driving the big American car with Texas plates. He had been in the area once before, but he didn't like this part of the country or the people who lived here. He preferred big cities, where everything was hurried and congested. It made him feel safe.

The traveler's first visit to Iowa was a short stay, but he remembered how easy it was not to get lost. Everything was a square, a right angle or a straight line. It couldn't compare to the challenge of snarled city streets, thousands of traffic signals and lengthy commutes. The Heartland's silence, open spaces and laid-back attitude made his feet burn.

The man had good reason to come back. It was the only reason for anything any more. And he didn't have to be in any rush. Why hurry when you're at the end of the road?

He parked his car away from the office of the Royal Motel in Highland, a tiny town nineteen miles south of Rockwood. The neon sign on top of the building had just been turned on and it stood out against the darkening evening sky. The sign read, "vacancy."

The Royal was the only motel in Highland. Its population was just four hundred and twenty-two souls. The dwindling number of salespeople traveling across northern Iowa still patronized the one-story, L-shaped business as did couples from nearby towns needing a cheap bed for a couple of hours. The real draw, for those who knew, was the Log Cabin Café next to the motel and was owned by the same people. Its reputation for the best road food around brought in people from a forty-mile radius.

"Just yourself?" asked the desk clerk as she looked up at her tall customer. Her round face displayed a friendly smile.

He pushed back stringy brown hair that matched his thin mustache and then rubbed his eyes. A light growth of whiskers covered his chin. He displayed no smile or pleasant look of any kind.

"Yep," he mumbled as he pulled a wallet from his jeans.

"How many nights?"

"Week . . . maybe two."

"One of our best rooms, which is still available, has a special weekly rate of just ninety-eight dollars in advance. Thirty for a single night. It has color TV, a nice shower and a new mattress. You also get a discount at the café next door. The room is only cleaned once a week at the special rate."

"How about a telephone?"

"Has a phone, too. Long distance calls, of course, are extra."

"Give it to me."

"Cash or card?"

"I've got the cash."

The desk clerk noticed the wedding band as her guest filled out the registration card. He hesitated when he signed his name.

The executive suite was decorated in royal blue wallpaper and dark woodwork. Cheaply framed and faded pictures of lakes with tall jack pine trees were glued to the walls, giving any guest a false sense of where they really were. Some of the furniture was chipped and the ceiling had water stains. But it was thoroughly clean and the mattress and bathroom were as advertised.

The man had placed his large suitcase on the dresser next to the television. The small canvas duffel had already been opened and sat behind a bottle of Johnny Walker on the round corner table under an ugly hanging lamp.

Waiting on the nightstand was a glass filled with a dozen dice-size ice cubes floating in brown liquid. The tired and thirsty traveler lay down and propped his head against the headboard. He sipped his medicine at first, finally gulping the last of it before his eyes closed in sleep.

uuu *chapter 19*

Rain kept area farmers away from their fields and anglers from Lake Emmet. They all converged on Main Street when that happened. Gentle, but steady showers kept the morning cool and dark in Rockwood and throughout most of northern Iowa and southern South Dakota and Minnesota. It was a day for lengthy conversations and slow motion. The cafes had already enjoyed robust business since the gray daylight appeared and the number of cups of coffee and donuts sold would be double that of a typical day. Every business except the bait shops loved a rainy day now and then.

Gravity pulled the water down over the awning that covered the front of Daytons Hardware. Phillip was protected by the store's blue canvas overhang until he made a dash to Corky's across and down the street. Once in the doorway, he pulled a folded newspaper from under his rain-soaked sweatshirt and searched for an empty booth. He was lucky. He saw a couple leaving a booth in the back. He quickly walked past the sit-down counter toward the booth.

People watched him as he made his way across the room. He figured everyone here thought they knew a little something about Rockwood's newest resident. Phillip was sure the rainy day coffee conversations would bring out considerably more speculation. But none of these really knew anything about the former university professor, ex-FBI informant, Federal witness and widower.

Greta was the only one Phillip had trusted with a small part of his story. It gave his residency some credibility. But he guessed she probably knew a little more than what he had told her. After all, she was a reporter and likely a good one. For some unexplained reason he didn't fear sharing a very tiny portion of his past with this woman.

After he passed beyond every patron's view, he was forgotten and they went back to their conversations. Williams chose the side of the booth that gave him the broadest view of the café. His jeans made a squeaking sound as he slide across the vinyl seat. He pulled a napkin from the metal holder and wiped his forehead and neck. Patsy Cline's "I Fall To Pieces" started on the jukebox but was nearly drowned out by loud chatter and the clinking of dishes being brought out and taken away. The noise was comforting.

"Coffee, Mr. Williams?" greeted the waitress. Her smile and blue eyes were a part of her service. She cleared the coffee cups, spoons and small plates from his table. He laid the folded newspaper on the seat beside him.

"Black," replied Phillip. He returned the cheery look. "Any muffins this morning, Sandy?"

Her smile got even bigger. She had been his waitress four times before, but this was the first time he had used her name. "Blueberry, and I think we might have some oatmeal ones left, too. I'll check."

"Three of whatever you have will be fine . . . and orange juice."

"Anything else, Mr. Williams? A side of bacon?"

"Just the coffee, muffins and juice."

Phillip sipped the iced water she left and glanced around

the café. Micki's Bar and Grill near the university campus popped into his mind. He didn't know why since there was such a contrast in the way the places sounded and smelled, not to mention the kind of customers. Things were so different now. It seemed like a lifetime ago that he had leisurely sipped beer and rambled on with other faculty members and students. He recalled the moment he'd seen John Kick for the first time. He forced himself to remember no further.

"We had both kinds," said the waitress. Her eyes revealed her desire to have a conversation. Even with his wet clothes and matted hair, Phillip looked good. He certainly stood out when compared to most other men of similar age in Rockwood.

"Is there anything else I can do for you?" she asked.

"I think I'm set for now. Maybe a refill a little bit later."

"I'd be glad to."

Phillip tested the hot brew from the thick, white cup and was pleased with the taste. He told himself he had to buy a different coffee pot soon. The blueberry muffin was delicious.

As he took a second sip he saw Greta and Ben come in. Seeing them instantly affected him. He didn't bother to analyze the feeling, but walked over to them as they stood talking with the cashier. Greta looked up in surprise as she saw him approach.

"Phillip!" said Ben in a big voice and smile.

"Ben," said Phillip with equal enthusiasm as he bent to greet him. "And Greta." He looked at her and found a warm and friendly smile.

"Good morning," said Greta. She wore blue jeans and a white sweatshirt. Her hair indicated she didn't have an umbrella either.

"Good morning to you, too."

A dozen pair of eyes watches the action.

"Ben and I are on donut detail," she explained. "We've got a hungry crew at the paper this morning and donuts were voted the number one cure." Greta ordered a mixed dozen from the cashier.

"What's going on at the paper this morning?" asked Phillip. "I thought George just printed this week's edition."

"He did, but we're finishing the work on a special section for the paper. I'll tell you more about it later."

"Then you don't have time for a cup of coffee?"

"Mom, can we stay and have a donut with Phillip?" Ben pulled on one of her jeans pockets pressing for a positive response.

"I don't think we have time right now, Ben. There's too much work to do at the office and everyone is waiting for donuts."

"How about if I stay and have a donut with Phillip?" pleaded Ben. "Phillip could bring me back when I'm done. Promise."

Greta didn't respond immediately. Phillip watched her work out her answer.

"It would be fine to have Ben stay with me awhile . . . if you feel comfortable with it. I'll walk him over to the paper in ten or fifteen minutes."

"Can I, Mom? Mom?"

"Sure . . . that's sounds okay, I guess."

Greta paid for the bag of donuts as Phillip requested two more on a plate along with a glass of milk. He gave the order to Sandy who had been standing behind the counter watching the threesome. Her smile had faded considerably.

"See you in a little bit," said Greta as she watched Phillip and Ben walk to the back of the café. Ben waved as his mother went back out into the rain. Whispering started in at several of the other booths.

"Ben. Tell me what's going on at the paper this morning. It sounds like really big stuff."

"Mom says there's this big water festival coming up in town and Grandpa has to print a big special newspaper about it for all the millions of people who are gonna come see it."

"Sounds like something we shouldn't miss. We'll have to ask your grandpa about all the fun when I walk you back."

Sandy put the additional order on the table and hurried off. Ben quickly sampled a donut and gulped some milk as Phillip finished his juice.

"Do you know how to dance?" asked Ben.

"A little, I guess. Why do you ask?"

"I heard Mom say she was going to ask you to go to a dance. But then she said to my Grandpa that maybe it wasn't the right thing to do."

"You wouldn't happen to mean dancing at the ballroom we saw by the lake when we were fishing, would you?"

"Yep. But it doesn't matter. She said you probably wouldn't want to go."

"I wonder how she would know that?" said Phillip.

"I guess moms are just good guessers. She always knows things about me."

"Moms are smart. And I think yours is very smart . . . and nice. But I don't think they are right every time."

"My dad isn't . . . I mean my old dad isn't nice. He's mean. He hurts my mom sometimes." Ben looked down at the last of his donut with a sober face and pushed it back and forth across the plate. "He hurt me once, too."

"I'm sorry that happened to you, Ben, and to your mom. But remember that most people are not mean. We just have to sort out the good people and the bad people."

"Are you a dad? You wouldn't hurt anybody, would you?"

"No, I'm not a dad. And I wouldn't hurt anyone, unless they hurt other people or tried to hurt me." Phillip felt he had better change the direction of the conversation. "Do you know any more about this big festival, Ben? What do you think it's going to be like?"

————

Fun and profit were on the minds of most Rockwood residents as the small resort-farm town prepared for it annual Summer Water Festival. The celebration this year would be extra-special, marking the centennial of the town's founding. Additional events were planned and the fireworks budget had been doubled. Although nearly everyone in Rockwood enjoyed the event, there were a small, but growing number of residents who fled for that weekend because they felt the festival had grown too big and was getting out of control.

Thirty-five thousand people were expected to converge on Rockwood for the two-day event. The festival posed big, but not insurmountable, problems for Chief Champ and his small force. He would have to rely on assistance from the county sheriff's office and the Iowa State Patrol again.

Rockwood businesses and most residents had forty years of practice in preparing for the annual onslaught. Every retail store in town stuffed its shelves and back room with extra inventory to meet the demands of the descending tourists. Every motel and the few B & B's in the area were usually booked months in advance. Some visitors arrived several days early with their travel trailers, campers or RV's, to be assured of space at the lakeside state park.

The chaotic event was always held the first weekend of August. Motorcycles, cars and vans with license plates from thirty or more states and Canada clogged the streets. Thousands of people pressed against each other on sidewalks and lawns to get a view of the mile-long parade that snaked it way through the town. Lake Emmet was crowded with watercraft of every description, and hundreds of anglers would be testing their luck.

Polka bands, rock bands and a variety of other talent entertained visitors at the park's band shell from noon until after dark both days. Arts and crafts dealers shared the downtown sidewalks with antique traders and wandering tourists. Water ski shows entertained lakeside viewers and a carnival extracted coins from the kids. A gigantic fireworks display was scheduled for Friday night, and the finale on Saturday evening would be an impressive parade of lighted floats on Lake Emmet and another, even larger, fireworks spectacular over the lake.

George Meyer, like most other business people in Rockwood, reaped a bounty from the town's yearly extravaganza. Advertising expenditures increased three-fold the week of the festival as businesses in Rockwood and surrounding villages promoted their wares and services at a fevered pitch.

———

"It stopped raining," announced Ben as he and Phillip entered the newspaper office.

"That's the best news I've heard all day," said George. The editor was rushing around the front office giving Peg and Lucy instructions for the distribution of the *Visitor's Guide*. He hurried over to Phillip, greeted him briefly and returned to Peg's desk.

"I hope you came to help," kidded George with his back to Phillip.

"Put me to work."

George took Phillip up on his offer and sent him off to the back room to help Greta with the bundles of guides. Ben sat in an over-stuffed chair in the corner playing a hand-held video game.

Phillip and Greta counted the guide bundles and marked their destinations before stacking them into boxes by the rear entrance. Greta filled him in on the coming festival and told him what he, as a lakeside resident, should expect with over thirty thousand extra people descended on the town. Phillip was amazed that this obscure little town in Iowa could put on such a show and draw so many people from so many places.

"The other day when George and Ben took me fishing, we went by the ballroom on the other side of the lake. Your dad said there is usually a dance there every weekend."

"Every Saturday night, as far as I know. Dad and Mom used to go to the Surfside all the time. Dad still goes once in a while. He enjoys the big band music and likes the ladies flirting with him. He's still very handsome. What about the ballroom?"

"Oh, after hearing your dad talk about it, I thought it might be an interesting experience to go Saturday night."

"By yourself?" she teased.

"Nope. But I thought if you, Ben, your dad go, I might tag along . . . not a big deal, just something I thought might be interesting."

"It might. Do you dance?"

"I was accused of being a dancer once. I won't say if it was good or bad, though."

"Let's do it. Dad, and especially Ben, will be tickled."

"Like I said, it wouldn't be a big deal.

The two stood back and admired their work. Twenty

thousand copies of the *Visitor's Guide* were boxed and ready for delivery to various locations around the county.

"By the way," she said. " I told Ben he and I were going somewhere special after I finished here. Would you like to go along?"

———————

Greta led Phillip up the grassy hill to Emma Meyer's grave. Their shoes were wet from the morning rain as they made their way to a particular oak tree, where Greta pointed out where her mother was buried. Ben was not far away, walking in front of a row of headstones looking for the oldest birth date. Emma's grave was marked with a large, but simple marble headstone. It wasn't as elaborate as many in Rockwood's only cemetery, but Greta and her father always said it was one the most attractive plots there. George had already purchased the space next to his wife's and had left instructions with Greta for his burial. She had wept when she received his requests in a letter two years ago.

Phillip held a small bouquet of flowers and a container of water as Greta emptied shriveled flowers and brown water from an urn at the base of the headstone. George visited the cemetery nearly every week and during the gardening season, he frequently brought freshly cut flowers for his wife's grave.

Greta read aloud the inscription her father had chosen.

Emma Louise Meyer
Born 1935   Reborn 1999
You live within everyone you touched

Tears glistened in Greta's eyes. Ben asked her why she was crying. She didn't speak, but cradled her son's head against her side and stroked his arm.

Phillip momentarily stepped back in time, re-visiting the winter day Caroline was buried. He'd thought his tears were going to freeze that day and his broken body shatter in the bitterly cold air. His despair was so deep, so wide, so . . . . He thought again about returning her body for reburial in Minnesota once he was finished with business in Rockwood.

He now watched Greta standing at the foot of her mother's grave. He knew there were differences in how people lost someone. Some died in peace, in expectation. Others, like Caroline, were violently ripped away without warning. He empathized with Greta's loss, and he thought she might understand some of his feelings. He hoped she would never have to endure the kind of horrific loss he had experienced and the depth of soul-scarring he knew.

"Who's buried over there?" asked Phillip. He pointed to a section of majestic-looking markers and started walking toward them.

Greta and Ben followed him. "The rich folks," answered Greta as she and Ben caught up. "The founders, the pillars . . . the heritage of Rockwood."

Greta pointed out a group of Hansen monuments and mentioned Phillip's house and how the Hansen dynasty had come to an end several years ago. They walked down another row.

"Here's the Jenkins family, of course," she continued as they walked through a corridor between towering stones.

Phillip stopped and stood in front of two large markers. His eyes were fixed on the name of one of the stones. The one next to it bore the same last name.

"The Fords," said Greta. "They were part of Rockwood's history, too. This is Jeremy Ford," as she pointed to the older of two headstones. "I know he had a son, Jesup, because I went to high school with *his* son, Barry. Barry had a younger brother, too. Very traditional family, although I heard they were involved in some kind of trouble a while ago. I think they were quite well off from a business they owned. The other grave is Jesup's wife."

"What happened to her?"

"Dad told me once that Barry's mother was killed while they were out-of-town on vacation. Barry and I were in the same class. After we graduated his dad sold his business and the family moved out west someplace . . . everyone except Barry's grandmother . . . Jeremy's widow. She's got to be over eighty now. I think she still lives across from the park on Hillside.

ﻠﻠﻠﻠ *chapter 20*

The bandleader leaned into the microphone on the stage. Applause from the sea of dancers on the basketball court-size floor almost drowned out his booming voice as he thanked the crowd. An alto sax hung from his neck and he smiled and acknowledged the warm reception. The evening's first number had just ended. With a sweeping motion of his left arm he presented his nine-piece band, The Ronnie Rogers Orchestra. "Thank you . . . thank you. Welcome once again to the Surfside Ballroom on beautiful Lake Emmet. It's great to be back playing the music you folks love to dance to."

The crowd whistled and cheered. The Rogers band played the Surfside one weekend a month and packed in the people. Ronnie always gave the crowd what they wanted.

"Keep your dancin' shoes on 'cuz here comes a little tune with a lot of kick, a standard by the old Glenn Miller band . . . "In The Mood"." He counted off four beats with his right hand, the band hit the familiar first notes with a punch, putting a hundred couples or more into motion.

The perimeter seating in the cavernous ballroom was lit with hundreds of small white ceiling lights. Nearly every chair at every table was taken tonight. The bandstand was outlined in red and white bulbs, and blue-filtered spotlights highlighted the musicians.

The dimly lit dance floor featured a shiny revolving globe overhead covered with tiny square mirrors reflecting darting beams of light throughout the building.

The music drifted through the open double doors, out into the warm, clear summer night. It mixed with the talk and laughter of the people outside. Neon lights lit the entrance canopy and the double row of soft sidewalk lights illuminated the path to a good time. The tradition of the Saturday night dance had not died in Iowa.

Greta, Phillip and Ben sat at a table close to the bandstand. Phillip sipped bourbon and soda as he watched George dancing with one of his many long-time acquaintances. George, he would learn, had willing partners for as long as he stayed at any dance. Many widows from Rockwood and its neighboring towns were regulars at the Saturday dances and they watched for the popular editor-in-chief to appear. He thrilled them all. George only danced the fast songs, though. The slow romantic songs he danced in memory only, with Emma.

"I feel like we're in another time," remarked Phillip. "And your dad . . . ."

"Isn't he great? I remember coming here as a kid with my parents. I loved to slide across the dance floor in my socks just after they sprinkled on the dance wax." Her head moved slightly to the rhythm as she watched the dancers. She watched Phillip, too.

"You look nice tonight," said Greta.

"So do you," returned Phillip.

"Thank you."

"I really like this music," added Phillip.

"So do I." Greta put her hand on her son's head.

Ben seemed a little bored with it all, and begged his mother for another glass of Coke. The last time he'd come, there had been a few other kids with their parents or grandparents. Greta gave in and Phillip offered to buy him a refill. He stood up and headed toward the bar.

"My Blue Heaven" ended and George escorted his partner back to her table, a scenario that would be repeated many times during the evening.

"Where's Phillip?" asked George as he sat down.

"He went to get me another Coke."

"Oh, you're not bored already are you, Ben? We've haven't even been here an hour."

"Are they going to play any rock and roll?" asked Ben.

"I don't think so, but I do know they sell popcorn. Maybe we can get some a little later."

"Can we get some now? I'm hungry."

"Later, Ben," cut in Greta. "We'll get some popcorn later."

The band started another up-tempo tune and the dance floor remained full.

"I'm going to sit this one out," said George. He tapped his fingers on the table to the rhythm. "How's Phillip doing? I was surprised that he wanted to come with us tonight."

Greta gave Ben a sly smile. "I think the little one here may have put that wheel in motion. But Phillip seems to be really enjoying it. Except for having dinner with us, I think this is the only social thing he's done in a long, long time." Greta had given her father a bare-bones version of what she knew of Phillip's past.

"I can tell you from experience, you can't ever forget the pain of the past, but you can sometimes put it in a corner at some point and store it temporarily. And you always have the wonderful memories. For some, I'm sure it takes a long time to adjust or go on with life. For others maybe it's not so long. Everyone is different."

Greta rested her hand on her father's forearm.

Phillip returned with a tray of drinks and two baskets of popcorn. Ben and Greta eyed each other and shared a silly look as Phillip set one of the baskets in front of Ben.

"Thanks for the popcorn, Phillip," said Ben. "And the Coke."

"My pleasure." Phillip put a glass of white wine in front of Greta and a beer next to George's empty glass. He raised his glass to them as he sat down.

George was soon back on the floor, and Greta wondered if Phillip would ever ask her to dance. Should she ask him? He was probably nervous. Somehow he didn't seem the dancing type. And she had observed that most men only dance to slow songs if they danced at all.

"Mrs. Donaldson," George panted as he joined them again. "She wears me out."

"You look so good out there, Dad."

"Thanks. Why don't you two give it a try? Ben and I'll stay here and watch you burn up the floor."

"What do you think," asked Greta leaning into Phillip's side.

"It'll be ad-lib for sure. I guess we can try it."

Phillip led the way into the middle of the pack as the orchestra started playing a fox trot.

They began to dance. Except when Phillip had brushed the raindrops from her cheek in her car, they had never touched. They moved awkwardly in each other's arms. And as they watched each other's reaction they burst into laughter. The song seemed to be over all too quickly and another started as Ronnie Rogers announced, "Moonlight in Vermont." Phillip's left arm was firmly around Greta's waist and his hand was on her back. She put her right hand on his shoulder, aware that beneath her fingers were flesh and bones that were violently broken not long ago. They moved in fluid motion to the simple and beautiful melody.

They were intently aware of each other, and the unison of

their steps improved with every measure. Greta closed the space between them and rested her head on Phillip's shoulder. Her dark hair was soft against his neck. It was an event.

The song ended too soon. As they broke apart and applauded the band, he watched her face intently. The theatrical lighting enhanced her engaging eyes and sensuous mouth. She looked stunning in the sleeveless summer dress next to her tan skin.

"I'm impressed," she said. "Dad told me there might be more to you than meets the eye."

"I'm surprising myself a little, too," said Phillip as a faster song began.

When they returned to the table Ben was leaning against his grandpa's shoulder.

"Our little fella checked out a couple of minutes ago, daughter," said George. "I'd better get him home."

"Oh, I hate to see you leave so early, Dad. Maybe we should all go."

"I won't hear of it. That's why I drove my own car. We both knew he wouldn't last too long. Besides, I really don't mind. It's been a busy week. A good book and my easy chair sound pretty good right now."

"Are you sure, George?" asked Phillip. "We could all . . . ."

"Yes . . . yes, I'm sure. You two stay and have fun. When's the last time either of you really had some fun . . . huh?"

George didn't wait for an answer. He routed Ben out of his chair, and Greta asked the people at the next table to hold their table while they went outside for a few minutes.

"Phillip and I will walk out with you, Dad."

They made their way around the edge of dance floor and walked from the ballroom into the warm Iowa night air. George located his car in the crowded parking lot and unlocked the doors.

"Ben, Grandpa will tuck you in tonight. "I'll come in when I get home." She kissed him on the forehead and secured him in the car. "Love you," she said through the partially open window.

Ben gave his mother a sleepy wave and yawn. Greta and Phillip watched until the car was out of sight.

They walked barely a half block to one of Lake Emmet's stone piers. Close by were the docks he'd seen from George's fishing boat. At the edge of the empty pier they stopped and viewed the lake.

"Dad says years ago there was a beautiful paddle wheeler that took passengers back and forth from this ballroom to the other side of the lake. And there used to be a small amusement park next to the ballroom."

Phillip gave her his full attention and imagination. He stared with her out into the distance where yellow lights from lakeside cabins dotted the shoreline.

"Dad says the boat was lit with hundreds of colored lights that could be seen from all the lake. And you could hear its horn all the way downtown. It would stop right here to let passengers off so they could go dancing or ride the Ferris wheel."

Phillip turned his gaze from the lake to Greta's face as she painted an image of a long-ago time. She remarked, a little wistfully, that it was a time when life was uncomplicated and nonviolent.

"It must have been quite a memorable experience," he agreed. "Tell me, why did you leave your world in Houston?" He watched her form a reply.

"Somehow, I feel you already know."

"I don't. I think it might have something to do with your ex-husband, but I really don't have any guess beyond that."

Greta faced the lake and took a deep breath. "Ben and I

escaped. I had become convinced that Richard was going to really hurt us . . . maybe kill me. I know that sounds pretty strong, but he could become very violent."

"Why would he want to harm you?"

"I divorced him and got custody of Ben. Richard couldn't accept it. He swore he'd never let Ben and me go."

"He threatened Ben, too?"

"Yes. I suppose I should have noticed how much Richard had changed. When I realized it, I honestly thought I could work it out with him. But then he lost his job and he just sank into this dark world of depression and erratic episodes of violence and hate. I wouldn't be surprised to hear one day that he had shot the boss who let him go. I do know once he sent the guy at his office a box of live cockroaches. He's sick."

"You don't have to talk about this, Greta. I don't mean to spoil the evening."

"No . . . no. It actually feels good to tell someone. Dad knows about it in a general way, of course, but I don't want to burden him with all of the details. He'd worry himself sick."

They moved away from the edge of the pier and sat down on a bench. The air had cooled slightly, and the night sky was dotted with stars. Music drifted faintly to the water's edge and beyond.

"So you just packed up one day and moved back here?"

"No. It got worse. One night over two months ago, I came home from work," she began slowly. "Fortunately Ben was at a friend's house. I was going out my front door for a swim at the place where I lived and Richard . . . he burst in . . . he beat me . . . and cut me with a knife and then hacked off all of my hair." Tears came to her eyes. Phillip moved closer and put an arm around her. Rage shot through him like lightening when he heard what Richard had done to her.

"He could have killed you!" He gently brushed away her tears.

"He wanted to destroy my career first. He'll go after the rest of me next time."

"What's that about your career?"

"He wanted to destroy my television career. He was extremely jealous of my success. He knew the TV stations were in their major ratings period and that I would need to put my best work and appearance forward. He battered my face. It was black and blue for a couple of weeks. That scared my father half to death when he first saw it when Ben and I arrived here. And he took the knife to my hair. I had to get it cut even shorter so it wouldn't look mutilated." Greta cried softly. "I couldn't go back on the air. I looked hideous. I guess it really didn't matter anyway, since Ben and I couldn't stay in Houston. We packed what we could put in my car and got out of there the next morning . . . before he came back. We ran for our lives. Fortunately my boss is very understanding. He is willing to give me a couple of months leave to get everything straightened out . . . something very rare in the TV world. But he needs me and I need the job. So I feel thankful about that."

"What about the police? Couldn't they have done something?"

"Ya, if they could ever find him. They helped as much as they could. But they couldn't watch him or protect us twenty-four hours a day. The same thing happens all the time to more women and children than anyone would suspect. The police tried, but it just isn't enough when it comes to someone like Richard."

They sat in silence for a few seconds. Greta brushed a tear away and took a deep breath.

"He hit Ben only once, many months before the last incident. He slapped him hard in the face and threw him to the floor. I called the police, of course, and I filed for divorce the next day."

Phillip asked Greta if she thought she and Ben were in danger now, in Rockwood. She replied that she was sure the risk was much less than in Houston. She told him about the restraining order, adding that it hadn't deterred Richard. She hoped they were safe, but she couldn't be sure. "Richard used to be a very charming man. I loved him. But he changed, or maybe he just finally revealed his true self. He became possessive, out-of-control . . . a demonic dictator."

Greta related how angry Richard had become just before their wedding when she told him she intended to keep her maiden name because it was part of professional identity. The confrontation passed but it foreshadowed what was to follow. She said Richard even treated his mother terribly now, something she could not understand because his mother was a very gentle and quiet woman. He was determined to control everything and everyone, and he had become increasingly mentally and physically abusive as her career flourished and his crashed and burned.

Greta stopped abruptly. "Enough of this," she declared as she stood up.

Phillip rose and stood behind her and put his hands on her shoulders. He looked where she looked . . . straight out, where the black water merged with the nearly black horizon.

"What do you see out there, Phillip?"

"Confusion. Conflict. Uncertainty."

"No hope?"

"When I think of young people, like Ben, I want to say yes. But I haven't been able to fully accept that yet. On nights like this I'm almost optimistic about the world. But when I wake up in the morning, it's gone. I know too much. I've seen too much."

"Some day tell me what you've seen and what you know." Greta put her hands over his and pressed gently.

"Let's go back inside," he said. "And if our table is gone, well, I guess we'll just have to leave or dance all night."

Greta searched his eyes, back and forth. She didn't know what she was looking for and couldn't define what she saw, but she decided she could trust this man.

"Thanks for listening. You're mysterious, Phillip Williams. I really don't know who you are or why you're here, but I do appreciate your kindness toward me and my family." She gave him a quick and soft kiss, then, locked her arm with his and they walked back to the ballroom.

————

The tall man with the Texan accent took a quick step back. Branches, thick with dark green leaves hid his body as the headlights from an approaching car lit the curb-side mail-box at the end of the driveway. He crouched and then parted enough foliage to give him an undetected view of the vehicle as it pulled ahead and stopped. His hiding place was no more than ninety feet from the Meyer house. The rest of the homes on the quiet street were dark, but here the front porch light was on as well as another in the kitchen. The sky was moonless.

The man silently cursed the mosquitoes and craved a cigarette, but he knew he couldn't swat or light up. He was pleased, however, that he hadn't had to wait long for his ex-wife to arrive.

He watched impatiently as she got out of the car. The view wasn't perfect, but it would do. The two photographs he carried in his worn billfold were tattered. He wanted to see her again, in the flesh, and see her beautiful body. While he waited, he fantasized about touching her and the way life used to be before, when they were all happy. Rage stirred in him. Nothing was the same now. He was ready to make his move.

The car's lights were extinguished as it stopped in front of the single car garage. The motor was still running. Several seconds passed before the driver's side door opened. Phillip got out.

"Shit! Who's that?" Richard whispered to himself.

Phillip walked around the car and opened the passenger's door. Greta was smiling as she got out.

From the bushes, bloodshot eyes with dilated pupils locked onto her legs. The hidden man wanted to charge at the couple. He wanted to scream, like a demon that had been challenged. But he didn't move or cry out. He sank back quietly and pulled a small, silver container from his back pocket. He unscrewed the tiny cap and nursed the opening with his eyes closed. His chin sank forward. He told himself he was cunning like a tiger, and had to pick the precise time.

Phillip walked with Greta to the porch steps.

"Thanks for driving me home," she smiled. "It almost feels like I've been out on a real date."

"I'm not ready to say that, but it was a very nice evening. Are you sure you want me to keep your car over night? I can walk home from here."

"Keep it. You probably need the practice," she joked. "Unless you're worried what your neighbors will think when they see my car at your house in the morning. We'll be the talk of the town next week."

Phillip simply smiled.

Greta searched Phillip's eyes again. She put her hands on his cheeks and kissed him. "I think about Ben, too, all the time," she said. "And I do see hope. I'm optimistic about the future of the world . . . at least Ben's world. It's just the present that's so screwed up."

"If I had a son, I'd want him to be just like Ben. He's worth fighting and dying for."

"Thank you. And thank you again for this evening. I had a wonderful time."

"So did I. Sleep well."

Phillip waited for Greta to let herself in the house and close the door. He heard the lock click and saw the porch light go out. He climbed back in the car, backed out of the driveway and drove through the quiet neighborhood toward his house.

The man in the bushes waited until the taillight faded from view. Then he staggered in the opposite direction toward the car he left parked two blocks down the street.

~~~ *chapter 21*

Monday morning's weather brought overcast skies and gusty winds to northern Iowa. Lake Emmet was choppy and all but empty of boats. The public beach was deserted even though the air was warm.

Phillip could see and hear just one boat on the lake from his bedroom as he looked through the double-door windows. The outboard was making crazy figure eights at full throttle. He assumed it was someone taking advantage of having the lake all to himself before tourists arrived for the water festival.

He had been up later than usual, despite the fact that he had worked at his laptop only until midnight. He had completed his manuscript about The Fort and he slept very soundly.

Williams was the kind of writer who revised and edited meticulously as he went. The process was slow, but the reward was confidence in his first draft, with subsequent ones going more quickly.

The manuscript, still untitled, was not overly lengthy, just two hundred fifteen pages. But it was a detailed and powerful account, not only what The Fort was, but of the dormant racist mentality with militant overtones that exists and how it can be aroused in some people with little effort. The book was not an indictment against first amendment rights, individual freedom or the desire of many Americans from all walks of life to restrict government's involvement in their lives. But rather, it was about the intense hatred, the intolerance and tragic violence that can sprout from such people like Jesse, Barry and Tommy Ford.

Phillip could almost recite his manuscript by heart. The document gave him purpose. It was an ace in the game he started the day he left Manitou Springs. He also held a wild card that he planned to play very soon.

Williams skipped his morning shave and dressed in his usual shorts, T-shirt and running shoes. Before making a pot of coffee, he decided to jog along the lake. He hoped UPS would deliver his package that day.

————

Morning television shows didn't interested Ben at the moment. He sat in Grandpa's chair looking at the blackened screen and told his mother he wished he could have brought his video game set from Houston. She agreed but reminded him again that they didn't have room in the car for everything they wanted to bring.

"Maybe after lunch we can go down to Dalton's Hardware Store and look over the sporting goods section," suggested Greta from the kitchen. "And maybe we might have to have some ice cream if it gets any warmer."

"Yes!"

"But right now I sure could use your help on the back porch."

"Doing what?"

"All of Grandpa's house plants are dying and I need someone who's very strong to help me pack down the new dirt in the pots."

"Does the dirt have bugs in it?"

"No bugs."

Mother and son worked side by side on a project they knew would please George. Greta listened to Ben talk about returning to Houston and how he missed his friends from school. He said the kids he'd met in Rockwood during the last couple of weeks of school were okay, but he didn't have time to really get to know anyone, except one kid just a little. Greta sighed deeply and thought about what Ben must be going through.

She had neither told her son they were going back to Houston to live again, nor that Rockwood would now be their home. She honestly didn't know what was going to happen by the end of the month. She still wasn't sure about her job in Houston anymore. If she moved back, would Richard find her for the final and fatal time? What about her townhouse and possessions? Should she look at other television markets, perhaps in Iowa or Minnesota? Did she even want to be a TV reporter anymore? And where and how was she going to support herself and Ben?

Greta usually saved these tormenting questions until she was alone in bed. Often, she would lay awake for hours trying to put her priorities into perspective and find a solution to her situation. Usually she would fall asleep from mental exhaustion, with everything left unresolved. She knew two things for certain each morning, however. That Ben was the most important person or thing in her life and that she would do anything to make his present and future the best they could be. She would not fail him.

Greta pushed away her deep thoughts as they started to fill the largest pot with the cool, black dirt from the plastic sack. Mom poured, son packed. No bugs. Finally, three white pots with tall green plants sat in a row on the porch waiting to be watered and taken back inside. Greta took a small bottle of plant food from a paper sack as Ben rinsed off his hands with the backyard garden hose near the bottom of the porch steps.

"There, don't you think they feel better now, Ben?" asked Greta as she took off her gardening gloves. She leaned over the short porch railing and affectionately mussed his hair. "Thanks for helping."

"Boy, will Grandpa ever be surprised!" Ben said, pleased with his work.

"Ben . . . why don't you go check the mail out front while I give these plants some food before we move them inside? Just leave it on the kitchen table."

Ben stopped at the neighbor's fence to say hello to the dog next door. Ben loved dogs and cats and said he wanted to have one or the other some day. He bent down by the fence and stuck his fingers between two boards to pet the Sheltie's nose as he slowly made his way around to the front yard.

"Good girl," Greta heard Ben say as she lost sight of him.

She read the directions on the plant food bottle and gave each pot the prescribed amount. Phillip Williams came into her thoughts as she swept loose dirt from the porch over the edge into a flowerbed. She had to learn more about him. He was becoming too important to her not to know his whole story. She debated calling Randy again. Would he know anything more?

After a few minutes, Greta heard the Sheltie bark.

"Did the mail come yet, Ben?" called Greta through the back screen door. When asked to get the mail, Ben would usually bring it through the front door.

There was no reply from inside. Greta put her nose to the screen.

"Ben? Did you get the mail?" Her voice was louder. She heard nothing but the gentle wind blowing through the trees. The dog stopped barking.

She looked in the direction Ben had taken as she walked quickly to the fence next door, the broom falling from her hand as she went. The dog pressed its nose between two boards hoping for a finger pat. Suddenly and intuitively concerned, she traced Ben's steps around the side of the house and into the front yard. Something was happening inside her head. Her heart accelerated, but, as panic gripped her, she felt as though she was moving in slow motion. Several envelopes lay scattered on the grass near the mailbox at the street's curb. A magazine was on the ground, its pages flapping with the breeze. Ben was not in the front yard. She ran into the street and anxiously looked both ways. Nothing. Terrified, she screamed Ben's name. She ran up the front steps and screamed for him, first through the front door again and then back toward the street.

"Ben? Ben!" No answer.

Through the house and into the kitchen she ran, pushing open the back porch door to check the backyard. Her voice filled the second floor as she cried his name up the staircase. Ben was gone. Greta was beginning to feel sick in her stomach and getting light-headed.

She hurried to the kitchen telephone and dialed 911. One of Chief Champ's officers answered.

"Give me Larry!" she yelled. "This is an emergency!"

"Chief's not here . . . had to go over to Highland . . . something going on there this morning. Who's calling?"

"Greta Meyer . . . someone just took my son!"

"What? Are you sure? Maybe he's just hiding or something. Kids do that."

"I'm sure! The mail he went to get is all over the driveway. Somebody took him!" Greta sobbed into the receiver. "Help me!"

"I'm on my way. I know where you live."

Greta hung up and rushed into the living room. Standing

at the front door, she scanned the street in disbelief. The telephone rang. The ring hit her like a bolt of lightning. She dashed back into the kitchen.

"Hello!"

"So you do answer the phone yourself after all," said a deadly calm male voice.

"Richard!"

"And you do remember who I am, don't you?" he said in the same manner.

"Richard! Where is Ben?"

"I tried calling just a few seconds ago ... Ben gave me your secret phone number, but I got your busy signal. Did you call the police, Greta? Did they believe you?"

"What have you done with my son?"

"My son!" he yelled back. "By the way, have you checked all of your mail today?" His voice was calm again.

"What do you mean?"

"Check your mailbox and don't call your boyfriend. Got that? Do not call your boyfriend." He abruptly disconnected.

Greta stood with the receiver in her hand trying to grasp what was happening. She hung up the telephone and ran out to the front yard. She frantically gathered the scattered mail, looked at the front and back of each piece, but found nothing unusual about any of them. She bent down near the mailbox and picked up the magazine. As she rose she noticed the red metal flag of the mailbox was pointing up. She walked to the front of the mailbox and opened it. Slowly, she put her hand inside and carefully pulled out a small glass jar with a lid loosely screwed on. She held it out in front of her. She screamed, but held on to the container.

The jar was filled with a dozen or more bees, a glob of what looked like honey at the bottom, and a folded piece of blue paper. Greta could make out the words 'Dear Honey' written on one side of the paper.

Without hesitation she smashed the jar on the sidewalk. Glass shattered and the bees were free. Some flew away, others buzzed over the sticky mess in a frenzy. She stepped on a few of them and then kicked the paper with her foot away from the pieces of glass. She grabbed it and ran into the house.

She unfolded the paper and read.

"Oh, my God," she whispered. "No!" she screamed.

Greta ran to the refrigerator, took a small piece of paper Phillip had given her from beneath a small magnet and punched numbers on the telephone. It rang once, twice, five times.

"Hello."

"Phillip!" gasped Greta.

"Greta?" he panted. "Just got back from a run. What's wrong?"

"Richard has kidnapped Ben!" Her voice was broken and loud.

"What?"

"Richard took Ben! I sent him to check the mailbox, Phillip!" Greta paced as far as the telephone cord would allow.

"Do you know where he might have taken him?"

"He left a note in the mailbox."

"What did it say?"

Greta opened the folded paper again. "Just crazy stuff."

"What does it say?" Phillip snapped.

"It says, *I talked to an angel near the water today and she said we could all go home now. You better join us.*"

"That's it?"

"And he signed his name."

"How did he sign his name?"

"*Richard Henry Black,* his full name."

"Greta . . . listen. Do exactly what I tell you."

"OK. I'm listening."

"Get in your car now and drive to the lake. Try the marina first."

"The lake. Yes, I think that might be right."

"Do not, I repeat, do not talk about angels or going home or anything like that when you see him. Talk about his old jobs, the ones he liked, and friends he'd had, your honeymoon . . . anything that used to make him happy. And then talk about how the future is always a chance to start over again. Just keep him talking! And do not show any panic even if it looks like Ben is in danger. Got it?"

"Yes."

"Now go!"

"But—"

Phillip hung up. Greta grabbed her keys from the kitchen counter and ran to her car.

Phillip raced upstairs to his bedroom, found the binoculars he had bought at Daltons and focused them from his window toward the lake. He couldn't see any boats on the choppy water. He panned his extended eyes to the right. The marina building was on the far side of a small point. He could see only part of the structure because of the natural obstruction, but the ends of the docks and the slips were in sight.

The area was void of people and activity except for a fishing boat bobbing in the water at the end of one of the docks. Phillip could see someone sitting in the back of the boat by the motor. Although his view was quite distant, he felt sure it was Richard. But where was Ben?

He continued viewing the area through the glasses and soon saw Greta driving into the marina area. He trusted she was thinking clearly. He was.

Phillip stripped his sweat-soaked shirt off as he ran down the stairs and dashed into the library. He took a half-dozen thick rubber bands from one of the desk drawers and threaded them on his left arm from his wrist to just below his elbow. He sprinted to the kitchen and took a large carving knife from a counter drawer. Its long blade was inserted into a plastic, self-sharpening cover. He fastened the weapon securely to his arm under the bands, ran out the back door toward the lake...a warrior preparing for battle on a minute's notice. It was a minute more than he'd had on Interstate 25.

———

Greta slammed her car to a stop just inside the entrance of the marina. There were just two other cars in the gravel parking lot. One had a Texas plate, although she didn't recognize it as one Richard had ever owned.

She flung the car door open and ran into the main building through the front entrance. Inside, she stopped and held her breath. She looked around and saw no one. She heard nothing but faint country music coming from a radio at the end of the sales counter. Behind the counter were large windows from which she could see the marina slips and one of the long docks paralleling the marina building down to the lake. A dozen or more moored boats bobbled up and down in their slips. Their owners were absent. The entire marina area looked deserted.

"Anyone here?" she finally called, letting her breath out. "Richard . . . are you here?"

She walked quickly between the aisles of marine supplies.

As she hurried by a new boat on display, she nearly fell over Bob Kelly, owner of the marina. He was on the cement floor. There was a sizeable gash in his head. The side of his face lay in a pool of blood. A canoe paddle was on the floor next to him.

Although the scene was not unlike what she had witnessed several times in Houston, she gasped at the sight. Kelly must be dead, or close to it, she thought. She heard him groan though, and saw his left arm move. She was relieved he was alive, but there was nothing she could do for him now. She had to find Ben.

Her movements were quick, but cautious, as she left the display room through a side door that connected with a long wooden dock. Straining her eyes, she tried to see what was at the end of it. She couldn't see anyone. She ran the length of the dock, looking from side to side. Her athletic shoes pounded on the wooden planks. She was running in a nightmare.

As she approached the end of the dock she saw the top of a fishing boat. Its bow and stern were tied closely to the dock posts. A man sat erect and motionless in front of the motor. She was close enough to see it was Richard. She didn't see Ben.

Before she could speak, Richard turned, looked at her through his sunglasses and put his finger to his lips.

"Shushhhhhh," he cautioned. "Ben's resting." Richard was calm and almost smiling. He was dressed in a long sleeved white shirt, long pants and was clean-shaven, unusual for him, she knew, during the last year.

With her hand to her mouth, fearful of what she might see, she walked closer to the boat. Ben's eyes widened as he saw his mother. He strained and struggled to scream for her help, but his mouth was taped. He was lying on the floor of the boat curled up at Richard's feet. His wrists were bound with duct tape, and his arms were tied together with nylon rope which had a plastic coated anchor attached to its end and was pressed into to his chest. He didn't appear to be hurt.

"Ben, Mom's here," Greta said with a shaky voice. "Everything will be fine."

"And Daddy's here too, Ben," said Richard. "We all get to go home today."

Greta stepped closer, not knowing exactly what to do next. She knelt down close to the boat hoping her presence would reassure Ben a little. She knew he must be terrified. She also knew she couldn't allow herself to feel the same, if there was to be any chance at all of surviving whatever her mad ex-husband had planned.

She moved closer to Ben, but the boat drifted back a little in the wind. In the space between the boat benches she saw a coil of rope, a roll of duct tape and two heavy anchors. She fought to control her trembling. Richard watched Greta's reaction as he rested his hand on a pistol lying next to his leg.

Gathering every ounce of control and courage she could muster, she forced herself to remember what Phillip had said . . . "talk about the good things." Stall him. But what was Phillip planning to do? Could he be here already, hiding . . . watching?

"Please come aboard, Greta. It's been a long time since I've taken my family for a cruise. Wasn't the last time in the Gulf off of Galveston?"

"That was a nice time," she said. "You're looking well."

"I would like you to sit on the first seat . . . facing me. And then I want you to untie the bowline from the dock."

Greta followed his instructions. Richard released the stern line. With quick glances he adjusted the setting on the motor and pulled the cord. The motor hummed in neutral. The boat began to move out onto the lake once Richard put the motor into forward gear. His left hand was on the tiller throttle and his right clutched the handgun. The water was choppy and the ride bumpy.

Richard propped one of his feet up on the seat in front of him once the boat passed the slips.

"Isn't this relaxing?" he said. Enjoy it, cuz we don't have far to go."

Greta saw that his shoes were covered with blood. It wasn't fresh, but it looked as if had dried only recently. The knuckles on his right hand and his sleeve also had blood on them.

Greta's mind was racing. What action could she take to end this madness?

She wished she had a gun and just one chance to shoot dead the man in front of her, there and now. She knew she would feel no guilt, or sympathy for his rabid condition. He was nothing to her . . . only a diseased animal that now needed to be destroyed.

The boat made its way slowly over the rough water toward the center of Lake Emmet. Greta found she could gradually inch her way toward Richard as long as she kept him thinking about the better times in his life.

"Richard?" she said. "I talked to your mother not too long ago. She sounded pretty good. How's your dad doing?"

Richard's eyes were fixed above her head. He didn't answer.

"I hope to stop in and see them if I go east sometime this fall. I would love to have some of her fried chicken again. Wouldn't you?"

She didn't think he realized she had moved slightly again. She was sitting directly in front of him on the middle bench. She hoped her closer presence was more comforting to Ben who could see her now. Greta watched Richard and the gun, hoping he would put it down when he stopped the boat. She knew she must be ready immediately for any opportunity.

––––––

Under the boat's bow, Phillip Williams held onto the nylon bowline with all his strength. Hidden from the passengers' view, he straddled the V shape of the hull pressing hard with his inner knees and feet. The force of the water helped press him against the hull and kept his head out of the water enough so he could breathe. One of the large jolts however, had smashed his head against the hull leaving a bleeding gash above his right eye. The shoulder and arm that had been crushed nearly nine months ago ached with ripping pain. The muscles on his other side strained and would have to compensate until the boat stopped. As soon as it did, he would cut the bowline.

––––––

Richard twisted the throttle and the boat began to slow. He didn't want to talk anymore. He strained his neck, concentrating on the lake. He searched for the sacred spot.

Greta watched his movements closely. She was confident she would be able to save Ben's life, at least. There would be no time to be concerned about any more than that. As long as Ben stayed in the boat he would survive.

She decided her only chance was to rush Richard while the boat was still moving and pull him overboard with her. That way, she thought, Ben would be carried away from the area and would be safe until help arrived.

She pushed the balls of her feet into the aluminum floor and set herself like a hurdler in starting blocks ready to lunge, but Richard cut the motor abruptly and she was thrown off-balance. He pointed the gun at her and waved the barrel back and forth. He took off his sunglasses and Greta saw that his eyes were glassy and streaked with red. The skin around them was wrinkled and dark. He had the face of a creature that might have crawled from underground. His eyes pierced hers.

"The angel said you might be reluctant to come home," he said calmly. "I told her I wouldn't let that happen. She's expecting Mr. and Mrs. Richard Black and family very soon. I promised." Shifting the pistol to his left hand, he grabbed Ben with his right and stood him up next to his mother. "Please don't try anything. It would spoil everything."

Richard released Ben with a jerk.

"Grab the tape and rope behind you and give it to me . . . slowly," ordered Richard. He held out his right hand.

She told herself she had to do something in the next fifteen seconds.

———

The bowline was no longer attached to the front of the boat as it bounced in its own wake and Phillip was no longer pressed to the hull.

With maximum effort, Phillip pushed off with his right leg from the short loop of bowline he had tied to one of the stern handles. He lunged up into the boat and clamped his hands around Richard's neck. He let out a monstrous growl as he pulled Richard into the lake with the relentlessness of a Great White shark. The boat rocked violently, spilling Ben into the choppy water. Ben sank at once. Greta dove after him.

Phillip and Richard struggled under the surface, Richard trying to position the handgun anywhere toward Phillip's body. Phillip managed to clasp an arm across Richard's neck and pull back on the hand with the gun. There was no opportunity to get to the knife fastened to his arm. Although Richard was the larger, Phillip felt he was the stronger one and had more lung capacity than his enemy, and he more mentally focused than Richard, which would be his advantage. If he could just keep Richard submerged long enough.

Richard struggled violently to free himself from Phillip's clutch. Phillip began to feel the kill, but a hand grabbing his shoulder interrupted him. He turned and saw Greta just behind him under the surface frantically motioning for his help. Phillip's grip slipped and Richard fought free. Greta saw the knife attached to Phillip's arm and she pulled it from its sheath and swam away. Phillip pushed off the bottom of the lake and swam after the heels of his enemy.

Greta sawed furiously at the anchor rope that kept Ben tethered under water. Her lungs were ready to burst as the last strands of the rope came apart. With her arm locked around Ben's waist, she pushed off from the lake's floor and shot through fifteen feet of water toward the surface. She gasped as they broke the surface next to the boat.

Ben was conscious, but looked as though he might pass out. Greta treaded water and managed to free his wrists with the knife. She stretched and grabbed the gunwale. The boat rocked with her weight, but she knew it would buoy them.

"Ben? " shouted Greta, "wrap your arms around my waist and keep your head out of the water."

She peeled the tape from his mouth and together they breathed the sweet air.

All was quiet on the water for a second until someone broke the surface somewhere on the other side of the boat. Greta heard a frantic struggling for air. She clutched the kitchen knife and remained silent, motioning to Ben to do the same.

"I know you're over there, Greta," came a ragged, almost tearful voice from the boat's opposite side. "Didn't I tell you not to bring your boyfriend? I've still got the gun."

Where was Phillip? The thought of him dead sent icy fear through her already cold body. She tried to locate Phillip's head somewhere above the surface. She saw nothing. She said nothing.

"I didn't want it to end this way, Greta. I just wanted all of us to go home today and be happy forever." There was a small splash on the other side of the boat and then silence.

Greta looked frantically from side to side, bracing herself for an attack. Instead, Phillip's head broke the surface directly in front of her and Ben. His index finger pushed against his lips. The boy almost blurted out Phillip's name when he saw him, but Williams quickly, gently, capped Ben's mouth with his hand.

"Talk to him," whispered Phillip close to Greta's ear. "Keep his mind occupied."

"Richard? It doesn't have to end this way," said Greta throwing her voice over the top of the boat. "There are people who can help you."

There was no reply from the other side. Phillip quickly slipped beneath the surface.

Two Rockwood police cars, moving fast, approached the marina on Lake Road. Their sirens cut across the lake and through Richard's ear as he surfaced near the bow of the boat. He turned to see one of the cars stop at the dock. The sirens cut off.

It must be Champ or one his officers. The thought gave Greta little comfort considering the immediate circumstances. There was too much distance and time between them and the boat. She wanted to know where Phillip was.

She heard violent splashing on the other side of the boat, but no voices. The boat rocked. There was a pop, then silence. Greta prepared herself for the worst. She felt something in the water brush by her legs.

"Ben!" she screamed. "Climb up my back and get in the boat now!"

Before he could do as he was told, Phillip appeared beside them.

"It's over," he said.

———

George Meyer drove into the parking lot and found Chief Champ and one of his officers talking with Greta and Phillip. He could hear bits and pieces of the story they were telling as he rushed to them as quickly as his legs would allow. He hugged Greta.

"Are you okay?" asked George.

"Yes," she replied adding a nod. George grasped Phillip's shoulders and pressed them, but found no words.

Bob Kelly was stretched out in a lawn chaise in front of his building with a bloodied towel over the side of his head. He acknowledged his long-time friend, George, with a weak lifting of his arm and a tiny smile.

George found his grandson in the back of the Chief's car wrapped in a blanket and eating a candy bar. He climbed in next to him and hugged him. Tears fell from his eyes.

The scene was beginning to attract a sizeable number of townspeople and Grandpa insisted that he take Ben home immediately. Greta agreed and Ben didn't hesitate to accept the offer.

The county medical examiner drove up as George and Ben were driving off from the marina. Richard's body lay covered in the grass next to the dock. Onlookers split their gaping back and forth between the body, and Williams and Meyer.

Larry Champ told Greta and Phillip they were lucky to be alive.

"I was called over to Highland earlier this morning," related the police chief. "A women was found at the Royal Motel who was severely beaten and raped. A recent telephone company bill addressed to George Meyer was found in the room"

Champ told them that it was almost beyond belief that the woman was still alive. The housekeeper had discovered the Highland resident in the room's shower bleeding to death.

"The victim was found in the room registered to a man who drove a big car with Texas plates," Champ further explained as he pointed to Richard's car sitting in the lot. "That one."

Greta shivered at the thought of what could have happened on the lake a half hour ago. She asked Champ to please quickly finish any initial questions he had of her so she could go home. Ben was her priority. He needed her attention.

Greta held onto Phillip's shoulder as they walked to her car. She hugged him for a few seconds.

"Thank you for being there," she said looking directly in his eyes. "I don't know what else to say right now." Tears came to her eyes as she hugged him again.

"You don't need to say anything. We both did exactly what we had to do and we finished it. Ben needs you now. And I think George would like to be with you now, too. Take care of your family. There's nothing more important. See me . . . talk to me when you're ready. I have some important things to do, too."

Greta drove away from the nightmare scene. Her mind was filled with a dozen different feelings, like bouncing Ping-Pong balls, colliding at random. One of her feelings was, strangely enough, a sense of tragic freedom.

———————

Phillip answered questions inside Champ's squad car for nearly half an hour. He watched through the windshield as the body under the blanket was taken away in a fire rescue unit. He wished the madman had suffered more. The sentence had been carried out too quickly and the punishment lasted for only an instant. This was not an appropriate ending for someone who had caused so much terror and inflicted immeasurable pain on others, he thought.

Tommy Ford belonged in this same category as well. But his ending would be as it should be.

⚋⚋ *chapter 22*

That same afternoon, Greta spent several hours comforting Ben. She let him know that none of what had happened in the morning was his fault in any way. "No guilt allowed," she said, hugging him tight.

She explained that some people get sick in their mind and that sometimes these same people do things that, if they were well, they would never ever think about doing.

"Your father needed more help than the two of us could give him, Ben. You have to believe that. We tried for years but there was nothing more we could do. He needed doctors and special medicines, but he wouldn't go to get that help." She looked directly into Ben's eyes. "Ben? I promise nothing like this will ever happen again."

———

The incident was heavy on George's mind, too. He scowled off and on during the afternoon and into the dinner hour, saying he should have been there to protect his daughter and grandson somehow. He told himself he should have known something like this was bound to happen. He was a father, a grandfather, and a newspaperman, for God's sake!

Greta tried to chase those thoughts out of his head at

the dinner table. No one could have known Richard was in town, let alone what he was planning. "No guilt allowed," she repeated.

George confessed to his daughter when Ben left the table that he was relieved, as awful as it sounded, the situation between her and Richard was over.

He had never expressed any ill will toward his son-in-law, but finally related to her that he had never believed they would enjoy a happy life together.

"You are the most loving, independent person I've ever known," he said to her, "and I love you for it. It will be hard and it will take some time I'm sure, but I think we should work hard at just closing the book on this. I know you and Ben will never truly forget, but put it on your shelf and try to get on with your precious lives."

As his daughter listened and thought about his words, she knew her dad was right.

She talked with Phillip briefly by telephone that night, some ten hours after the incident on the lake. She wanted to know how he was and how it had gone with Champ. He asked her how everyone at the house was faring. He received a good report. Ben had been asleep for nearly an hour, and she was going to bed early, too. George needed her help at the paper for the next few days. The Water Festival was coming up soon and there was much yet to be completed for Wednesday's special edition.

"I'm going to be pretty busy the next few days, too," Phillip said. "I want to complete the revisions on my manuscript."

She asked him if she could read it when he finished. He responded, but didn't say yes or no. He was equally non-committal when she mentioned getting together for some of the festival events during the weekend. Greta didn't allow him to be vague on this, telling him she had planned something special for Friday. Greta let a few seconds of silence pass and then began to express what his help that morning meant to her. She wanted to elaborate, but decided to save it until they could be together.

"Goodnight, Phillip."

"Goodnight."

———

Tuesday morning, in addition to working at the Ledger office, Greta talked with Larry Champ and the owner of Rockwood's funeral home. Arrangements needed to be made to send Richard's body back to his hometown of Clarksburg, West Virginia. Richard had been born there and it was the town where his retired parents still lived.

Champ had called them late Monday afternoon to notify them of their son's death. He related to Greta their initial hysterical disbelief, and the cursing accusations against her made by both parents over the telephone.

They had never been close, but Greta thought well of them and had always treated them with kindness and respect. Greta knew the Blacks would give her little chance to explain the real story of her marriage to Richard, and the final circumstances of his death. She would likely never see them again since she would not be attending the funeral. Yes, she and Richard had been married and he was the father of her son, and yes his death was tragic, but she had little now to give or do for this man who had tried to kill her and Ben.

Greta called Randy Quarve in Houston a little before eleven. She caught him as he was hurrying out of his office to a homicide scene. Their conversation took less than a minute, with Greta relating the important points of the incident with Richard.

Quarve had already heard of Richard's death. The police

chief in Highland had called Houston PD after Black's iden-
tification was found in the bloodied motel room. He apologized for being in such a rush, and they promised to talk
longer and in more detail soon.

Greta called her attorney in Houston next. She asked him
to call Richard's lawyer and tell him of Richard's death. She
also felt Richard's parents should to be called by his attorney
regarding his will and any other legal matters that needed to
be concluded.

The following morning, Phillip sat at his desk flipping through
the white pages of the thin telephone directory until he
reached the letter F in the Rockwood section. There were
thirty-eight names starting with that letter, four of which
were business listings. There was only one Ford. He hoped
the old lady was home.

"Hello," answered a woman. The voice was old, but
strong. The caller could hear a television game show in the
background.

"Hello? Mrs. Ford? Good morning," announced a friendly,
tenor voice on the other end. "My name is Dennis Robertson.
I'm helping out with the Water Festival committee this
year?"

"Yes?"

"We wanted to ask you, Mrs. Ford, if you planned to be
in town for the festival this weekend. We're looking for vol-
unteers to help out at the new information booth on Main
Street and we want you to consider volunteering this year.
You know this town so well. It would only be for five hours
each of the two days."

"Not on your life whatever you said your name was. I
wouldn't give one damn minute to be pestered by those rowdy
tourists . . . gets worse every year."

"I see. Then you really don't care for the festival?"

"I did many years ago," she answered with an even stronger voice. "There are just too many people anymore. And more weirdoes, now. They walk all over my yard last year and messed everything up trying to see the parade when it goes by here. You can't even get waited on in a store and you can't get any sleep at night because of all the racket. I can hardly take it anymore."

"Then you won't consider helping us out?" asked the polite, but persistent caller.

"No, I won't! And no I can't!" Her voice developed a definite edge. "In fact, I'm planning not even being here. My friend, Evelyn, and I are going to Lake Okoboji for the weekend to stay with her daughter. We're going to have a quieter and more peaceful time there. Evelyn can't take the noise either."

Phillip liked what he heard. "So you won't be here to see any of the new festival activities we've planned this year . . . for the centennial and all?"

"They'll just bring in more rowdies. We're getting out of here Thursday!"

"Well, Mrs. Ford, I do thank you for your time. I hope you enjoy your weekend away."

"I will. Say, you talk funny."

Phillip hung up the cheap telephone Ruby Jenkins had given him and pushed it to the far corner of his desk. He was pleased the woman would be out of town. His original plan would have worked fine, but this was even better. It was perfect.

He turned on his laptop and then the small printer that he purchased through the mail with a money order and had finally been delivered by UPS. The writer loaded paper in the printer and brought up his Fort document. His final draft totaled two hundred six pages, not including the cover page, which still lacked a title. Everything was on the computer's hard drive with a back-up flash drive. But he needed to see the finished product on paper. Phillip wanted to hold it and feel its weight. He compared all of the months he had worked on this manuscript in Colorado and Rockwood to a pregnancy, and now the work was ready to be born. Phillip went to the print command and with the click of his mouse and the printer went into labor.

At just over two hundred pages, the manuscript would not make a lengthy book, something most mainstream publishers frowned upon, but university and small presses might welcome. But he knew the work was too important, regardless of length, to be considered just an academic piece. Many people could be killed because of people like Ford and his recruits. America needed to know how they thought, the intensity of their beliefs and how deadly they could be. Sweet Caroline had been killed. He also might die by their hands.

The book had punch. The author's hunt for truth was relentless. The book began with Lund's decision to turn down an acceptance into the FBI training program. It would end with this weekend's events.

If Phillip didn't survive into the next week, a letter taped to his body would be discovered. It would instruct Greta Meyer to locate, and send an addressed package to, Elgin Duff, Phillip's trusted colleague at the University of Minnesota.

He sat back and watched the printer do its work. He scribbled possible titles for the book on a pad of paper. He was confident he would have the right one by the end of the day.

~~~ chapter 23

The weather forecast for the Water Festival promised a warm and humid weekend. The prediction also included thunderstorms, but not until late Saturday night or early Sunday morning when the celebration would be nearly over. Rockwood residents and the swelling number of visitors settling in for the two-day event heard the good news from the nearest radio station twenty-five miles away.

Main Street had been cleaned from end to end, curb to curb. Storefront windows were spotless and a half dozen shops sported new awnings or freshly painted entrances. Giant circular pots thick with red and white geraniums sat at each corner of the three-block business district. A banner, stretched above the street between two lampposts, welcomed one and all to Rockwood's annual Water Festival and the town's one hundredth anniversary.

A carnival set up on the eastern edge of the lake was in full operation Friday morning, as were the four beer gardens and a variety of food vendors in the city park and around the public side of Lake Emmet. It was the biggest event in the history of the town and county. Rockwood was prepared to make a lot of money.

Police Chief Larry Champ estimated the crowd had grown

to over twenty-five thousand people by noon. At least another ten were on their way.

Every unplanted field within five miles of town had been converted into a gigantic parking lot. School buses were shuttling herds of fun-seekers to the downtown area and to drop-off points near the park and around the lake.

Champ was in constant radio communications with the Iowa State Patrol, county sheriff's officers and personnel from neighboring police departments recruited for the weekend. The bumper-to-bumper nightmare was law enforcement's priority.

There were vehicles from Pennsylvania and Idaho, Manitoba and Arizona, and every state in between. A car, truck or van occupied every possible public parking place. Local kids waved yardsticks from their driveways at passing cars, offering the drivers a parking space on their lawn for just ten dollars a day.

Phillip couldn't escape the influx of humanity, nor did he want to. The more people there were, the more confusion, so much the better. He had never seen such a gathering in such a small place before, except for Big Ten football games, or the stadium concerts he and Caroline had attended.

In front of his house, Lakeside Drive was lined with parked cars and vans. From a window in one of the smaller bedrooms, he saw the public green space to the north covered with hundreds of tourists. The row of thick bushes and trees provided a barrier between his house and the people, however. The stone fence in front also added to the security. The wooden yard vane, staked firmly into the lawn, kept its guard near the front porch. Philip debated whether to leave it in the yard or bring it in during the festival.

Williams became accustomed to the bird waiting for him when he returned from a jog. He had applied a few drops of oil to his wooden friend from a can he'd found in the garage and now the hawk's wings twirled like a fan when there was a breeze. He decided to leave it outside and take a chance.

Phillip stood on his back porch wearing a black T-shirt and dark blue shorts. His feet and legs were tan, as was much of the rest of him. Recently, he allowed himself a little time each day to briefly lounge on his deck overlooking the lake and absorb sunrays and the smells and sounds of summer. It took him back to his summers when he was a youth, before he was so aware and so affected by violence in society. Was there more now than back then? As a man, his gut and emotions told him it was so. As a professor, he could only rely on logic and statistics to answer the question. What he knew was that, within the last year, his wife had been killed, he had discovered deadly plans by an organization for human destruction, and a psychotic father had lured his son and ex-wife into a death trap. He also thought of himself and his own vindictive plan. His philosophical reflecting did not affect his agenda in the end, however. Phillip Williams won. Professor Lund lost.

He watched a small armada of motorboats traverse the lake. Buzzing speedboats were pulling skiers in formation, practicing for their performance later that night. It was not a good time to fish.

He turned away from the deck and went inside to the library and sat down at his desk. He left the French doors open to let in what little breeze there was to help cool the hot room. He connected his digital camera to his laptop and viewed several images. He selected two photographs and downloaded them to the hard drive. He then brought up an e-mail program, selected his recipient from the address book and wrote a short message. Phillip had been waiting months for this moment. He was ready to dangle the bait in front of Tommy Ford. It was designed to set in motion a deadly game Phillip had been planning since just after Caroline's death. The revenge was what had given him purpose since then.

He was surprised Dr. Carrie McGaw, his psychologist in Colorado Springs, hadn't caught on to his strategic thinking. Or had she? She may have suspected his game, but her patient had left town before she'd learned where and when it would be played. Surely the FBI must have questioned her to attempt to learn more about her grieving client.

Phillip reviewed the cyber package he was ready to send. This was the first of two messages he would send, just minutes apart from one another. He clicked his mouse on the send command and he knew surprise number one would be on its way to the Wallowa Mountains.

—————

Twelve hundred miles away in the Pacific Northwest, a computer sitting on a desk in the library at The Fort made a chime sound, alerting the computer's owner that an e-message had just arrived. It was a half hour before Tommy Ford entered the "command center" and noticed he had a received new e-mail. The address the sender had used was an old one, but still active. It was initially created to correspond with potential recruits, until the FBI planned cyber eavesdropping program made it unsafe to use.

Tommy opened the document and read:

Dear Jesse, Barry and Tommy,
I just wanted to say good-bye to all you boys. I must now pay for your sins. I'll be joining your grandpa on Sunday.
Love, Gram

His reaction was confusion and disbelief at first. He read it again, slowly, and clicked on the first of two attachments. Up came a picture of Grandmother Ford standing in front of her house. It was the same woman and the same house Tommy, his brother and dad all felt very close to. "What the . . . !" Tommy yelled. He launched the second attachment. "Shit!" he screamed when he saw a picture of his grandfather's tombstone from the Rockwood cemetery. His boot heels made thuds as he kicked hard at the central communications desk that Jesse Ford normally occupied.

Tommy read the message a third time and then looked at the two photographs again. He stood up and screamed every obscene invective he knew. He then kicked into the air as he frantically pulled a key from one of his tight jeans pocket. He unlocked a thick cupboard door that covered part of the bookcase, exposing a wide drawer and a black briefcase on a shelf.

Another e-mail alert sounded. Tommy ran to the computer and opened the second document. There was only an attachment. It was the cover and the first three pages of a manuscript. In the center of the paper were the title and the author's name. In the upper right hand corner was the book's word count of 55,000. No telephone number or address was indicated on the cover, however. Tommy got the message.

"I'm gonna kill you, you bastard!" he screamed. "Daddy's gonna kill you!"

In a frenzy, he flipped through a small black book he had taken from the drawer. His eyes locked onto a telephone number his thick index finger had found. He grabbed a portable telephone from his father's desk and punched in eleven numbers. The number he was trying to reach rang three times. "Dammit, Grandma, pick up the phone." It rang four times more. "Dammit! Please be home." There were twelve unanswered rings in all. "I swear I'm gonna cut your heart out, you son of a bitch!" he promised out loud.

Tommy turned to another page in the small book and found the number he was looking for. *. . . have to reach Dad and Barry.* He pushed eleven more buttons. After two rings, it was picked up.

———

Greta glanced at the clock on the kitchen wall as she stood near the table. It was close to four-o'clock and almost everything was packed. A large basket held a bottle of wine, two glasses, cheese, a French loaf she had baked that morning, cold deli meats, cookies and a corkscrew.

She hummed as she covered the top of the basket with a white kitchen towel. She delicately tucked it in to conceal the contents. Satisfied with the way it looked, she pushed it to the center of the table next to a gift-wrapped package.

She smiled as she thought how surprised Phillip was going to be when she knocked on his door. Although he had seemed a little distant during the week, she firmly dismissed any and all speculation.

Greta's expectations for the evening were few. She just knew she wanted to spend some time with Phillip, to listen to him and learn more about him, if he would open up. She felt there might be a chance he needed to confide in someone. She felt some surprise that she wanted to show him that she cared. She had no idea how he would react to that.

His wife had only been dead about nine months. Kindness and friendship, even though from a woman, should be permissible, shouldn't it be? She felt she could be a kind of ointment to help heal a wound, if he would let her.

She was pleased with her basket of delights and surprise gift. She still needed to change clothes and call Jason Bing's mother to check on Ben once again. There was a sticky note on the kitchen telephone with Bing's number. Nancy Bing answered the telephone on the third ring.

"It's me again, Nancy," said Greta. "You probably think I'm nuts."

"Not at all. I'd be doing the same thing if I was you." Nancy's voice was warm and understanding.

"Thanks. I just wanted to check and see if Ben was still doing OK over there."

"Things couldn't be better. The boys are getting along just great."

"I'm so glad to hear that. Ben has really missed playing with other kids. Our lives have been a little crazy lately, coming in at the end of the school year. It was wonderful that Jason asked him over."

"It's great to have him. I feel guilty for not having him come over sooner. Ben is a delight."

"Well, you have the two numbers in case you have to call."

"They're right here by the phone. Don't worry about a thing. We'll have dinner here and then my husband and I will take the boys to see the water ski show and go to the carnival . . . if that's alright with you."

"That's fine."

"If they're not too tired, we'll watch the fireworks, too. We'll bring them back here and get them into bed. Jason has bunk beds and Ben said he can't wait to try one."

"I know Ben will have a wonderful time. Thanks again," said Greta sincerely.

"So we'll meet you in the morning in front of the newspaper office?"

"Yes. It's a really good place to see the parade."

"See you at ten."

"Bye, bye."

Greta ran upstairs happy that Ben was having a fine time playing with a new-found friend. The invitation from Jason and his mother had come at the perfect time. It would remove Ben further away from the tragic lake incident, although he seemed to be handling the whole experience much better than she'd thought he would. She turned on the shower, undressed and stepped inside, closing the glass door behind her.

Fifteen minutes later, she stood before the large mirror in her bathroom. She applied the finishing touches of her subtle makeup. Her eyes always dominated her face whether or not she was wearing cosmetics . . . big, beautiful and clear, under dark, well-shaped brows. She then studied her hair, which she was pleased to tell herself was looking much better than two months before.

She wore delicate silver earrings, and a thin silver chain circled her neck. A dab of perfume went below each ear. Her black pants went perfectly with her white linen blouse. Classy sandals matched her pants and complimented her ankles and feet. Even though it was a warm evening, she chose a white lightweight sweater from her closet and took it downstairs with her.

Greta set the basket, the gift-wrapped box and her small purse on the car seat next to her. She sat for a moment making sure she hadn't forgotten anything. The note to her father with Phillip's number and Bing's number was on the kitchen table. He would be home from the office shortly. All the house doors were locked and Ben had everything he needed for the night. That should be everything.

There wasn't any way to avoid the snarled traffic on the way to Phillip's house. It was heavier than she had expected. She resigned herself to the fact that it would be a snail's pace all the way. She would have walked if it hadn't been for the special cargo she carried with her. She was reminded of Houston rush hour traffic, something she had learned to live with.

At five-fifteen she pulled into Phillip's driveway. The side of the street Phillip lived on was lined bumper to bumper with parked cars as far as she could see. She felt privileged she had a private parking place as she stopped her car next to the house. She hoped Phillip hadn't seen her drive up. Greta wanted her visit to be a complete surprise.

She took the picnic basket and her purse as she got out of the car, but left the box and sweater. She heard the boats on the lake and the commotion of people beyond the bushes and trees to the north.

———

Forty-five minutes earlier Phillip had sent his surprise package to The Fort. He was now sitting in the library sipping a bottle of beer, wondering if Tommy had received his present, and if so, what his reaction was. He visualized Tommy screaming and kicking furniture, then packing his guns and looking for the keys to his truck.

Phillip was taken completely off guard when he heard a knock and answered his door. Greta stood before him. She looked stunning. She smiled with a touch of prepared slyness. His eyes didn't leave her face as he joined her outside on the front porch. Once again, he was jettisoned into a totally different frame of mind and behavior because of Greta's presence. The contrast from one moment to the next was a shock, but he played it well, as usual. He noted the basket she held and smiled.

"If you're from Meals On Wheels, then this must be Beverly Hills," Phillip said, complimenting her appearance.

"Well, this place *does* look like something out of a Hollywood film," replied Greta, gesturing to his house.

"It's only a front. Everything inside is an illusion, just like in the movies."

"Good. I brought you an imaginary dinner."

They laughed as he invited her inside. He left Greta standing in the hallway for a few seconds as he pulled closed the double doors to the library.

"This is a real surprise," said Phillip.

"Good."

"What's the occasion?"

"The reason . . . well, it's Friday, the Water Festival started today, and I just wanted to have dinner with you. I haven't seen you in a while."

Phillip was now at a loss for words. Only a few minutes before, he had sat in deep thought, thinking about his secret life as a former FBI informant who discovered something very ugly and who lost everything because of it. And he had just sent a cannon shot that would start a battle but end a personal war. Greta's presence jolted him out of that world and into one that made him feel like he was in a tug-of-war with himself.

"I'm glad you're here," he finally said. "I've been working hard all week and this will be a nice break. You look wonderful," he repeated.

"Thanks . . . again. I'm glad to be here."

"Let me take your basket," he offered.

She followed him into the kitchen and watched as he set the basket on the table. There were a half-dozen coffee cups on the counter and the same old percolator on the stove. A perfectly formed line of empty beer bottles sat on the floor next to the back door. Phillip leaned over the table and sniffed the basket.

"No peeking," said Greta.

"Smells great. When's dinner?"

"Later."

"And until then?"

"I thought we might take a walk and see some of the festival. I just want to walk and talk, and of course eat . . . but later. I thought you might feel the same. It's a perfect summer night." Greta had a hopeful look on her face as she waited to hear what Phillip thought of the idea.

"How can I say no to such an invitation?"

"You really want to? Great! It'll be fun, I promise," she beamed.

"But first . . . " added Phillip. He stood directly in front of her and looked into her eyes. "I want to know how you are."

She watched his eyes as she formed her answer. "I can't fully explain this because I know that day could have been the end of Ben and me, but I'm doing fine. I really think I'm okay. It's like a burden has been lifted and I can go on with my life now. I feel free. Does that make sense?"

"Yes. I'm glad to know you're surviving so well."

Greta leaned back and searched his face. "Thank you for caring." She then gave him a quick, but firm kiss. "Let's go."

Phillip walked upstairs to put on shoes and change his clothes. Meanwhile, Greta put the cheese and meats from the basket into the refrigerator. He closed the doors as they left the house, but left them unlocked as usual. Within a few minutes they were negotiating their way through a sea of people.

They first walked to the city park, passing the stage where a five-piece polka band was tuning up for an early evening concert and outdoor dance. The major activities for this first night of the festival were in the park or on and around Lake Emmet.

Food vendors were busy grilling burgers, brats and hot

dogs for the crowds of hungry people that waited in front of their portable stands. Hundreds of blankets, occupied by families with their coolers and picnic containers covered most of the grassy areas of the park and the lake's bank. Dozens of vendors barked their souvenirs to anyone within twenty feet.

Phillip and Greta found the atmosphere entertaining and the food almost too inviting. They didn't yield to temptation, however, except for a cup of beer at one of the tents.

When they reached the water's edge, they took the path part way around the lake. The stone piers were crowded. People took pictures of kids and parents next to the towering stone columns at the end of each pier. More people were working their way to the lakeshore to get the best view of the ski show.

"I assume Ben is with George tonight?" said Phillip as they turned back the way they had come. "I wouldn't think he'd miss any of this."

"He won't," said Greta, "but he's not with George. Believe it or not, he was invited to stay overnight at a friend's house."

"That's great. Who's the friend?"

"Someone he met in school. We arrived here with only three weeks of the school year left, but this boy, Jason, was in his class, and he and Ben hit if off. The family lives close to school. I've met them and they're very nice people."

"Everybody needs a friend," said Phillip.

"His family knew about the incident on the lake and called to see if there was anything they could do. And they wanted to know if Ben could spend tonight with Jason. I didn't know if he was ready, but he jumped at the chance."

"I'm glad to hear that."

"And Ben, Jason and his family are all going to see the water show and then go to the carnival for awhile. They might stay for the fireworks, too, depending on how sleepy the boys are. Tomorrow, I'll meet Ben at Dad's office at ten so we can see the parade together. And then, of course, there's the parade on the lake tomorrow night, with more fireworks afterward. I was hoping you might join us."

Phillip didn't want to hear that. "So how is Ben doing?" he asked abruptly.

"Ben is incredible. He's only seven, but I think he's already sorted a lot of things out. I think he's doing great . . . because of you."

"Me?"

"Yes. I truly think he never had a doubt that you would save us. He told me he knew you wouldn't let us die. He said you could never let anything bad happen to people you really like."

Phillip's looked down and knew that was not true. "I'm not the super hero he thinks I am. Besides, you deserve the credit. I'm just a man trying to survive like everyone else."

"Maybe, but I believe children see very clearly. They sense the truth about people and situations more than we realize." Greta changed the subject. "So . . . will you join us tomorrow?"

He had to tell her. He had to make it clear that he could not be with her, Ben or George for the next few days. He had to make her understand how important it was to him that he must be alone and that no one could come to his house. Maybe the reason was nothing more than that he had to work non-stop for at least the next three days in order to polish the manuscript for an editor's deadline or something, but he needed time to think it through before he said anything at all, whatever it might be.

"Let me think about your offer over dinner."

Phillip and Greta sat on a plaid blanket in the middle of his backyard, not more than fifty feet from the edge of the lake. Their seats were perfect for the water ski show that was in progress. Dinner was spread out before them ready to be devoured.

Thousands of spectators thronged close by, beyond the trees and shrubs marking his lot line. Greta said they would all be back the next evening for the water parade and fireworks, but they would scramble as fast as they could to their cars to try and beat the traffic once they were over.

They sat and enjoyed their food and the water show, mixing them with shared stories of their youth. Phillip carefully told her about his summers at Wisconsin lakes. And they traded stories about the first time that they had gone skinny-dipping.

"I can't believe all the crazy things I did as a kid," said Phillip. "If my parents had only known, they would have chained me to the kitchen table."

"They probably knew."

"Probably." He tool off his sunglasses and put them in his shirt pocket.

Without thinking, he shared that he was an only child, too, and that his father had died of a heart attack at a young age, years ago. Greta moved closer and put her hand on his shoulder.

"In spite of all the hard things you've lived through, you seem pretty mentally healthy. I've run into a lot of corkers as a reporter." She took the bottle of white wine out of the basket again and refilled their glasses. "You know, when I was growing up here," she continued, "the big thing my parents worried about, I think, was 'the boy thing'. I suppose all parents are concerned about that if they have a daughter."

"I'm sure you were as pretty then as you are now," Phillip smiled.

"You know, I haven't had a man say that to me, in a nice way, I mean, in a long time, except my dad. When you're on TV, you wouldn't believe the kind of people and comments you attract. It's absolutely incredible."

Silently they finished with their food and watched the end of the water show.

"What's next on the agenda?" he asked. He stood and surveyed the distant spectators to the south.

"Fireworks over the lake in about a half hour," announced Greta. "I thought we could stroll through the crowd for a while and have dessert before they start."

Phillip turned to her and said, "You know, I have a great idea . . . at least I think it is. Wait right here." Phillip jogged around the side of the house and disappeared from view.

She wondered what he was up to. It was like closing your eyes and holding open your hands.

Loud banging, thuds and a groan came from the direction of the garage. She wondered if he needed any help, but decided to wait before offering. Within a few minutes, Phillip appeared, dragging a small aluminum fishing boat into the back yard. He pulled it to the lake's edge, letting the stern down part way into the water.

The craft was a twelve-foot Mirror with wooden seats. The boat appeared to be of quite old, but clean and looked seaworthy.

"Be right back," said Phillip as he ran back to the garage. He flashed her a big grin like a college kid in the midst of a prank.

Greta was enjoying his antics, even though she knew now what his intentions were. She walked to the middle of the back yard and waited. Phillip emerged again, this time with a wooden oar resting on each shoulder. The oars were weathered gray and covered with small cracks. They had undoubtedly stroked the water of Lake Emmet thousands of times. He put them down in the grass by the boat.

"There," he said, pleased with his efforts. "Now, unless this has a hole in it, you and I will have the best seat in the house for the fireworks. We'll be sitting right underneath them. So what do you think?"

"I think this is a perfectly enchanting," she responded warmly. She inspected the inside of the boat and then spread the picnic blanket across the stern seat. She took everything out of the basket, except for the bottle of wine and the two glasses. She placed it inside the boat with care.

"I discovered this boat one day, all covered up against a wall in the garage," he said. "I guess it was just left by one of the owners somewhere along the way. The garage is full of old tools, a bicycle and boxes full of all kinds of things. It smells like another time in there."

He pulled off his shoes and socks and tossed them in the boat. He fit the oars into the oarlocks and pushed the boat part way into the water. Greta climbed aboard. Phillip pushed the craft further out and when it cleared land, he hoisted himself up and into the boat, taking the middle seat and assuming the duties of the oarsman.

The boat quietly eased out from the shore as the oars dipped and pressed against the calm water. They joined several other boats, whose occupants had the same idea.

Phillip rowed out about two hundred yards on to the lake and commented that their boat didn't have any lights, nor an anchor, but they wouldn't drift very much. He put up the oars and they sat in silence for a moment, listening to the soft conversations from their boating neighbors and watching the cabin lights circling the shore. Greta soon poured two glasses of wine and offered a toast to a perfect summer night. They waited.

Three thunderous explosions shook the sky and the audience a few minutes past ten. They were followed by faint streaks of white smoke speeding skyward. Within a few seconds, shells exploded into dazzling light that reflected off the water. Cheers from over thirty thousand people were heard around the lake.

Phillip and Greta raised their glasses to the spectacular display from their front row seat. They sat on the blanket side by side on the floor of the stable boat. Their shoulders and bent knees touched in the tight quarters. They leaned against the seat behind them and let the fireworks entertain.

Greta finished her wine and put the glass in the basket. She turned to him and traced his eyebrows and nose with her finger. He looked at her, then looked straight ahead, looking somewhere at the center of the multitude of colorful explosions in the sky. She watched his face for a few seconds and then turned to join the sight.

"I think we should go back before all of these boats scramble to get off the lake," Phillip said.

"That's fine with me. We can watch the end as we row in."

The fireworks finale filled the entire sky above them in an immense volley of thunder and light as Phillip slowly rowed home. At the shore behind his house, Phillip hopped out of the vessel and offered his hand to his passenger. The final volley ended and the air was filled with smoke and cheering of an appreciative audience.

Greta took Phillip's hand as they made their way up the wooden back porch steps and into the quiet house. It was warm and dark, except for the streams of faint light from street lamps coming through the front windows. It was private and safe, a sanctuary Phillip admitted he had come to enjoy over the past couple of months.

They stood in the darkened hallway at the bottom of the

steps that led to the second floor. Greta put her hands on his shoulders and then around his neck. She kissed him. He accepted the feel of her warm lips and then cupped her head in his hands, his thumbs brushing across her eyebrows for a second.

"Greta?"

"Yes?"

"You are a beautiful woman . . . in many ways. I think you are a very loving mother and a good daughter to George and a good person. I've grown to like you very much."

Greta stood in front of him, her hands now at her sides and looked deep into his eyes. "Thank you. That means a lot."

"And you tempt me." He let go of her. "But I can't submit to that temptation on this night or this weekend or until I don't know when. It's hard to explain and maybe I'm a fool, but . . . "

"I think I know. I should apologize for not respecting more of what you have been through. Your loss. Your pain. I've grown to like you, as well, but, showing that, as I'm doing, is probably not the best thing right now. I thought I might be able to give you some comfort and to be closer, but I may have been off base."

"You have been a comfort, but there are things you don't know."

"Like what?" she asked seriously.

"Things I can't tell you."

"You're too mysterious, Mr. Williams. Is that a good thing?"

"That's just who I am."

They shared a few seconds of silence looking at one another and then slowly walked toward the front door. "I think I should be going, Phillip. Can we talk tomorrow?"

Phillip turned to her and took a deeper than normal breath. "I won't be able to see you or Ben at all for the next couple of days or so," Phillip told her, looking directly into her eyes. His voice was determined. "I have to be out of town."

His revelation caught Greta off guard. "Where are you going? You don't even have a car."

"One of the gas stations had a couple to rent."

"Why don't you just borrow mine?"

"Don't need to. I already have one reserved. Not a luxury vehicle, but it'll do. Thanks, though."

She looked surprised and a little disappointed at the same time. "I was going to suggest Ben and I meet you tomorrow for the parade and night show on the lake, but if you're tied up with business, that's really okay."

"I have an editor friend I have to see . . . book business stuff."

"Then you're finished with your book?

"Finished, until my editor says it's not."

"That's great! Am I going to get to read it?"

"Yes . . . absolutely."

Greta retrieved her purse from the hall tree and pulled out her car keys. As Phillip opened the front door, she hugged him tightly and then searched his eyes as she had done before, trying to see more than he was willing to show.

"Is everything okay?" she asked. "I mean, if there is anything I can do to help you, although we've just been down that road a few minutes ago."

"There's nothing," he assured her. "Everything is as it should be." He held her close, cradling her head against his chest. "Your concern about me means a lot. Most of the world out there is a living hell. You saw it every day in Houston. And it can invade someone's life and destroy everything so quickly. But here . . . here, I found a little bit of heaven. You've already helped me."

Greta held him tighter. Her eyes glistened as she fought

to hold back tears. "I just wanted to let you know that if you are in trouble or need anything, you can tell me . . . you can count on me, whatever it is."

"I know."

On the front porch they kissed goodnight and Greta walked to her car. The neighborhood was quiet. The lake was still calm and the shore was mostly deserted. Phillip waved as she got into her car. He walked back into the house and closed the door.

"Damn," Greta said to herself as she noticed the forgotten gift on the front seat. She was two blocks from Phillip's house and didn't turn around.

———

Phillip stood in the doorway of the darkened library, looking outward toward the lake. His mind was divided between Greta and the reality of Tommy Ford's impending visit. He hadn't thought much about Ford that evening since Greta had surprised him at his door, but now he had a vision of maniacal Tommy speeding across Wyoming or South Dakota in his truck packed with rage and weapons. He could imagine the fire and panic in Tommy's bloodshot eyes, and hear, even smell his foul loutish mouth. *Would he be alone, or with some recruits?* Phillip knew he had to be prepared. He had to make sure the few people he cared about would be nowhere near him or his house when hell started to break loose.

———

George Meyer fixed coffee at eight-thirty. He had already read the main news section of the Saturday morning paper and had poured his juice. A stick of butter was softening on a plate next to the half-empty glass.

The atmosphere of the house felt strange as he shuffled around the kitchen. The noise of cartoons would ordinarily be coming from the living room, but Ben wasn't there. And Greta, usually as early to rise as he, was just getting up.

Things were changing in the house. He could feel it. And all for the best, he finally decided. The rest of his life wouldn't change very much, however. He didn't want it to, especially now that he felt his daughter and grandson had a new chance for a better life, wherever they might start over again. Rockwood was a wonderful little place for him, but it didn't offer the challenges and opportunities Greta and Ben needed.

Greta came down the stairs and into the kitchen. She was barefoot and wore an oversize T-shirt.

"Seems odd not having the cartoons on this morning, doesn't it, Dad?"

"I'm sure Ben's just fine, if that's what you're thinking, Greta. Mrs. Bing called about ten last night to say everything was just great. And that they would see you today."

"Oh good. I thought a lot about Ben last night. This was a good experience for him. Seems like things are changing a bit around here. For the better, don't you think, Dad?"

George affirmed her question with a mumble as he turned to check the coffee maker.

"Why does coffee always smell so much better when someone else makes it?" she asked as she inhaled the kitchen air. "Oh, I forgot. I've got to run a quick errand, Dad. Keep the coffee hot. I'll be back before you know it."

Greta took just six minutes to slide into some Saturday clothes, brush her hair, scrub her teeth and back her car out of the driveway. She put on sunglasses as she drove off.

She was surprised to find traffic lighter than it had been on Friday. Most of the tourists had already found their parking spot for the day and were on foot now, jockeying for position along the parade route.

As she pulled into Phillip's driveway, she was pleased that it had taken less drive time than she had anticipated. Parked ahead of her car was an older, dark blue Buick with Iowa plates. The front of the house was shut, but she figured he hadn't left yet. "Good."

She took the wrapped box from her front seat and walked toward the back of the house. As she approached she heard a splash on the lake nearby. Someone was surface diving and swimming hard not far off shore. It was Phillip. She didn't know the yellow trunks, but she recognized the body when he stood up in shallow water. He had his back to her.

Greta almost yelled out his name, but immediately had a better idea. She retraced her steps to the front of the house and hurried up the front steps. The door was unlocked. She would make coffee for him with a new coffee maker in the gift box, and then slip away unseen, leaving just a cute, short note. She thought he would certainly enjoy the surprise and the better tasting coffee. Maybe he could take some with him on his trip if he was leaving soon.

She quickly unpacked the maker and found an already-opened can of coffee in the refrigerator. While the tap water ran, she put the filter in place, measured out enough coffee for four cups and found space on the counter for the maker. She poured water, plugged the appliance in an outlet and hit the 'on' switch.

She glanced out of the kitchen window and saw Phillip swimming further out in the lake. She smiled broadly, pleased with her impromptu plan.

As she was getting the instructions out of the box to leave on the table, she heard a telephone ring. She had never seen

one in the house before, but knew Phillip had one somewhere. The only place she hadn't been was the basement and
the library, the doors of which had always been closed.

The telephone rang twice again as she began to search for
the sound's origin. Her best guess, the library, was right. An
old princess style telephone sat atop a large executive style
desk. The computer equipment on the desk caught her attention, too. The doors were open.

She stood in the doorway, unsure. Should she run out
and yell at Phillip that someone was calling him? That would
spoil her surprise. And he'd never make it back to the house
in time. What if it was an emergency? Maybe it was his editor friend calling him to say not to come today. Would he be
angry if she answered it, no matter who was calling.

Greta made her decision. She walked quickly to the desk
and answered the telephone after the sixth ring.

"Hello." The line was quiet. "Hello."

"Is this the Williams' residence?" a male voice finally
asked.

"Who's calling?" Silence.

"Oh, excuse me, I'm sure I have the wrong Williams." The
caller hung up.

Greta was puzzled by the call, but was distracted by what
she saw on the desk.

She noticed a neatly stacked manuscript next to a printer.
The cover page read,

"*The Fort: Death's Boot Camp,* by Michael Lund". She
stared at the author's name. Her index fingernail underlined
the title as she read it again. Next to the manuscript was
a small note pad showing an E-mail address and the name
The Fort.

Her stomach felt nervous. She vaguely remembered a
couple of news stories about a place called The Fort some-

where in the Northwest, and that someone she had known had been arrested. Yes! Dad had mentioned it about a year ago. Something about Jesse Ford being arrested. The story had come and gone quickly, without much media fanfare, at least not in Houston, that she could recall. What could Phillip have to do with that?

The laptop computer on the desk was turned on. A moving screen saver image she was familiar with occupied the screen. Should she hit the space bar to see what would come up on the screen? With little hesitation, she press the long bar. A message on his e-mail program displayed a small amount of copy. Greta read the message addressed to Jesse, Barry and Tommy. She stood in disbelief and confusion as she read it again. She then noticed the attachments and click on the first one. She shook her head as she recognized Mrs. Ford, Jesse's mother who lived in town. The second attachment she viewed reinforced what she gathered from the first. And then she remembered the pistol in the suitcase upstairs. It didn't take long to piece together a shocking scenario.

"My God," she whispered to herself. She turned toward the open library doors, half-expecting Phillip to be standing there. *What horrible thing is he planning?* What had he already done? Why would he do this? How could he do this? Who was Michael Lund?

Greta's confusion turned into anger, pain and disbelief as she walked out of the library. She heard someone in the kitchen.

"What another great surprise." Phillip said as Greta entered the kitchen. His hair was wet and drops of water fell from his swim trunks. He'd left footprints on the tile floor.

"The coffee pot idea is great. I bet the coffee is, too."

As he took a sip from his cup his eyes narrowed and grew

cold. He watched Greta march directly toward him. Her lips were tightly pressed. He lowered the cup.

Greta pushed him backward as hard as she could, and steaming coffee splashed across his arm and on to his leg. He gained his footing and then stood perfectly still and quiet, failing to react to the hot liquid on his body. He scanned her face and he knew. She had been in the library. He knew what she had seen. He braced himself.

"Bastard!" she screamed. Her face contorted and her body trembled. "And all along I thought you were the one being hunted and haunted . . . the poor victim . . . the one who needed refuge and help. I saw the photographs! I read your message!"

She stared hard at the man before her. "*You're* the spider!" she said. "And this town is your web . . . and the manuscript and those pictures are the bait! You plan to kill somebody and maybe you already have!" She slapped his face hard.

"You don't know anything about me!" he said back loudly. "But then you're the ace investigative reporter from Houston, right?" He put his empty cup on the counter and dried his arm and leg with a kitchen towel.

"I don't have all the facts and I don't know who was on your telephone just now, but I have enough to know that you're planning something very violent."

"There was a telephone call?

"Yes. I answered your goddamn phone in your *private* library. That's where I saw everything."

"Who called?"

"He didn't say. And maybe you've already killed old lady Ford!"

"I haven't killed anyone!"

"But you're going to, aren't you? Is your need for revenge that strong?"

"It's justice."

"It's murder!"

"No! I'll tell you what murder is. Murder is what took my wife away from me. You should have seen her die, Greta. Look. See the driver's ugly face, the gun, the shots fired and the screaming and the blood of my innocent wife. That's murder. The Fords murdered my wife!"

"And now you're going to get one of them."

Phillip turned and looked at the lake from the kitchen window. "No comment."

She folded her arms and shook her head. "You can't just kill people because they are killers. That would make you no better than they are. And you'd have to live with it all your life, Phillip, that is, if you even survive whatever it is you have planned."

He turned and took a step closer to her. "And what about Richard?"

"What?"

"You would have killed Richard six days ago without a second thought if you'd had a gun. Wouldn't you?"

"Yes . . . but he was a threat. Our lives were on the line."

"So was my wife's. So is mine. I'm the one they really wanted to kill. The only difference between your situation and mine is time . . . time, Greta."

"But mine would have been self-defense."

"Mine will be, too."

"What do you mean? What the hell are you planning?" Greta followed Phillip out the back door onto the porch where he looked out to the horizon.

"Do you have any idea what The Fort is, and who the Fords really are?" he asked.

"Only a little bit I remember from last year." Greta's voice was somewhat more controlled. "Some compound out west where Jesse Ford was arrested on gun charges. I don't remember the story ever being that big."

"The Fort was . . . is, a training ground for death and destruction. I was there for two months . . . as an informant. And do you know what I discovered? Jesse Ford and his sons had plans for bombings and shootings all over this country." Philip's voice quickened. "They followed civil rights cases from all over the country, and if the cases didn't turn out the way they wanted them to, they made more plans. They made sophisticated remote control bombs and modified assault weapons . . . all illegal. The morning of the raid by federal agents I was to leave on a mission along the American-Mexican border . . . to shoot at Mexicans trying to cross the border at night! Anyone who isn't straight and white is their enemy."

"And they went to prison."

"Yes, but only Jesse and Barry. And they were only convicted on weapons charges. That's it. All the FBI wanted was a good solid conviction they could stick up congressional noses. There was a conviction because of me. They didn't seem to give a crap about the Ford's plans and mentality, but I did. Everything I learned at The Fort is in my book. The Fort is still alive and well. And my book is going to tell this country about these hate mongers!"

"And now that they know you've written this book and they're coming for it, and you."

"Let 'em come."

"That's just great! Start a war in little Rockwood."

"It's not a war . . . it's justice. Tommy killed my wife and now he is going to do himself in."

"You can't do this, Phillip."

"This is none of your business."

Greta pushed hard at him again. He barely moved from the force. Her eyes were hard as she looked directly into his. "When you saved my life and Ben's you made it my business. When you held me and we kissed, you became my business. I'll go to Champ if I have to."

"If you do that, only more people will get hurt. It will be a war then. Do you want that?"

Greta moved away from him and stared into space. "Did you really intend to drive out of town and see a colleague today, Phillip?"

"No. I wanted to keep you and Ben away from here and me."

"So this is where you plan to end it all?"

"The Fords started it. I only picked the final battlefield."

Greta turned quickly to him. "Great answer. Go ahead! Kill and be killed. Just don't forget to leave a note for Ben explaining why you're not around anymore, Phillip, or Michael . . . or whoever the hell you are." She turned and ran down the steps, around the house to her car.

Phillip heard the car door slam and the car squeal out of the driveway. He ran down the steps and across the backyard toward the lake. His body hit the water in a dive.

———

Tommy Ford locked his customized pick-up before he went in to pay for the gas he had just pumped. He thought the leather briefcase on the floor on the cab would be too tempting for any gawkers checking out his unusual truck. He pulled his jeans up under his belly and pulled a fat wallet out of his back pocket as he approached the front of the truck stop. The heel of his cowboy boot made a "chink" sound as he scuffed the metal threshold at the door.

His fancy truck sported an exterior roll bar lined with short, wide spikes. A double-decker row of spotlights was mounted on top of the cab roof. One set faced forward, the other to the rear. Flared rear fenders covered the giant tires. The entire truck body was painted white except the hood, which was covered for a forty-eight star flag. The windows were heavily tinted. A cellular telephone was holstered to the dash, one he had used several times since the start of his journey to call his grandmother. She never had answered his calls.

He returned to his truck with a large container of coffee, a Coke and a paper bag stuffed with junk food from the I90 Truck Plaza. It was several hours past his breakfast time and he was hungry. He had driven almost fourteen hours, taking just one two-hour nap in western Wyoming. There was no comrade to share the driving. He calculated he had about eight to nine hours to go before he'd arrive in his old hometown. He was stocked up on gas and food, and was refreshed enough for another long stretch of driving. He ignited his truck's V8 engine and rolled on the interstate highway heading eastward to South Dakota.

Ford wasn't used to traveling near the speed limit. In Northeast Oregon, he never gave it a thought. But he grew more cautious as he came closer to the upper Midwest. He would never get to Rockwood if stopped by a highway cop. If there was a search of his truck it would turn up a modified semiautomatic rifle, two handguns, a Blackjack knife and several rounds of ammunition. All but one pistol and the knife were well concealed deep inside the custom-made truck box behind the rear window.

He set his cruise control at a safe four miles an hour over the limit. Driving slower than usual gave him fits, so he used the extra time to fume over his enemy. Had Willams killed his Granny? Or was he holding her hostage at a motel in town or some place nearby? The stool pigeon was gonna die!

Ford decided he would check his grandmother's house first and then talk to the neighbors, asking about any strangers that might have been seen there. Maybe someone had heard about something strange going on someplace in town. It was a start.

As an absolute last resort there was the police station. But Tommy hated Larry Champ. Years ago, when the Ford family had lived in Rockwood, he had seen Barry come home after a high school football game with his face bloodied. His brother and Champ had fought over a girl in their class. Larry had been the bigger guy and not afraid of Barry. Barry was the smarter and aggressive one, also unafraid of Champ or anyone else. He wouldn't back down no matter what the odds were. The fight was just one episode in the long-term, on-again, off-again feud between the Fords and the Champs that lasted until the Fords moved away.

Tommy set his large coffee container in the cup holder molded into the center console. He tore open a pack of Twinkies and pushed the scan button on his stereo system. He listened for a better country station. His eyes were glued to the Interstate as he lit a cigarette after inhaling the spongy, yellow cake. Fatigue started to kick in a little once again, but he trusted the nicotine, caffeine and the anticipation of getting to Williams would keep him going.

He also thought about his dad and Barry sitting in separate federal prisons. They were going to be proud of him. And, once they were released in couple of years, they would all be back at The Fort in no time at all taking care of business as usual.

Tommy enjoyed being in charge of a new operation. And if all went well this time, he would take home major trophies . . . the manuscript and Williams' scalp.

He pitched the hot butt from his window and lit another cigarette. Sioux Falls, ninety-two miles.

~~~ *chapter 24*

The parade's first marching band was playing Stars and Stripes Forever as Greta found Ben, Jason Bing and his mother in front of *The Rockwood Ledger* office. She gave Ben a quick hug and kiss. It was ten past ten.

Onlookers lining Main Street were shoulder to shoulder. The boys and Mrs. Bing could see very little except for the backs of heads until Greta suggested they watch the parade from the top step of the office entrance.

She unlocked the door and invited everyone in. The boys stood in the doorway listening to the brassy music, waiting for the first float to come by. Greta flipped a wall switch and a bank of fluorescent lights suspended from the high ceiling lit the cluttered office.

"I hope everything went all right last night," said Greta.

"Everything was fine," replied Jason's mother. "The boys had a great time at the carnival and they were in bed by ten-thirty . . . pretty early for a sleep-over. They were up by seven for cartoons though."

"I can't thank you enough for having Ben over. It was just what he needed, I think."

"Don't mention it. The boys really get along well. I think they'll want to do it again."

Greta excused herself and walked to the furthest desk in the office and picked up the telephone receiver punched in seven numbers.

"Hello?" answered George.

"Dad, I'm at the office with Ben. Just wanted to check in with you. Everything OK?"

"Well, good morning again. I'm still keeping the coffee hot." George had a chuckle in his voice. "Yes, everything is fine. Why wouldn't it be?"

"No reason, Dad, I just dashed out of the house so quickly after I got up that I didn't ask how you were doing this morning. And then I got caught up with my errand so I didn't get back."

"I couldn't be better this morning. Hey, though, you got a call from your detective friend in Houston about an hour ago. He said you might want to call him. He said he would be in his office until about noon today. What's up?"

"Nothing, really. I think he's just concerned about me."

"It never hurts to have good friends at the police station. Do you need his number? He left it with me."

" I know it. Thanks."

Ben and Jason covered their ears as the town's volunteer fire department demonstrated their fire truck sirens as it passed in front of the office. Following close behind were two mammoth farm tractors from the local implement dealer and a shiny convertible carrying the Little Miss Rockwood pageant winner.

Greta stood behind Ben with her hands on his shoulders. She bent down and kissed the back of his head. He turned and smiled.

"I really had a great time at Jason's last night, Mom," yelled Ben over the parade noise.

"That's what I heard," said his mother. "Maybe we can have Jason spend the night at our house sometime."

"Great!"

Clowns throwing candy to the crowd diverted his attention. A handful thrown over several heads reached the steps in front of the boys. They scrambled and shouted for more.

Greta excused herself again. Mrs. Bing said she would keep an eye on the boys.

Greta walked to an office in the back of the building where it was quieter. She repeated Randy Quarve's office number aloud as she entered the numbers on the telephone.

"Quarve."

"And you probably thought I couldn't remember your number anymore," said Greta. "What kind of reporter do you think I am . . . was . . . whatever."

"The best, Greta," said Quarve, recognizing her voice. "The best. How's my Iowa connection?"

"Fine, I guess. What's up? Dad said you called."

"I've been digging on this Williams guy a little more. I wanted to tell you what I found. You're sure everything's all right?"

"Things are a little hectic here, but I don't think Ben or I are in any danger, if that's what you mean."

"That's what I mean. I told you before this guy's wife was killed in Colorado last year and that it was murder, right?"

"Yes."

"I found out he was a federal witness at one time and was under their protection program. And, well, his real name is Michael Lund. Professor Lund . . . University of Minnesota. Professor Lund . . . FBI informant."

"Anything else?"

"I found his car. It's sitting in long-term parking at Des Moines International. No one knows this now but you and me."

"Good."

"It's been there since the first of June."

"The day before he arrived here."

"He's going to have one helluva parking tab when he gets it out."

"If he ever planned to get it out."

"What?"

"Nothing . . . just talking to myself."

"One more thing. I got a call from the FBI two days ago . . . a Raymond Stacey. Somehow he got wind of me digging around. He wanted to know why I was asking about the Williams guy and his wife's death. He grilled me pretty good, but I didn't tell him much, certainly not where Lund was. I wanted to talk to you first. Seems this guy with the gun is more than a professor on the run."

"You've been a great help, Randy."

"I have a feeling you know more than I do."

"Maybe."

"Just play it careful."

"Don't worry, I'll play it smart."

"Call me if you have to."

"Thanks again, Randy. Say hello to your family."

Greta replaced the receiver and realized she didn't know what to do next.

———

One hundred and seven miles past Iowa's western border, Tommy carefully surveyed the road ahead. He was on Highway 18, which ran east and west across the northern part of the state, and he was watching for the turnoff that would take him within twelve miles of Rockwood. He was getting close.

It was four years since he was in Rockwood to see Grandma Ford. It was her seventy-sixth birthday and he had come with his father and brother. It was also the last time he had visited the grave of his mother. Although a younger teen-ager at the time of her death, the memory of her lived within him, almost in a twisted sense, thanks in part to Jesse, who wouldn't let his sons forget the details of the day she was killed in Washington D.C.

Nine miles off Highway 18, flashing lights from a police car not more than a half a mile ahead surprised him. He cautiously hit the breaks and slowed well below the posted speed limit. "Dammit," he growled.

As the speedometer dropped even more, he saw a high-way patrolman walk out from near the patrol car that was parked on the right shoulder of the asphalt road. The officer waved his arms in a crossing motion. The length of a football field now separated them.

There wasn't any accident that he could see, or any other car, people or activity around anywhere. He and the patrol-man were alone in wide-open farm country on a hot sum-mer day. *What the hell was going on?* He began to panic. He slapped hard on the glove box to assure it was tightly closed. He also made sure the contents inside a small rolled blanket under his seat were secure. He pushed the blanket back as far as it would go. He smashed his half-finished cigarette in the ashtray and turned the radio off. He knew he couldn't turn around. That was sure to bring on suspicion, if not a possible chase. There were two other options for him. He chose compliance, not confrontation.

Ford lowered his window as he slowly drove up to the of-ficer. He couldn't read the officer's attitude because of the dark sunglasses and the wide-brimmed hat pulled down on his forehead. The patrolman approached the driver's side of the truck with a calm and confident stride. His firearm was holstered.

"Afternoon," said Tommy as he took off his yellow

sunglasses. He grinned and leaned out the window slightly. "I can't believe how hot it is." He prepared himself to retrieve the handgun in the glove compartment at a second's notice if necessary.

"Good afternoon. We're stopping all vehicles here to let drivers know that traffic is very congested just outside of Rockwood. If your destination isn't Rockwood, I suggest you consider turning off at the next intersection and go around the town. If you're going into Rockwood, you should know that parking in the town is almost impossible."

Tommy listened intently. His panic lessened. "That's where I was headed . . . Rockwood. Visiting a relative and then headed further east. I guess I'll just have to deal with it."

"Good luck." The trooper stepped back.

"Thanks for the information . . . and stay cool," replied Tommy as he put the transmission in gear.

The patrolman waved him back on the road. Tommy grinned and waved back. He lit another cigarette as he continued on his way.

Traffic started to slow down two miles outside of Rockwood. Hundreds of cars and trucks were parked single file on the sides of the highway providing a metal corridor for Tommy and his white truck.

He thought back to when he was a kid in Rockwood and his anticipation of the annual Water Festival. He was surprised it turned out that he was coming back to Rockwood during the festival after four years. He and Barry had always had a great time. It was almost better than Christmas. He missed those exciting days and simple times as a child. They had come to an end when his mother was taken from him.

Ford's memories brought him back to thinking about the fate of his aging grandmother and what he was going to do to informant Williams when he found him. Once he had the manuscript and computer in hand, Mr. Undercover Scum Sucker wouldn't escape again. Ford grabbed the brief-case from the cab floor and put in on the seat next to him. Grandma's house was not far away.

———————

As Tommy's customized truck came closer to Rockwood's city limits, Phillip sat inside the parked Buick on the side of the highway facing oncoming traffic. The car melded into the wall of other vehicles. He held field glasses to his eyes as he observed through the windshield. His arms were tired and his stomach growled.

"Bingo." Phillip held the binoculars perfectly steady. His extended eyes, shaded by a cap pulled low, picked up the roll bar spikes and the roof-mounted spotlights that he new so well. The truck came closer. The familiar face in the cab came into focus.

When Ford was less than two hundred feet away Phillip replaced the binoculars with an unfolded state map that cov-ered his face. He remained unnoticed as Tommy drove past. Ford looked preoccupied with the sea of traffic he had to navigate. Straight ahead of him was Rockwood's landmark, the town's water tower in the shape of a bobber.

———————

Greta's eyes were unblinking as a hot breeze blew her short hair. She sat on her front porch, oblivious to the sounds drifting from all over town. She had told George and Ben she would catch up with them in time for the boat races that were scheduled to begin at five.

Until then, she needed some time to be alone and think. She hadn't told anyone about Williams and what she thought he had planned. She needed to focus on Phillip and what she should do about the pending violence she felt certain would happen between Williams and Tommy Ford and maybe others. She knew Chief Champ would drop everything else to prevent a tragedy, if he could believe with certainly that some deadly event was about to take place. But, if something tragic did happened, when would it occur? Tonight? In two days? Just when? And where?

Greta debated whether informing Champ now would be a wise move. Rockwood would still be overflowing with thirty-five thousand people, at least until the night water parade and fireworks were over. She was trying to convince herself Williams wouldn't carry out his private battle in such a public place. Informing Champ was an option she had to decide about quickly. It was now more than seven hours since she'd left Phillip's house.

Greta went inside and returned to the front porch wearing casual summer clothes and sunglasses. She tested the front door to make sure it was locked and put her cell phone in her pocket as she walked past her car in the driveway. She turned down the sidewalk at a brisk pace in the direction of Lake Emmet. It was nearly five o'clock.

———

Tommy found the house key to his Grandmother's house in her unlocked garage. She still kept it under a red coffee can next to her garden tools on the workbench. Mrs. Ford's favorite straw hat banded with a wide yellow ribbon rested on the wooden peg above. Her old, but immaculate white Oldsmobile was parked inside.

She had never, ever locked her garage as long as Tommy could remember. And it was only when her family moved away that she had started locking the door to her house. He locked his truck and, after knocking on the door, let himself in.

Tommy went through every room in the house, including a thorough search of the attic and basement. He used a flashlight from his truck to check the dark cellar corners. He found nothing to suggest anything violent had taken place there. But then, Ford knew Williams was fully capable of deception.

Further investigation revealed the refrigerator was well stocked, and the homemade cookies in the cookie jar she had used forever were still fresh. Everything was as he remembered it, except that his grandmother was not there, nor was her purse to be found. (As a child, Tommy had never had trouble finding her purse. He was convinced she never noticed any change missing from the coin holder inside.) Then he noticed the daily calendar on her writing desk in the dining room. The page facing up was Thursday, two days ago.

It looked like she had simply vanished.

He spent the next few minutes checking out the neighbors on either side. No one was at home. In her mailbox he found a garden magazine and envelopes addressed to Mrs. Jeremy Ford. As he looked through the mail inside the house, the telephone on the desk rang. The sound startled him. It rang again . . . and a third time. He grabbed the receiver on the fourth ring.

"Hello," Ford said in a low voice.

The line went immediately dead.

"Dammit!" He threw the mail against the wall and kicked the air with his pointed boot. He then stormed out of the house through the back door and again checked to make sure his truck was locked.

He headed in the direction of downtown, which was not more than two blocks away. He was angry and hot. Someone in town must know something about the man he had to find.

Sweat dripped from under his western hat. His legs were sticky and irritated under his heavy jeans, and he felt beads of sweat rolling down his chest under his shirt. He was tired and hungry. He swore under his breath at the oppressive Iowa heat as he looked at the watch on his thick wrist. Five minutes after six.

The downtown was filled with people looking for a place to have dinner. Lines formed outside the three cafes on Main Street and food vendors on the sidewalks had all the business they could handle. Ford stopped and looked at the front of the town's only hardware store. A sign on the wood and glass door said it was still open. The bell above the door jingled as he entered. Tommy was greeted by Henry Dalton, who was reading a set of three brass weather gauges mounted on the wall behind the counter. Tommy muttered a soft reply.

"The fishing is going to be great tonight . . . if you can get on the lake, that is," said the storeowner. He said he was about to close, but asked if he could help his last-minute customer.

Tommy remembered Dalton, but he knew the owner didn't recognize him. Too many years had passed since he was in Dalton's store, and Ford had gained height and even more weight. The light-colored western hat setting low on his brow and the yellow sunglasses added camouflage.

The smell of the store hadn't changed. Although he had never known what the scent was, he had always enjoyed it. The tin ceiling and worn wooden floor were unchanged, too. He had liked going to Dalton's Hardware as a child to look at BB guns, fishing lures and the candy display by the cash register. He was only caught stealing once from the store. It happened to be when he was with his dad. The tube of BBs stood out too much in his pocket and Mr. Dalton apprehended him. Tommy felt the belt on his rear when they got home. The next day Jesse bought him a BB gun and a dozen tubes of BBs.

"I was wonderin' if you might be able to help me." Tommy looked squarely at the owner.

"I'll try." The owner didn't recognize him.

"I'm lookin' for an old friend that might have moved to town not too long ago. Lean, strong-lookin' guy . . . about thirty-five or so . . . likes to work with his hands and fish. Name's Williams. Just thought I'd ask in case you might have seen him around town or here in your store. I wanted to stop and surprise the guy since I was passing through. We've kinda lost touch over the years.

"I do know him."

"You do?" Tommy faced Dalton across the same wooden counter he had stood at dozens of time before as a kid.

"I mean I've seen him . . . a few times. I guess I really don't know him. No one in town knows much about your friend, except maybe Greta. Kind of a loner, but friendly. He doesn't let on much about himself. I think I heard over at the market he was a teacher. Does that sound like your friend?"

Tommy didn't immediately reply, but started looking around the store instead. Henry Dalton straightened up the counter and locked the cash register as Tommy's eyes found the place where the BB and pellet guns had been displayed on the wall years ago. The shelves were now lined with small electronic items. Ford finally turned back to the storeowner.

"Oh yes, Professor Williams. He used to outsmart everybody. So does he live here in town?"

"He moved into the old Hansen house down by the lake, about four blocks from here. That monster was on the market for more than a year. I can't believe that anybody very smart would want it. Anyway, he's been there since around the first of June, I think."

"When did ja see him last?"

"Monday or Tuesday, I think it was. He came in and spent

a lot of time looking, but ended up buying just some rope and a big hunting knife."

"Who's this Greta my old buddy is seeing? Girl friend? I wouldn't want to just barge in on them or anything, if you know what I mean."

"Greta Meyer. Her dad owns the paper down the street. From what I hear, again, over at the market, yeah, I guess you could say they're pretty good friends."

Ford knew the name and remembered Barry talking about her when he was in high school. Larry Champ's name came back to him again, too.

"Well, thanks. You told me what I needed to know. And I like your store. I'll come back and shop when I have some time.

"You bet. Enjoy your stay in Rockwood. If you're still around, don't miss the big show on the lake tonight."

Ford left the store, pleased with the information he had extracted from Dalton. His next destination was the Sunshine Market where he knew his grandmother always shopped for groceries. The owner might remember the last time Mrs. Ford had been in. And the clerks might know something useful about Greta Meyer.

The aroma of food from the vendor's booths teased him as he made his way down the sidewalk to the market. He began making a mental list of what he would carry back to his grandmother's house to devour as he rested and planned his next move.

"How much longer before the water parade and fireworks, Mom?" asked Ben. He yawned as he laid his head on Greta's lap. He stared at the moving clouds in the dimming sky and told his mother and grandpa that he could make out the image of Mickey Mouse's head.

"Not too much longer, maybe a half hour or a little more." Greta gazed across the lake in the direction of Phillip's house. Boat floats were assembling for the water pageantry. Yellow lights on some of the lake homes reflected faintly on the water. She could not see Williams' house, but she could visualize it and its occupant.

Greta hadn't told anyone yet about Williams' private war with the Fords and the battle that might erupt at any time. Sitting at the lake's edge with her son and father on a peaceful summer night made such a scenario seem absurd. Yet, she knew from her professional and personal past that violence can rear its ugly head any time, any place. It had been nearly ten hours since she'd fled from Phillip's house, feeling ready to explode.

Ben waggled his feet back and forth impatiently on the blanket and rubbed his eyes. She smiled at her handsome son as she ran her fingers through his hair. He needed his mother. She wouldn't do *anything* to jeopardize that.

"I think we've got a tired little fella here," whispered George to Greta. "He's had a couple of busy days."

"I know," said Greta. "I'm not sure he's going to last until the fireworks."

"I heard you guys," said Ben with another yawn. " I could stay awake until midnight if I wanted to." He curled up on his side.

Greta watched, as his eyelids could no longer support themselves. Within minutes Ben was asleep.

Empty spaces along the lake's shore were becoming scarce as the anticipation of the festival finale drove people to find a good view. A thousand others surrounded the Meyer blanket. Someone had lit a cigarette nearby and the breeze carried the cloud of smoke to them. She turned around to give the inconsiderate lout a furious look, but the smoker nearby in the cowboy hat and yellow-tinted sunglasses was not looking in her direction. She watched him for a few seconds as he plucked at the grass and bounced on his haunches. He was staring across the lake. Small binoculars dangled on a strap from his thick neck, and a soft leather pouch hung from his right shoulder. Their eyes did not meet.

He finally stood up and walked away with the cigarette dangling from his lips. A final swirl of smoke passed and dissipated.

George realized Greta's mood had been tense ever since she and Ben returned home from the parade. She was impatience and easily irritated. She seemed distant and preoccupied.

"What's been eating at you all day, Greta? You've been troubled about something since this morning. I'm here to listen if you want to talk about it."

Greta gave her father a rueful smile and patted his hand. "You know me too well, Dad."

"It has something to do with Phillip, doesn't it?" he asked.

Greta took a deep breath and looked at Ben to make sure he was still sleeping. "Yes."

"I thought things were working out well for you two lately."

"They had been . . . until this morning. Dad, I think Phillip might be in serious trouble. And I don't know whether telling certain people about it will make the situation better or worse."

"How serious?"

"Very."

"Police serious?"

"Yes."

"Is there anything you can do?"

"I tried. He listened, but it didn't change anything. He suffered a terrible tragedy last year and he's still carrying all of that pain with him. I think he's ready to do something terrible, thinking it will make his life better, or at least even things out."

"You care about him a lot, don't you?"

"I think I do . . . and I'm really surprised that I do. A couple of months ago he frightened the daylights out of me. And he's scaring the daylights out of me again . . . now."

They remained silent for a minute and watched the gathering crowd. She straightened out a corner of the blanket that the wind had blown up.

"How does he feel about you?"

"I think he cares about me . . . and Ben. As much as he can, considering the tragedy he's been through. But it's apparently not enough."

"If it's as serious as it sounds, maybe you should call Champ in to find out what it's all about."

"That's what has been eating at me since this morning. I truly don't know what's the right thing to do. I've almost convinced myself to confront Phillip again and try to prevent something terrible, and then I'm almost convinced to call Champ first and talk to him about it."

"When?"

"As soon as I convince myself."

Loud, brassy fanfare music from out on the lake signaled the start of the most spectacular event Rockwood and its Water Festival were known for. Thousands of eager spectators clapped and whistled in anticipation of seeing the many-lighted water floats on their choreographed parade around the lake.

Greta's gentle tug on Ben's arm, and the music, were enough to wake him. He looked around a moment to recollect where he was and then showed his delight at the sight of the first float coming in close to their side of the lake. The design was a gigantic American flag made from brilliantly-lit red, white and blue bulbs. The reflecting lights danced on the choppy water as the float made its way past the cheering, standing crowd. A rousing recorded version of "Stars and Stripes Forever" accompanied the spectacle.

People sat down after the flag float passed by. Over the years it had become an unspoken rule of courtesy to remain sitting after the flag had gone by, so all could see. Newcomers learned quickly from their neighbors. Small children were usually exempt from the rule.

Ben snuggled on Greta's lap and settled in for the rest of the parade. The second float was a sixty-foot tall replica of the Rockwood bobber water tower. Spotlights directed up from the bottom lit the structure and a huge "Happy 100th" logo outlined with bright red light bulbs blinked on and off.

Without warning a sudden strong gust of wind blew across the lakeshore. The surprise briefly distracted the spectators as people reacted to the sound of leaves flapping on the giant oak trees that ringed the lake. Several older folks simply raised their chins to the southwest and studied the sky.

George straightened the blanket again and moved a little closer to Greta and Ben. All eyes were once again fixed on the extravaganza in front of them . . . all but Greta's, whose vision carried across the lake in the direction of the stone house. She tightened her arms around Ben and squeezed, then turned to George and whispered in his ear.

Greta sat with Ben on her lap, gently swaying back and forth as the parade of water floats glided across the water. By the time the last float was in sight, Ben was resting his head on his mother's shoulder and yawning again.

"Ben?" said Greta. "Mom has to go do a quick errand. You and Grandpa can stay here until the parade is over."

"But it's nighttime, Mom."

"I know it's late sweetie, but this errand is important." Greta caressed her son's cheek. "Grandpa will take you on home after you watch a little bit of the fireworks. They're the same ones you saw last night and Grandpa thinks you guys should get started for home before everyone else tries to leave."

Ben rubbed his eyes. Greta and her father looked at each other and nodded. George scooted close to Ben and hugged him. "We'll be just fine."

"Grandpa will tuck you in and I'll come in and kiss you good night when I get home."

"I'll expect you or your phone call within an hour or so. I think you know what I'm saying," said George.

"I do. You'll see me or hear from me soon. Love you both."

Greta stooped to stay out of the crowd's way and quickly began to weave her way through the sea of people. She walked away from the lakeshore toward Lakeside Drive. Her slim figure and attractive face caught the attention of many as she passed. She felt their stare and heard a few comments but she stayed focused on the pay telephone stand she knew was straight ahead, across the street on the parking. It wasn't the telephone she needed, since she had her cell phone, but the light emitting from the stand made would made her feel more secure.

When she reached the sidewalk there were only a few other people walking around the back of the crowd. Attention was fixed on the parade's coming finale. No one probably notice her quick jog across the street to the public telephone. It was unoccupied as were the sidewalks and the grassy parking areas nearby. Lights were on in a couple of nearby houses, but few other signs of life on this side of Lakeside Drive were evident. She could hear the leaves fluttering in the trees and music coming from the water floats.

She pulled her telephone from her pocked and punched in a recently saved telephone number from her address. She had no idea what she was going to say. Greta hoped the appropriate words would come when Phillip answered. She stared into the telephone stand light and concentrated on the first ring. The rise and fall of her rib cage was more pronounced than usual. After the eighth ring she hung up the receiver. "Dammit." she said to herself. "I'm going to call Champ."

As she brought up her address book again, she felt a presence close by. She turned to see if anyone was waiting to use the public phone. Her pupils were still constricted from staring into the stand's light, but she could make out a person in a cowboy hat. In less that a second she connected the hat with the man who had earlier been smoking near her blanket. He still had his black bag slung on his shoulder. Immediately Greta knew.

Tommy Ford grabbed the cell phone from Greta's hand and pinned her to the telephone stand with his body. "If you make a sound, you are gonna die," Ford said slowly with gritted teeth. He flipped her cell phone closed and stuffed into his left jean pocket.

He had a small paper bag in his right hand and shoved it into her ribs. The shoulder bag blocked the sack from view. There was no one around close enough to see.

She felt the hard blunt object through the sack. Ford pressed his sweaty face into her ear. His breath smelled almost as foul as the rest of his body.

"If you try to run, I will put a big hole in your nice little body, and your nice little boy over there won't have a mommy anymore. Do you want to take that chance?"

Greta shook her head back and forth.

"And my comrades will make sure he doesn't have a granddaddy either. That's a promise." Ford straightened his torso and tried to act natural as if he were talking to a friend in case anyone came near.

Greta did not speak.

"Let's move away from the phone and you just start walking half a step ahead of me . . . real natural like," he instructed.

She heard the rustle of the sack behind her, but the object was no longer jabbing into her. They began to walk down Lakeside Drive.

A single explosion detonated high over the lake, signaling the start of the fireworks display. Within seconds a half dozen gigantic balls of colored light glittered against the cloudy sky. The symmetry of the illuminations was distorted by the increasing wind. Regardless, the fiery introduction inspired the spectators to show their approval with applause and whistles. Ford took advantage of the noise and distractions.

"Hey, the timing's just right, ain't it, in case I have to use this." Ford waggled the sack back and forth. "No one would hear my little friend here, would they? But you're not gonna run, are ya? Sure a cute little boy you got."

Greta's mind was working full speed. She was afraid, but not enough to cripple her ability to think. She knew she could escape, although probably wounded . . . at least get away from him. But were the comrades he mentioned real? Or was he bluffing? Could she afford to gamble? *Not now.*

They continued in the direction of the stone mansion. There was no one else on the sidewalk. The spectators were glued to the lake and the space above for the moment.

"Where are you taking me?" demanded Greta.

"I thought we would drop in on the professor. Didn't you just call him?"

"What are you talking about?"

"Cut the crap, bitch. Everybody in town knows you and Mr. Whosit are a 'thing.' Those two old bags at the market know everything about you . . . and that sure helped me. They told me about you and your family, your Mr. Professor, and even what you looked like. Hey, I found you as easy as flies find shit."

"What do you want with him?"

"More crap. Maybe *you* know what the bastard did with my grandma. The old ladies at the market said they hadn't seen her in four days . . . didn't know why she hadn't been around lately. Did he kill her? Did you help him?"

"Your grandmother is alive."

"Then you do know where she is . . . maybe tied up in his house . . . booby trapped maybe."

"I don't know anything about it." She turned her head to see him and he poked the object in her back again.

"Well, you and me are gonna make a little visit and find out all about it."

———

The wind's velocity increased again and it was having an affect on the spectators. Several groups gathered their belongings and began to leave the wide grassy areas as the fireworks continued. The brilliant sparkles and the patterns were becoming even more distorted because of the wind. Blankets flew up into people's faces and pieces of paper became airborne, swirling overhead and through the crowd. Caps and hats flew off heads. The evening's festive atmosphere was changing quickly and becoming unpleasant.

Families with little children were the first to scatter to the cars. Groups of out-of-town visitors stood and nervously looked for buses and other vehicles that would shuttle them back to the parking fields. None had arrived yet for boarding. The temperature had dropped.

———————

Tommy held onto his hat and prodded Greta in the back to move quickly down the street. She hoped George and Ben had left early and were at home safe with the doors locked. The approaching storm and the thoughts of Ford's threats and his friends replayed in her mind. She was in the middle of another nightmare and she didn't know how to get out.

Greta could tell Ford's calmness was changing in tandem with the exodus of people that had begun. He picked up the pace and cautioned her tersely not to even think of taking advantage of the situation. He assured her he was skilled at his profession and again wouldn't think twice about putting a hole in the back of her head if she ran.

Several hundred people milled up and down and across Lakeside Drive in their rush to beat the bad weather that was rapidly approaching. No one noticed the kidnapper or took time to recognize his hostage in the windy darkness. Ford walked beside Greta now, his arm around her. No one would suspect anything abnormal.

As they approached the wall of oak trees and buses that separated the stone house from the public green space, Greta looked through the bouncing branches for any sign of light from Phillip's house. Nothing but black windows. Is this how Phillip planned it? A hostage in the middle. Was she another piece of bait Phillip counted on like the manuscript and the

photographs of Mrs. Ford and the tombstone? Was he waiting in the house with a gun, or was he behind them, right
now, watching? Dammit! She should have called Champ.
Stupid! Dammit!

The sidewalk in front of Williams' house was thronged
with hurrying people looking for their own vehicle. Drivers
pulled out from spaces one by one at a fast pace, intending
to beat the traffic out of town.

"Keep walking," ordered Ford. There were too many people
around to approach the house yet. Greta cautiously looked
across the street and again saw no sign of life at Phillip's
house. The dark blue Buick, however, was still parked in the
driveway. Ford's massive hand pulled her in tightly. She felt
hard objects through the soft leather of the shoulder bag.

"So what are we going to find over there?" asked Ford.
"Are you scared?"

"What do you think? What do you want from Williams
anyway?"

"Do you know he also went by Ted? Who knows what
else he used."

"Yes, I do." Greta sensed Ford's confidence growing as the
area became more deserted. She knew she had to play something out with him. Delay him. Distract him if possible to give
her more time to think or hope fate my be on her side.

"And do you think he's responsible for putting my daddy
and brother in prison?"

"How is Barry?"

"Don't give me that crap. He's rotting in the pen 'cuzza
your boyfriend. What do you care anyway? You probably
treated him like shit in high school like everybody else did,
just like that chicken-shit Champ did."

"I didn't know Barry that well, but I thought he was very
smart. I just didn't agree with some of the things he said. I

never treated him badly ... and I don't think most of the other kids did either. Barry had a lot of potential."

"He ain't got shit now."

Ford guided Greta across the street and slowed the pace. The last of the cars were leaving on that block and there were eight houses between the corner and Williams' house. Ford's ears and eyes were on full alert. He looked carefully up and down the street, in between houses and even up into the trees. He listened intently for anything beyond the wind and blowing leaves. "Boy, is Teddy gonna be surprised," he cackled.

"How is your Dad, Tom?"

"Shut up. No more talking."

Tommy released his grip slightly and walked a half step behind Greta as they approached the house. The space between the two homes was vast. On the lot line was a row of low-cut bushes and tall oak trees with thick trunks. The wall provided as much privacy on the south as there was on the north side. Except for the front, the stone house was quite secluded. The back yard ended at the lake's edge.

"Stop," ordered Ford. He scanned the second floor windows. His eyes analyzed the porch, the first floor and basement windows. The house was completely dark. He resisted crouching and waving his weapon around as they did in training and practice at The Fort. The only movement he and Greta saw was the yard vane with it wings spinning rapidly.

Tommy tipped the brim of his hat like a baseball pitcher and told Greta they were going to walk slowly along the side of the house. He told her to stop again just before they reached the edge of the foundation. They stood motionless.

"What are you waiting for?" said Greta.

"Shut up."

"What do you really want from Phillip?" she asked in an even louder voice.

"Shut your goddamn mouth," he said through his teeth. He poked her hard in the back with his gun, which was no longer concealed inside the paper sack. Greta grimaced in pain. "He's got my granny... that's one. And I want that computer and all the disks and the book he wrote about my family and The Fort. And don't tell me you don't know anything about that. Ain't nobody gonna read that book, ever! And I want his scalp. My daddy and Barry are gonna be proud of me."

"And what if you lose this battle?"

"I won't lose." Ford unzipped his leather bag with his left hand. He pulled out a handgun twice the size of the one he had pointed at her. A silencer was attached to the end of the barrel. He quickly exchanged pistols and the small one went into the leather bag.

"This is gonna help me a little, don't you think?" he said as he brandished the large gun in front of her face.

For the first time since being abducted, she started to feel paralyzing fear. She fought panic and the urge to scream or run. Ford seemed so confident in his mission, yet he was all alone, or was he? She couldn't convince herself one way or the other. She had no idea what Phillip had anticipated, or if he would be capable of saving himself. She felt exhausted as they waited at the corner of the house. She closed her eyes and wished she would wake from the nightmare.

"Let's go see if anyone's home," he said. Ford put his left arm around her waist and they walked into the open backyard. His hat spun away in the gusting wind. Light gray clouds sped across the dark sky and white caps rushed inward toward the shore. The bushes and trees bent and whipped as the air howled.

Tommy used Greta as a shield as he walked backward toward the lake. The barrel of his gun rested against her right ear. They stopped close to the edge of the lake so he would have the widest possible view of the house and driveway. Phillip's rowing boat lay turned on its top and not far away.

Ford approached the beached boat carefully, still holding Greta in front of him. He called out, "Hey, Teddy . . . Mr. Williams . . . whoever you are, you wouldn't possibly be making this easy for me, would you? I thought we trained you better than that at the Fort."

As Ford fired his silent hand cannon into the side of the boat, the boat jerked with the impact of two exploding shells. The gaping holes showed the power of the weapon. Greta covered her eyes.

"Lift it up!" shouted Ford above the roar of the wind and surf. He pointed the gun at her and repeated the command.

Greta gripped the gunwale, bent her knees and flipped the fishing boat over. The straw hat banded with a thick yellow ribbon that belonged to Grandma Ford lay on the grass beneath. It blew away but quickly became water logged from the rain and fell to the ground.

Ford screamed for Williams, threatening to kill Greta if Phillip didn't show himself and tell him where his grandmother was. As he forced Greta toward the house again, they could see that the back screen door was open and pinned against the house by the wind. The heavier interior door was open, too. *Was it an invitation or only a result of the storm?* Ford's face turned ugly and looked as if searching his options. He also looked tired.

"Williams!" Ford yelled at the open door. His voice was little match for the gale winds. He and Greta moved closer. "Williams . . . you've already lost one, 'cuzza all this . . . you wanna lose another one? Here's the deal. First, I want to know what you did with my granny. And then I want you to bring out your book, and your computer and everything that goes with it, and lay everything at the bottom of the steps. Do you hear me, Williams?"

The door banging in the wind was the only reply.

"Just do what I say, and I'll let your nice little lady friend go. Williams! Do you hear me?"

Behind Ford and his hostage, a dark figure slowly emerged from the turbulent black water. A head and broad bare shoulders rose from the lake's gray surf. Then muscular legs appeared as the man stood and began to approach Greta and Tommy unnoticed. In his right hand was a handgun. Strapped to his left forearm was a large hunting knife. His eyes were unflinching and focused intently on the back of Ford's head as he moved forward out of the water. Greta was a foot from her captor, which would make for an easy, clean shot once he got a little closer. He aimed.

Before Williams could fire, a speeding police car with bright headlamps and flashing roof bar lights blasted around the Buick and came to a sliding halt in the backyard. An officer, firearm drawn, bolted from the car and took cover behind the north corner of the house. Ford immediately positioned Greta as his shield.

"You! Don't do it! Williams! Don't do it!" boomed an amplified voice from a second squad car that had arrived. "Both of you! Drop your weapons! Now!"

Ford spun around and saw Williams hit the ground rolling. Tommy's hurried first shot missed him by a yard. His immediate second and third shots took out the headlights that flooded the backyard. The police car rocked. Ford dragged Greta to the fishing boat for cover. They dropped and hugged the boat's hull. Williams was not in sight.

"This is Police Chief Champ. Throw down your weapons. There is no way out."

Tommy popped up over the side of the boat and fired at a squad car again, exploding the windshield. "That one was for Barry, you son of a bitch!"

Greta covered her head with her arms, expecting a volley of fire from Champ and whoever was with him. She expected to die within the next few seconds.

"Hey! I've got a certain pretty lady here with me! I think you both know who I mean. Let's put it this way . . . if I don't get out of here with what I want, she won't be leaving either. Understand?" The only answer was the raging wind mixed now with large drops of pounding rain.

From the corner of her left eye, Greta caught a slight movement on the back porch of the house. She stared and didn't know how to react. Tommy seemed totally unaware of it. She thought she could make out a rifle resting against one of the horizontal porch railings. And yes, there was a man's face behind it. She was sure of it.

"Tommy!" the man behind the rifle yelled.

Tommy turned his head in the direction of the voice. It was not that of Williams. The man crouching on the porch squeezed the trigger. The large caliber slug entered Tommy's forehead, throwing him backward against the boat. Blood oozed and mixed with the falling rain.

"FBI! Hold your fire!" shouted the man from the porch. He was still crouching. "Hold your fire! I'm standing up."

The tall man faced Chief Champ who had now taken cover behind a thick oak tree. One of his officers ran to the bottom of the porch steps and crouched with both hands on his aimed service revolver.

Phillip Williams appeared out of the darkness from behind Greta and the now dead Tommy Ford. He ran quickly up to Greta. She sat with her head between her knees, crying and drenched. He knelt between her and the dead man. "It's over," said Phillip as he cradled Greta in his arms.

Oddly, the large man on the porch said the same thing, only in a louder voice, as he lumbered down the stairs with his hand raised. Phillip recognized the voice despite the distortion from the wind. It was John Kick.

The police chief ran to the fishing boat, gun still drawn. He ordered Williams to hand over his gun and remove the knife from his arm.

"Now, move away from Greta." Williams complied again. "Jesus!" said Champ as he got a better view of the dead man. "That almost looks like Tommy Ford! I went to school with his brother. You remember, Greta?"

"Yes, it's Tommy," she said.

"Jesus Christ! What the hell is going on around here?"

Greta took a deep breath as she stood up straight. "Phillip was trying to save my life, Larry. You can put your gun away." She took a few steps away from the bloody body to have a private word with the chief. Phillip waited as the brief conference took place. Champ handed Williams' gun and knife to Greta. She finally joined Phillip but held on to the weapons.

As he walked toward the man who claimed to be with the FBI, the chief talked to the station on his hand-held radio, asking for a rescue unit. He also ordered one of his officers to go check out old Mrs. Ford's house and report back ASAP. The dispatcher informed him that traffic was thinning out on the highway and that Rockwood seemed pretty quiet according the latest reports.

Phillip and Greta walked together to the lake's edge. They hugged tightly. The wind had diminished slightly, but the rain continued as before.

"My plan never included having anyone else here," he

said. "This was strictly supposed to be between just Ford and me."

"But you knew I might come here, or try to find you, didn't you? Greta asked.

"I thought you might. And my worst fear was confirmed when I saw that Ford had you hostage across the street. When did you call the police?"

"I didn't. I'll bet Dad did. We both felt something terrible was going to happen."

Another patrol car pulled onto the scene and the town's rescue unit arrived a few seconds later. Champ pointed out the body and told the paramedic to hurry up before the whole town showed up to see what was happening. He then continued talking with Kick.

"Who's the guy up there?" asked Greta as she walked with Phillip back to his house. She still held his knife and gun.

"The man who got me into this mess in the first place, John Kick."

"And he really is an FBI agent?"

"Yes."

"Looks like the G-Man kinda saved the day, just like in the old movies."

"He did, but the outcome would have been the same even if he hadn't shown up."

"I'm very glad it didn't come to that. Why is he here?"

"Good question. I plan to find out right now. I didn't invite him."

Kick was finishing with Chief Champ at the bottom of the porch steps. He greeted Williams like an old war buddy and asked him if he was all right. Then he asked to be introduced to Greta. Champ turned away from them to talk to one of his officers.

"I doubt if Phillip's plan worked out the way he really

wanted it to," said Kick to Greta, "but I think Phillip had everything under control until that grand entrance by your local police. They really know how to stir things up, don't they?"

"They were just doing their job," Greta quickly countered.

"Just what was your original plan, Phillip?" asked Kick. "You got Ford here, but then what?"

"It doesn't matter any more, does it?"

"How in the hell did you ever find your way here, Kick?" asked Phillip. "And then showing up here tonight, of all nights."

A call coming in on the chief's radio briefly interrupted Kick's reply. Champ moved away from the conversation as he told the office to go ahead with the message.

"You have been a son of a bitch to track, Phillip. But a little, teeny break finally came when I learned that someone at Houston PD made an inquiry at the Bureau and then at the Denver PD. He was asking about an unusual traffic incident last year on Interstate 25 south out of Denver last year. Anyone know a Randy Quarve?"

Greta excused herself and said she was going inside out of the rain and to call her father.

"No, I don't." Phillip's eyes followed Greta as she walked up the steps.

"Doesn't matter. Anyway, we did some checking and then some thinking, and presto, the pieces seem to fit. Stacey sent me out here to find you and see what the hell was going on. Just got lucky on hitting the right night, I guess. Glad I did, though. I got into town just a little bit ago and managed to locate your house."

"Thanks for good timing."

"You're welcome, but you would have bagged him first if it hadn't been for the Iowa Rangers coming to the rescue.

If that was your original plan, it will always be just between you and me."

The chief returned and announced that a pickup with Oregon plates registered to Tommy Ford had been found at his grandmother's house, and that it looked like it had been broken into. One of the windows was smashed in. "All they found were some clothes and hidden weapons. And I guess Mrs. Ford wasn't home . . . probably gone away with her friend to Lake Okoboji again."

The rescue unit left the scene with Tommy's body. The wind and light rain had died down considerably now, replaced by sporadic lightning and thunder.

Champ wrote down a few more details from Williams for his initial report but suggested they finish at the police station in the morning at ten. The chief told Kick to be there, too. Kick assured the police chief he would have all of his questions fully answered.

"Let's call it a night," said the exhausted Champ. "I'm glad this damn festival is over for another year. Say, where are you staying, Kick?"

"I found a motel out on the highway that actually had a vacancy tonight," replied the agent. "Sure glad I didn't come into town yesterday. Calling it a night sounds good to me, too. Ten sharp."

"Ten," confirmed Champ.

Phillip watched the remaining squad call pull out of his muddy back yard and then offered to drive Kick to wherever he was parked. Kick replied he'd found a spot only about a block and a half away and said he would walk, since the rain had now let up and he was already soaked.

"You're lookin' good," said Kick. "It's great to see you. Say, how's that book coming?"

"It's finished."

"I'll bet it's real explosive."

"It just might be."

"By the way, do you always leave your doors unlocked? I mean I'm glad you did tonight, since I had to come through the front, but . . . "

"This isn't Washington. But I may have to reconsider after tonight. See you tomorrow."

Kick chuckled, said goodnight and disappeared around the corner of the house.

Phillip, wearing just his soaked swim trunks, found Greta inside, sitting on the stairs leading to the second floor. She looked exhausted and she toweled her hair. Two glasses and a half bottle of Jack Daniels she had found in a kitchen cupboard sat next to her. She invited Phillip to join her if he didn't mind sitting by a drowned rat. She rubbed her forehead and pulled her hands down her face as she took in a deep breath.

"How are you doing?" asked Phillip.

"I'm shook up, but I'm glad all of this is all over. It's hard to believe all of this has happened. I used to see violence all of the time as a reporter in Houston, but it was always involving other people . . . until it started happening to me with Richard and now here. I don't know what to think or how to feel about it anymore."

"I know what you mean. I'm sorry for what you've been through."

"Thanks." She poured the liquor into the two glasses. "I called Dad. Everything is fine there, but he was worried out of his wits about me. I told him what happened and that I was perfectly safe now."

"So he called the police?"

"He called the station when I didn't return. We were all

sitting by the lake watching the water parade. I left to call you, but you didn't answer. And then I was going to call Champ, but that's where Ford grabbed me."

Silently they sipped their drinks.

"Tell me where Mrs. Ford is," said Greta.

"She's alive and well with her neighbor friend at a lake called Okoboji or something like that. She left on Thursday."

"How convenient. Then Tommy knew?"

"Knew what?"

"Tommy told me he wanted three things . . . your computer with your book in it, your scalp, and I do think he meant that literally, and he wanted to know what you did with his grandmother."

"Looks like he struck out all three times. "It's over."

Greta took a large gulp from her glass. "Do you think Tommy came to Rockwood alone?"

"What?" he shot back.

"He mentioned comrades . . . maybe he came with some of his buddies from wherever this Fort is. Wouldn't he have brought help if he wanted your manuscript so badly, not to mention getting rid of you?"

"I don't think he brought anyone else. His dad and brother are both in federal prison, although not long enough to suit me. I think he needed to prove to them that he could handle this operation all by himself. The kid was really insecure and he needed a victory to take back home. If he brought someone else with him, they would have been here by now."

Phillip put his glass on the step above him and stood. He tugged at his wet trunks and pulled them down a couple of inches. Surprised and curious, Greta watched as he began to remove two wide pieces of packaging tape that held a small, clear plastic bag to his outer left thigh. It took a good pull to separate the tape from his skin. "Damn!"

Greta brushed the area with the back of her hand. "Ouch!" she empathized. "Can I ask why you have a bag taped to your butt?"

"Instructions."

"Let me guess," she said sarcastically. "Instructions for your body. You're really an android. Is there a warranty card inside?"

They both chuckled and then Phillip explained.

"It was to tell you what to do with my manuscript and my belongings . . . just in case."

"In case Ford got you first?"

"I had to prepare for all options. The coroner would have found it." He pulled his trunks in place and sat again on the step next to Greta. "Are you still mad as hell at me?"

"I haven't decided. I almost got killed tonight. And I still don't know if it was my fault or yours."

Phillip cradled the back of Greta's head in his hand and gently kissed her.

"Would you like to stay tonight?" he asked. "I not suggesting anything more that just being here with me. I think we could both use some close company."

Greta made him wait, just a little. "I'd like just that."

"You'll have to call George again then, won't you?"

"No." She made him wait some more.

"And . . . "

"And I already told him I might be staying. But I said I'd be home before Ben wakes up."

They walked slowly up the stairs and into the bedroom.

⚓ *chapter 25*

The lighting and the rain that began again were less threatening this time, as Greta slept soundly on Phillip's shoulder.
They didn't make love. They had showered and then crawled
under the sheet on his bed, simply wanting to be next to one
another. They gently kissed and touched, both agreeing that
this was all that was wanted and needed for tonight. Greta's
exhaustion led her quickly into a sound sleep. Phillip skillfully
moved his arm out from under Greta's head and propped
himself up on his elbow facing her. He caressed her body as
he replayed the events of the night in his mind. The big red
numbers on the alarm clock said it was almost two AM.

Phillip Williams lay on his back and stared at the slowly
revolving fan blades above. His mind was still going full
throttle. He thought about Greta. When he saw her in
Tommy's clutches, he realized that she was very important
to him. He wondered what would have happened if Kick had
not been there. Phillip knew, that, not by design, he had been
responsible for her being put in fatal jeopardy.

He turned his eyes away from the blades and expanded
his thoughts to the events in his life during the past fifteen
months. A tear rolled from the corner of his eye and was
absorbed by his pillow. Before that time, his life seemed so

distant and like a dream. He didn't want to revisit any of his past right now. He didn't want to think right now. He just wanted a little peace, but his mind kept churning. It was twenty minutes until three. He was wide-awake.

Phillip slid out from under the sheet. The bedroom was warm and its air humid. Something cold to drink sounded good. He stood for a moment at the bedroom window looking out at the street. His front yard was littered with small broken limbs, tattered oak leaves and some litter from the festival visitors. The rows of cars parked at the curb for the past two days were now gone, replaced by a steady stream of rushing water obeying the law of gravity. The deserted street was black and shiny. Phillip calmed as he watched the cleansing process.

He walked across the bedroom to see the lake from the French doors. Although he could barely see further than the bullet-riddled fishing boat, he knew Lake Emmet was still rough. The rain seemed to gain intensity as he stood watching branches on nearby trees begin to dip and sway just a little.

Returning to the front window of his bedroom, he pulled on the handle to let in some cooler air. He thought opening the window an inch or so would be safe. As he put his hand at the opening to feel if rain was coming in, he noticed a car parked at the curb on his side of the street where one had not been just a minute before.

It wasn't directly in front of his house, but close enough so that he could see the front end of the vehicle . . . American made, most likely he guessed. It wasn't very distinct due to the rain, but he was sure it wasn't a car he had seen before. Its lights were off, and no one was on his lawn or standing outside the vehicle. He hadn't heard any slamming car doors or people's voices, but the rain might have muffled any sounds, he concluded.

Phillip quietly slipped on a pair of running shorts and shut the door carefully as he left the bedroom. Greta hadn't moved. She was in a deep sleep.

Curious, he peered through the blinds on the front window in the darkened parlor. Everything was the same as he had seen from the second floor. He surveyed as much of the front yard and street as his limited angle of view allowed.

He didn't like what he was sensing. His stomach began to tighten. His arms and shoulders tensed and his mind shifted from curiosity about the car to concern. Greta had mentioned comrades. He told her Ford surely had acted alone and he still thought so. *Perhaps the car belonged to friends of neighbors who were staying over. Maybe.*

Phillip peered out the windows of every room on the first floor. He listened with a tuned ear. Nothing unusual, but he decided he had to investigate. Otherwise, he knew he would never be able to sleep.

The hunting knife he had strapped to his arm earlier in the evening was on the counter next to the kitchen sink. He had no idea what Greta had done with his gun. He picked up the knife and went out on the back porch, pulling the kitchen door quietly shut behind him. His trunks were soaked within seconds.

He decided to go across the back yard and follow the thick row of bushes out to the street. From the top window, he had seen that the hood of the car would line up closely with the end of his property. The drenched grass felt good on his bare feet. His toes dug into the soft earth to avoid slipping.

Crouching, Phillip moved as swiftly as he could between the two houses. He gripped the knife tightly in his left hand, ready for combat if that became necessary. He knelt near a bush by the sidewalk. From there he had an unrestricted view of the entire right side of the car. The motor was off and the tinted windows yielded no clue as to anyone inside. He had to see a license plate.

He eased himself between two other bushes and edged his way toward the back of the car. He was only about ten feet away and he could get a look at the back plate without a problem. Still moving in a crouch, he saw a flicker or flash of light inside the car. As if in a time machine, he was hurled back to the wintry night on I25 in Colorado. He saw again in his mind, the flash from the gun's first shot, the flash from the second and then there was a third. But had the third flash been from a gun? The third light had been longer . . . it glowed more . . . just like the one in the car now. Heart pounding, he wiped the rain from his eyes and focused on the car's front window. The orange light appeared again through the blackened glass. *It's the same light! Christ! It's the same!*

Phillip dashed to the front passenger door, lifted the handle and yanked it open. The dome light didn't go on but the side door panel light did. He could see a fancy cigarette lighter being held up in front of a big cigar. It was John Kick.

John Kick immediately threw the lit cigar at Phillip's face and grabbed for something in an open briefcase next to him on the seat. Phillip slammed the case lid down on Kick's hand and went for the ignition keys. Struggling to protect the keys, Kick managed to knock Phillip's knife away, but Phillip had the advantage of leverage and was quicker. Phillip struck at Kick's face with his fist and the sharply cut keys. The strikes drew blood immediately and a groan.

"*You* killed my wife, you son of a bitch! You!" Phillip pounded the agent's head mercilessly.

Kick swung his large frame around enough on the seat to use his foot as a weapon. He cocked his leg as far as he could and kicked Phillip in the center of his chest. Phillip found a good grip on the lip of the briefcase. What looked to be banded packs of money and a handgun, spilled from it. The pistol and some of the packets fell to the floor and more packets dropped out of the car into the water rushing along the gutter. Phillip staggered backward and fell out of the car, taking the briefcase and what was left in it with him. The pain was severe. Maybe a broken rib . . . maybe two.

"I'm going to kill you, Kick! Phillip yelled, breathing with agony and slightly hunched over. Adrenaline kicked in.

"No, I don't think so." Kick wiped away the blood running into his eyes and reached to the car floor for his gun.

Closing the briefcase with the remaining contents, Phillip ran. He knew the agent would follow him since he had his keys and a good portion of the money.

Kick steadied himself as he got out of the passenger side. Gun in hand, he moved into a defensive posture, taking cover along the thick bushes. He had gained weight since Phillip saw him in Colorado and he was out of shape. He lumbered rather than moved with agility. The blood still trickling from his head wounds ran down onto his clothes with the rain.

Kick couldn't spot his prey anywhere in the front yard, but he doubted Phillip had escaped into the house. He knew Williams was bent on revenge and wouldn't run away. Williams would fight. He would also use the environment and the weather to his advantage. But Kick didn't think he'd pull the same coming-out-of-the-lake surprise.

Emboldened, Kick ran to a large oak tree close to the front of the house. Stopping to catch his breath, he surveyed the yard and the house. To his surprise, he saw the black-briefcase lying in the middle of the yard near a yard vane. Before he could decide on his next move, Phillip leaped from behind and landed on Kick's back. The gun flew from the large man's hand. He hit the ground hard with Williams clutching him around the neck.

"*Why?*" demanded Williams. He struck Kick's head as hard as he could with his first, but his ribs felt as though they were coming through his flesh.

Kick sensed his weakness and pushed off the ground, bucking his enemy off his back. A hard strike to the chest by Kick's fist, Phillip groaned as he fell to the rain soaked earth. He managed to get to his knees and there he stayed, hunched over, unable to move further. He was vulnerable . . . a perfect target. Kick charged Williams like a soccer player ready to score a goal with his foot. Phillip summoned all the strength he had left and grabbed Kick's foot before it connected. He twisted the ankle and the desperate agent fell to the ground again. This time Kick was damaged.

"Why did you kill my wife?" He cradled his ribs as he again demanded an answer.

Kick struggled to his feet but did not speak. He limped toward the briefcase. His wet clothes clung to his body, and his paunchy belly and fleshy sides were distinctly visible. "Business!" he yelled back to Williams.

"You won't get far without these," taunted Phillip, jangling the set of keys.

John Kick had nearly reached the briefcase when an exhausted Williams again tackled him. Kick rose slowly to his feet and finally reached the briefcase. Bent over, Phillip followed. Instead of picking up the case, Kick grabbed a broken tree limb the thickness of a baseball bat. As he landed a powerful blow to William's left shoulder, Phillip's sharp cry of pain pierced the dismal night. He staggered forward and dropped to the ground near the yard vane. The bird's wings whirred next to his face. Phillip fought to stay conscious. He knew he must, or the killer would never pay for murdering Caroline.

Kick, limb in hand, towered over Phillip. The briefcase lay at his feet.

"It was the money, what else," Kick panted. "Tommy and I made a nice deal. I wasn't after your wife. I was paid to get rid of you. She just happened to marry the wrong guy. And she paid the price for your FBI fantasy. I'm sure you'll be very happy together. So long, Lund."

Kick raised the club above his head. Williams took a painful deep breath and mustered what strength he had left. In a quick, continuous motion, he pulled the yard vane out of the soft earth, turned it over and delivered the pointed metal tip deep into Kick's chest as the limb was heading for its target. Kick's eyes glazed and the limb fell from his hands. He staggered and fell to the ground. The impaling hawk, wings spinning, witnessed death quickly overtaking John Kick, special agent for the Federal Bureau of Investigation.

Phillip sat hunched over next to Kick, rocking gently back and forth, trying to stay conscious. Somehow he had to get Greta's attention. But he could barely move. He managed to turn enough to face his bedroom window. The room was dark.

"Greta." The call was feeble, more of a whisper than a shout. He couldn't expand his chest. Maybe she had heard the sounds of the struggle and she was on her way. But the rain was so muffling. Maybe he would have to wait until she missed him in bed and came looking for him. At least he was alive and Greta was safe. He could survive the rain and the pain. Phillip told himself he would try again in a few minutes. He carefully lay on his side, still close to Kick, and groaned. He closed his eyes.

Opening his eyes what seemed like minutes later, Phillip thought he heard someone talking behind him. He didn't know if he had been asleep or unconscious for just a few seconds or several minutes.

"Tired, Mr. Lund?" came a man's low voice. "Busy night, isn't it . . . all the bad guys are getting killed."

Phillip tried to wipe away mud and rain from his eyes and turn his head to see who had spoken.

"Here . . . let me make it easier for you." A round-faced man with a ponytail walked around in front of him waving a large handgun from side to side. In his other hand he held a trash bag that looked like it contained something heavy. He dangled the bag in front of Phillip.

"I've been doing some late night shopping," he said. "And I think I found just what I was looking for." He inched open the bag with the barrel of the handgun and pretended to peer inside. Let's see. Oh, here's a little, but very fancy computer . . . I bet its hard drive is just full of wonderful stories." His voice was a sing-song. "Extra flash drive comes with it, too. And looky here, a book, excuse me, a man-u-script about The Fort. He cinched the bag and bent down to Phillip's face.

"Remember me?" he said in an ugly voice. The man laid the bag on the grass. He turned his yellow baseball cap around on his head so the bill was in back. Then he put his left index finger under his nose to imitate a mustache. "Bang, bang."

Phillip's eyes opened wide and his teeth clenched as he recognized him, the driver who fired the gun that killed Caroline. His attempt to lunge at the man was worthless. The man pulled the set of keys from Williams' weak hand and stuffed them in the pocket of his rain-soaked jeans.

Lund attempted another strike at his wife's killer but it was as futile as the first.

"You look confused, Mr. Lund. I don't think you know what the hell's going on here, do you? Well, to start with, me and John have been partners for a long while. John always had a night job, if you know what I mean. He wanted to re-tire early. The Fords hired us to take you out in Colorado.

I'm sure you know why they'd wanna do something like that don't you? We didn't want to do your wife in, we just wanted you, but, hey, so we never got our money."

Phillip tried to dig his heels into the slippery grass and grab at the man. He could muster little strength and collapsed.

"Hey, I ain't finished. With all that protection you had in Colorado and then you disappearing, we was worried about you." The driver-trigger man laughed. "Then the Ford kid calls us in a panic and tells us he knows where you are and that if we back him up and get the book you told Kick you were writing, he'd double our pay. But then the woman is here and the cops show up and things get messed up. It really doesn't matter, 'cuz things are turning out pretty good for me. Kick killed the crazy kid and you took out my partner, so that leaves all of the money for little old me."

Williams managed to prop himself up and painfully tried to get to his feet. He couldn't get past his knees. "If you and Kick collected the money tonight, why did you come back?"

"Insurance, professor . . . business insurance. And we didn't collect our pay, we had to steal it out of the kid's truck. Anyway, old man Ford was sure to be after John's ass because he killed his kid . . . but if we had the book about this Fort of his . . . It's insurance. John also thought Mr. Ford would feel better about the whole thing if he knew you were taken out. The best part is that no one *alive* knows I was Kick's partner. Nobody knows I exist . . . ha! It may be raining like hell, but it feels like heaven to me!"

The killer walked behind Phillip and stopped. "Sorry I can't tell you any more stories, professor. I've got a plane to catch." He pointed his gun at the back of Phillip's head. "I don't think we'll see you later."

Phillip heard the shot but didn't feel anything pierce his skull or flesh. He turned and saw Greta holding his handgun, still aimed at her target who was laying on the ground next to the plastic bag. She cautiously approached, both hands gripping the gun. She looked fearful and brave at the same time. Blood flowed from the killer's head mixing with the mud around him.

"He's dead," Phillip struggled to say.

"Are there anymore?" she asked.

"No."

Greta ran to Phillip and knelt beside him. She gently cradled his bleeding face and asked if he was hurt anywhere else. She wanted to hug him tightly, but he told her that would have to wait.

"Tell me it's over this time, Phillip. Tell me."

"It's over."

chapter 26

X-rays revealed two cracked ribs and a simple fracture of his left clavicle . . . re-injury. Industrial strength Motrin, rest and limited motion for at least four weeks were prescribed until the shoulder was strong enough to start therapy.

Greta had driven him to the emergency room of the Algona hospital an hour after Chief Champ and one of his officers arrived at Williams' house for the second time in six hours. Phillip insisted his pain could wait. He felt almost driven to tell Champ everything, and to assure him that no one else in Rockwood was in jeopardy.

Before sunrise, the rescue unit took the two muddied and bloody bodies away. The car parked in front of the house was not Kick's after all, but his partner's. It was towed to the rear of the police station and parked next to Ford's pickup truck. The rain had stopped and the forecast was for a sunny and humid Sunday.

Phillip slept until mid-afternoon. He severely hurt only when he tried to roll over onto his left side. Greta helped him downstairs where he sat in a stuffed chair next to his desk in the library. He asked Greta to hand him the telephone and a small, black book that was taped to the underside of the desk. He held the receiver with his right hand and waited.

"Yes," announced a sober voice.

"Almost a year ago you gave me this number and told me to use it only in case of a major situation. I'm doing it now."

"Who's calling?

"Haven't you heard yet, Stacey?"

"No."

"About Agent Kick."

"Mr. Kick is no longer employed with the Bureau."

"What?"

"Please identify your operation and code name."

"The Fort . . . Sucker."

"Lund . . . I mean, Williams! It's good to hear your voice. We've been very worried about you. What's your status?"

Phillip moved slightly in the chair and winced as pain shot through the left side of his chest and his shoulder. "You mean how's my day going? Or how's the world been treating me lately?"

"Phillip. I just want to know if you're all right. Then tell me about Kick."

"Yes. I'm alive. And you tell me about Kick first, right now, or I hang up!"

"OK. OK. All I can tell you is that Mr. Kick was suspended from the Bureau less than a week ago. If our investigation turns up nothing, he'll be put back into service. He was actually in the middle of tracking your whereabouts when this happened."

"I don't think so."

"What do you mean?"

"Never mind . . . continue. Tell me about the investigation."

"Kick recruited an informant for us two years back for a multi-state drug operation out of Miami. We hid the recruit very well after the operation was over and the indictments were out. But somehow, his identity and location were discovered by the wrong people and he was hit."

"Yeah! You hid him about as well as you hid me and my wife."

"Now, Phillip. Your protection was as it should have been. We still don't know how you were found. Anyway, last month one of our people in Miami overheard John Kick's name mentioned on the street in connection with a recruit from some three years ago. We've been doing some digging. It could turn out that Kick and the other guy we used were moonlighting for the other side. But remember, I said he was only suspended. We have to have proof."

Phillip started by telling Raymond Stacey that Kick was dead . . . that Kick's recruit friend was dead . . . and that Tommy Ford had bit it, too . . . all in Iowa. Stacey was stunned and upset.

"Dammit!" he growled. "The Bureau is supposed to be informed immediately by any local law enforcement agency when an agent goes down." He pressed Phillip for full details. Williams drew Stacey a brief picture of the preceding eighteen hours and said he was available should Stacey want to come out to Iowa and hear more. Phillip knew the FBI would be at his door the next morning.

He gave Stacey his telephone number and mentioned Police Chief Larry Champ as the person to call if he needed more information immediately. Jesse Ford would have to be notified of his son's death.

The Washington Bureau Chief offered Phillip his regrets for the misery he had been put through, but added that America and the security of Americans had benefited from his service, and reminded him that he had, after all, volunteered, and had been paid very well for his work. Phillip told him he had a new life to begin and hung up.

He smiled at Greta. She had brought him a glass of water and more pain killers. "Does the Bureau know about your book?" She handed the medicine and glass to him.

"I doubt it . . . not unless Kick told them."

"So what happens now? You want it published, don't you."

"Yes. People need to know."

"So when you get better, you'll be leaving?"

"I have something to do in Colorado Springs and then Cross Lake, Minnesota, first . . . a promise I made nearly ten months ago." Phillip swallowed the pills with a gulp of water.

"And after that?" Greta walked to the window and looked out to the lake.

"I don't know, Greta."

She turned from the window and formed her words. "This may not be a good time to think, let alone talk, since I haven't had much sleep and you're full of pain, but I'm trying to see what the future might hold for me . . . and you." She walked over and sat on the arm of his chair.

"The biggest crisis in my life so far is over," she said. "Now I'm free to choose almost any future for me and Ben that I want. We don't have to run anymore or fear any one anymore. We could move back to Houston and do very well. I know the station would take me back or I could find another good TV job there. Or we could stay here for a while with Dad and live a quiet, good life."

Phillip watched her expressive eyes and mouth as she spoke.

"What I'm trying to say," she continued, "is that I have to choose where I go from here, and you do, too. I'm afraid that now that we are free to choose our new destinies, we will no longer be together. And I don't think I want that to happen."

Phillip studied her in silence and knew he wanted her to be a part of his future, somehow, somewhere. It made him happy that she felt that way, too. They understood and shared each other's pain and fears. Their history together was brief, but encompassing.

"For a long time I've tried to shut everything out of my life that would distract me from my mission . . . to see Caroline's killers destroyed," said Phillip. "Nothing else mattered. Nothing else was important, or so I thought until I met you and Ben. You put a hole in my wall of revenge."

"And look what came through," said Greta with a smile. She moved around in front of Phillip, offered her hand and suggested they go outside and sit by the lake or on the back porch where it was cooler.

"You saved my life last night, Greta."

"Just returning the favor."

They slowly moved to the back deck and found the breeze coming off the lake made the humidity more tolerable. The grass in Phillip's backyard was a deep lush green and the sky was endless, unclouded blue. Lake Emmet and its shore were back to normal . . . quiet, soothing and beautiful. Phillip spotted three boats on the still water.

"Now that this is over, I don't know what I want to do, or when I want to do it," he said from a deck chair in the shade. "I really like working with students who want to learn, so some day I may teach again. Know any good universities in Houston?"

Greta chuckled at what she thought he hinted at, but then her eyes turned more serious. She leaned in toward him and put her hands on his knees.

"I'm not sure how this is going to sound to you, but . . . Ben and I would like the three of us to be together when and wherever we all start up our lives again." She lowered her head slightly and her eyes became misty. "I think I fell in love with you somewhere along the way. I can't explain what kind of love, or if it will grow even deeper. I just know that being with you feels right and good. I know you had a wonderful wife you loved and a tragedy that caused so much pain. I understand that and know these things will always be with you."

Phillip put his fingers under her chin and leaned forward as far as he could. She met him the rest of the way and they gently kissed.

"When I met you, I didn't have a future," he said. "I hurt so badly that I didn't want one. But now, I think it would be even more painful to go into the future without you and Ben. I have a lot of healing inside and out that's needed, yet. But now I feel like I am able to start something new, something productive."

Tears shone in Greta's eyes. Phillip wished he could wrap his arms around her. He touched her face with his fingers instead. "I think I fell for you, too."

Another kiss was interrupted by the sound of a boat coming in behind Phillip's house. The motor stopped and someone yelled as the craft bobbed in shallow water just off shore. Greta and Phillip peered toward the boat and saw George and Ben waving to get their attention. Phillip was surprised. Greta wasn't.

"Hi, Mom!"

"Hi!" responded Greta. "Hi, Dad!"

Phillip waved as best he could with his good arm and he and Greta walked slowly down the steps.

"Hi, Phillip!" yelled Ben.

"Good morning, Ben. Morning, George. How's the fishing?"

"Pretty lousy because of the storm, but it'll get better, always does," said George. "How's everything on shore this morning?

"Everything is fine, Dad. I'll be home in a couple of hours."

"See you later then." George smiled as he started the motor.

"Bye, Phillip. Bye, Mom"

Greta and Phillip watched as the boat slowly made its way out to deeper water. Hand in hand they walked through the damp grass back to the big stone house. The colors of summer in Rockwood were vivid in the bright sun.

"What name shall I use?" asked Greta. "Phillip or Michael?"

He put his lips to her ear. "My name is Michael."